Missing 1

Daniel Ca
Sean Cam

CW00433658

Missing Persons
First published in Great Britain by De Minimis 2017
© Sean Campbell 2017
The moral rights of Sean Campbell & Daniel Campbell to be
identified as the authors of this work have been asserted by
them in accordance with the Copyright, Designs and Patents
Act 1988.
Cover Art designed by Nadica Boshkovska, © Sean Campbell
2017
All characters are fictitious. Any resemblance to real persons,
living or dead, is purely coincidental.
First Edition

Chapter 1: Freedom

Sunday 5th June

The world was beautiful once more. It didn't matter that it was raining, or that Faye was pallid, gaunt, and ungroomed. It didn't even matter that she only had forty-six pounds in the bank. She was finally free.

Four years had felt like a lifetime inside the walls of HMP Holloway. It was a dubious honour to be one of the last women ever to be incarcerated there, for the prison was due to close shortly after Faye's release.

Though legally an adult, Faye hadn't felt that way when she was convicted. Eighteen seemed to be an odd age: no longer a child, yet not quite a woman. Faye had never been to prom. She'd missed out on university. She'd never had a real job. As her boyfriend Mark always said, doing nails part-time on a Saturday didn't count for much. Now she was free, and the future had never looked so bright.

Today was the first day of the rest of her life.

'Faye! Faye! Are you paying attention to me at all?' Mark waved a hand at her.

Faye twisted against her seatbelt to look at the man speaking to her, Mark Sanders. Mark had been her rock, the one person she could rely on. He'd visited her every week without fail, unlike her so-called friends, who had almost all stopped coming entirely within a year or two. He'd even taken in her precious cat, Fabby, when she was locked up. Without Mark, she'd have gone crazy on the inside.

'I'm listening,' Faye said. 'What were you saying, again?'

'I said, you'll have some adjustments to make now that you're coming to live with me,' Mark said. 'Living on a narrowboat isn't like being in a flat. I just know you'll love it.'

'Mark, I'm not too sure about this,' Faye said hesitantly. 'There's room at Mum's.'

Mark took Faye's hand in his and looked into her eyes. 'I've told you, babe. You can't go back. Not while *he's* there.'

Faye snatched her hand from Mark's and then turned away to stare out of the taxi window. When she turned back towards Mark, her mascara was smudged. 'Ilford's all I've ever known, Mark.'

'Then it'll be an adventure. You used to love Dad's old boat! Remember that time we snuck on board with that bottle of vodka you'd pilfered from your parents' cabinet? It'll just be us. You and me against the world.'

Faye bit her lip. 'It's not the same, though, is it? Hiding on a boat for a night isn't like living on one.'

'You'll adjust. Life on a boat is so freeing. We can move around as much as we want, even take off to the country for a weekend if we like.' Mark gave her hand a gentle squeeze.

Faye hesitated and then squeezed back. 'I guess you're right.'

'She's moored in Poplar at the moment. She's a real beauty, you know. Seventy feet long, a traditional stern, and made by Kingsguard. Money can't buy a better boat. Dad's life insurance was good for something, after all.'

The Thames came into view as the taxi passed Limehouse Basin. They travelled in silence as Faye stared out at the overcast sky, the window open despite the rain.

Faye's eyes suddenly lit up. 'Can we visit Laura later? I haven't seen her in forever.'

Mark glowered momentarily, and then he turned away. When he looked back, his face was a mask; emotionless. 'I don't think so, babe. Not today.'

'Please?'

'I said no. We've got to move the boat tonight.'

'Why?'

Mark's polite demeanour melted. 'I've already explained all this. Weren't you listening the last time I visited you? We have to move every two weeks, otherwise the Canal and River Trust will be all over me. We're heading down to Victoria Park.'

'How far is that from home?'

'Not far,' Mark said. 'I've got you an Oyster card and put twenty quid on it so you'll be able to get around a bit. Is there anything else you need me to pick up for you?'

Faye thought for a moment. She'd been given her old purse back, but other than a few scraps of paper, an old lipstick, and some copper coinage, it was nearly empty. 'I could do with a mobile.'

'I'm way ahead of you there, darling. Here.' Mark fished inside a carrier bag at his feet. 'All yours.'

The phone Mark handed her couldn't have been any cheaper. It looked like the sort of mobile phone a child might be given in case of an emergency. It wouldn't play games or go online, and it was chunkier than Santa at Christmas. At least the battery would last for weeks rather than hours. 'I've put my number in there already, and Jake's. I'm afraid I don't know Laura's number, so you'll have to look that up on Facebook.'

The taxi pulled to a halt. The driver turned in his seat to open the plastic window between the front of the cab and the back and then glanced at the meter. 'Fifty quid, please.'

'Daylight bloody robbery,' Mark muttered as he stretched to free his wallet from his jeans pocket. The taxi sped away as soon as the doors had shut behind the pair, and soon they were trudging down towards the canal towpath where *The Guilty Pleasure* awaited them.

***

The Guilty Pleasure was an enormous boat, nearly twice the size of the next boat over. She was sleek, olive-green, and modern, with windows along the length of her. Mark took Faye by the hand and helped her onto the bow. Faye noticed a pair of frayed jeans hanging from the rail with the legs going into the murky water.

'What's that for?' Faye asked.

'The jeans? Oh, that's for Fabby. She loves jumping into the water, but she can't get out easily without something to sink her claws into.'

When Faye went inside, the first thing that struck her was how spacious the boat was. The second thing she noticed was the pile of takeaway leaflets by the sink in the small kitchenette. Her nose crinkled disapprovingly.

'I don't get to cook much,' Mark said sheepishly. 'Work has been crazy lately.'

'That's okay. I haven't had a takeaway in years.' Faye riffled through the leaflets until she spotted one for the Bengal Kitchen in Canary Wharf. 'Do you fancy Indian?'

'Oh, no. If you're staying with me for free, you're earning your keep. I've bought in everything you need to make spaghetti Bolognese. The veg is in the fridge, and the meat is defrosting on the counter. If you can't find something, look again.'

Faye scowled.

'It's just tonight, okay?' Mark held up his hands as if in surrender. 'I really need some me time, as I've got to go prep for work.'

'You work too much.'

'This isn't normal. I'm pitching for a new client next week. It's the biggest deal I've ever worked on. The company is huge, and we'd be looking at a seven-figure service contract. If I can land it, my commission would be more than my salary. This one could be huge for me. For us.'

Faye looked sceptical, but she began to search through the fridge.

Mark kissed her neck, his aftershave lingering in the air. 'We could go on holiday somewhere warm and sunny. Haven't you always wanted to go to Paris? Give me a shout when dinner is ready, and we'll move the boat after we've eaten.'

Faye turned, ready for a fight, but Mark had already disappeared through the narrow doorway out of the galley kitchen, heading towards their tiny sitting room. Gnashing her teeth, she took an onion and began to chop. Her eyes began to water almost immediately. She hoped it was the onions.

***

The ropes were untied, and the mooring pins had been placed safely on the roof of the boat. Mark kicked against the towpath to push the boat off. It was late afternoon, and the boat had to be moved before it got dark.

'Normally, I move on Saturdays, every other week. Limehouse is a short stay, just twenty-four hours. Think of it like parking a car. Some places we can stick around for a while, and some we can't.'

'How long will we be able to stay in Victoria Park?' Faye asked.

'Two weeks, which is forever for central London. Assuming we can find a space. It's in demand this time of year. We'll be able to picnic in the park, take long walks along the canal, and sleep under the stars. Doesn't that sound lovely?'

It took a moment for the starter motor to warm up, and then they were off. At three miles an hour, the journey still took less than two hours' trundling along the Regent's Canal. Mark steered from above, obviously enjoying showing off his boating skills, while Faye watched him from the sitting room below. He didn't yet trust her to man the helm. 'It's not as easy as it looks,' he'd said. 'She's a big boat, and there's a lot of weight to manhandle. I'll teach you soon enough, just not tonight.'

In the end, they made it into Victoria Park long before sunset. Boats were moored two abreast all the way along the canal. For a seventy-footer like *The Guilty Pleasure*, there was no chance of mooring up.

'Damn!' Mark cried loudly.

Faye poked her head out of the cabin. 'What's wrong?'

'We're going to have to keep moving. There's not enough room for us here. We'll need to move on to City Road. It's a lot less pretty, but it'll do for work.'

Chapter 2: Work

Monday 6th June, 09:30

City Road was as dingy as Mark had promised. The tow-paths were littered with broken beer bottles, empty rubbish bags, and the occasional needle. The water was dirty, so Fabby was confined to the boat. Even the people seemed grubbier, more desperate. Everybody walked slightly hunched over in short strides, desperate to avoid eye contact with those they passed. Worse still, it meant Faye had to walk to the tube and then catch a bus just to get home to Ilford.

By the time the bus dropped Faye off on Ilford High Street just north of the leisure centre, her Oyster Card had taken a battering.

Ilford was familiar at first glance, with a mix of charity shops and places to gamble away the weekly giros. Then there were a smattering of boutique shops and fancy-looking restaurants that Faye didn't remember being there before her stint inside.

It was early on Monday morning, and a queue was forming along the pavement near a payday lender that Faye remembered all too well. Her eyes glazed over for a moment, and then she snapped back to attention. She was there for a reason.

Mark had given her a stack of curricula vitae he'd printed out for her at work. Not that she'd had much to put on there. Three GCSEs and half a GNVQ didn't qualify her for much. Nor would prospective employers be too enamoured of her ability to paint nails every other Saturday. Faye pulled the first CV from the top of the pile, swallowed her pride, and headed into the first building nearest the bus stop. The sign above the door read Ilford Building Society.

She waited in line for the customers in front of her to be served, and then edged towards the counter. 'Hi, I saw the sign in the window. Can I give you a CV?'

The woman looked down at her as if sizing her up. She homed in on the half-blank CV straight away. 'Let me see it.'

Faye handed it over, trying not to bite her lip.

'Hon, what's this gap? You did nails for a living four years ago, and then what?'

'I was in prison,' Faye mumbled.

The woman burst out laughing. 'Are you serious? You want me to give you a job where you'd be handling money all day? Get out of here.'

'But...'

'Out.'

Faye turned on her heel and headed for the door. It was going to be a long day.

***

Six hours later, Faye had only sore feet to show for her efforts. One or two businesses had promised to call her if anything came up. The rest had been as unsympathetic as the woman at the building society. Most of them had wondered why she didn't have a fixed address. It wasn't much of a CV: half a dozen lines, a huge gap, and no real skills or experience. Even Faye wouldn't have hired herself.

She almost stopped for a coffee before heading home, but one pound sixty-five for a small cup seemed too much to lose when all she had in the world was the forty-six pounds the prison had given her upon release. At least she had Mark to go home to.

As she headed to the bus stop to get the number twenty-five bus back to the boat, an older woman unexpectedly limped over to her and hugged her.

'Leah! It's been far too long, my dear. When did you get back to Ilford?' The woman was in her seventies, with blood-shot grey eyes and a tangled mess of white hair. A small flower was perched above her left ear.

Faye pried herself away from the woman's embrace. 'I'm sorry, I think you've mistaken me for someone else,' she said as gently as she could. 'My name is Faye, not Leah.'

'Oh, you are a minx, Leah. Always playing games with me, you are. You've been like that ever since you were a child, you know. Away with the faeries. Always away with the faeries.'

Faye crossed her arms. 'Ma'am, I really don't know you. Are you confused? Can I call someone for you?'

'You can call your mother once in a while. Poor sweet woman hasn't heard your voice in years. And you used to be such a nice girl.'

The arrival of the bus saved Faye from responding. She leapt on board, swiped her Oyster card, and looked out the window as the crazy lady with the flower in her hair disappeared into the distance.

***

Mark was unimpressed with her story about the old woman. They curled up in bed as the rain pounded down on the roof.

'It's Ilford, ain't it, babe? You're going to get weirdos all over town.'

'I like Ilford,' Faye said.

'I know you do, babe. Me too, but isn't this better? We've got our own space – our own very private space.'

Faye felt his hand traverse down the small of her back to caress her buttocks. She sat up sharply and slapped him hard across the face. He looked stunned for a moment and then drew back his hand and balled it up into a fist as if he meant to punch her. She froze, a deer in the headlights. Being free didn't feel much different from life inside. A sob escaped her, and then he began to apologise.

'I just... I love you so much. I can wait. Just not too long, okay? You've been inside for four years, babe, and I *am* a man. With needs.'

She shivered as he wrapped an enormous arm around her.

Chapter 3: Old Times

Sunday 12th June

The days blurred together, and before Faye knew it, she had been on the boat for a week. They'd moved on to a new mooring that Saturday, doing what Mark called his Saturday Shuffle, and were now moored up a little farther along the City Road Canal in Islington. Faye could now see the canal tunnel in the distance. Graffiti was all over the stonework, and some of it looked so familiar, it could have been her own handiwork.

Faye had barely seen Mark during the week. Each morning, he had woken her up with a cup of builder's tea and a kiss on the forehead, and then he disappeared to suit up and head to work. The only time he paid her much heed was when he trying to persuade her to have sex, or she'd done something wrong. Faye supposed she must have deserved it. He was good to her. He'd given her a home, a purpose, a freedom she hadn't enjoyed for years.

And she was finally going to get to catch up with Laura. Her best friend since childhood, Laura had always been there. Before prison, anyway. These days, she was dating a mysterious older man called Tim. Mark had agreed that Faye could invite them both over for Sunday dinner.

Five minutes before they were due to arrive, the smoke alarm went off.

Mark came tearing through from the sitting room, which doubled up as his study. 'Fucking hell, woman. Can't you get anything right? Don't you know I've got work to do? I told you, I'm pitching a new client tomorrow, and I cannot concentrate with that racket.'

'S-sorry,' Faye said as she turned out the oven. Dinner was a charred black mess.

'Throw that overboard,' Mark barked. 'I don't want it stinking up my boat. Then find something else for tonight. They'll be here any minute. And for fuck's sake, lock the cat in the bedroom. I'm not having her stealing table scraps tonight.'

He paused before he slammed the door shut. 'Have you seen my phone? I swear I left it on the table.'

'No, I haven't seen it,' Faye said. There was just enough time for her to coax their cat into the bedroom, fish a takeaway leaflet out of the drawer, and then call through her order before Laura and her boyfriend Tim trundled along the canal pathway arm in arm.

Faye flung herself from the narrowboat as they approached, narrowly missing the gap between the boat and the towpath. She skidded to a halt in front of Laura. Her best friend hadn't changed a bit. She was still slim, voluptuous, and perfectly made-up, with long blonde hair cascading over pale shoulders.

Laura pursed her blood-red-stained lips in an air-kiss. 'Hey, you. Long time, no see. How've you been?'

'Better now you're here. Who's this?' Faye looked at Laura's companion. He was an older man, a good decade older than the girls. Grey hairs had begun to show in his tawny mop. If it weren't for the Rolex prominently adorning his wrist, Faye would have wondered just what her best friend saw in him.

'This is Tim,' Laura said.

'Nice to meet you, Tim.' Faye shook his hand. 'Want to come aboard?'

The four were soon seated around a fold-out table aboard *The Guilty Pleasure*. The Chinese meal had yet to arrive, and the boys were knocking back the beers in no time.

Laura leant in conspiratorially. 'Any luck with the job search, babe?'

'Nothing,' Faye said, shaking her head. 'Nobody wants an ex-con with no skills and no fixed abode.'

'I hadn't even thought about that. Where does your post go?'

'We have to collect it from the post office,' Mark chimed in. 'I get everything sent POST RESTANTE Mark Sanders to the post office opposite my work.'

Tim drained the bottle he was holding and looked over at Mark. 'Couldn't you just get it sent to work?'

'The boss wouldn't like it,' Mark said. 'He doesn't even know I live on a boat, so I'd have to explain that to him. Want another beer?'

Tim nodded. 'You're still at Berryman these days, aren't you?'

'That's us. Berryman Financial Services.'

Laura looked confused. 'What do you do? Sell investment opportunities?'

Mark laughed. 'I'll give you the opportunity to earn me a fat commission selling you something. The market can go down as well as up. As long as I get paid, I'm fucked if I care which.'

'Remind me never to lend you so much as a tenner.'

Faye watched the conversation with a glazed expression. It felt forced. Thankfully, they were interrupted by someone tapping on the window. Faye looked out and saw a delivery bike on the towpath. She sidled away from the table to fetch dinner.

'Faye, I've been thinking,' Tim said. 'Laura said your dad is a chef? Couldn't you go work for him? He must need people all the time in the restaurant, and you're more than pretty enough to cane it in tips.'

Laura cut him off with a scowl. 'We don't talk about him. Faye, may I use your bathroom?'

'Sure. It's down the hall on the–'

'Left. I know.'

Faye watched her friend trail from the room. How did she know where the bathroom was?

'Babe,' Mark whispered into Faye's ear, 'I'm thinking we should have an early night tonight. It's been ages since me and you... you know... did it.'

Faye waved him off. 'Not tonight.'

She wasn't ready. Not yet. He'd asked every night since she'd got out.

'It's been four years, babe. When? Please tell me you didn't go gay for the stay.'

Faye said nothing.

Dinner idled on for much too long. By the time the wontons were gone and the beer had been finished, Faye was ready to collapse into bed. She bade the others goodnight and curled up in their tiny bed while Fabby the cat purred contently by her side.

Eventually, the voices of the other three drew quiet. An early night wasn't such a bad idea after all.

Chapter 4: Home Alone

Monday 13th June, 07:30

Faye awoke to a cold, empty narrowboat that Monday morning. Mark hadn't woken her up with her usual cup of tea. He had left without kissing her goodbye. The bed was cold where Mark should have been lying, and condensation was running down the windowpanes. Evidently, Mark hadn't put the generator on, either.

The generator was on the bank side of the boat, hidden behind a wooden panel. It was diesel-powered. Faye strained to recall what Mark had said about starting it. *Don't something something too long.*

It took her a while to work out, but eventually she fired up the generator, and the boat hummed to life. She turned on the hob, cracked two eggs, and set about making an omelette.

The sun was already up by the time she emerged onto the deck to look around. She pinged Mark a good morning text in the hope of putting the awkwardness of the previous night behind them.

By mid-afternoon he still hadn't replied. *Fine*, Faye thought. *If that's the way he wants to play it.*

Yet by teatime, her resolve had begun to weaken. He still wasn't home when she began cooking, or when she served up their chicken curry. His portion went into the microwave for later. As she finished eating her dessert, she cracked.

'*Mark, where are you?*' she texted him.

Thoughts ran through her mind. Was he late at work? Was he at the pub with his mates? But then why wasn't he texting? Was his phone dead? Was he with another woman?

'Mark, I'm sorry I said no last night. I won't do it again. Come home. Please.'

Still no answers came. A dozen more texts, and still dead air. She tried calling. His number went straight to voicemail. 'Mark, it's me. Please give me a call.'

Soon, it was nearly midnight, and he hadn't come home. She locked up and headed to bed. *Surely, he'll be home by breakfast.*

Chapter 5: The Other Woman

Tuesday 14th June, 12:05

The next morning Faye woke up late. There had been no sign of Mark. She'd tossed and turned throughout the night, trying to listen out for him. At one point, she'd thought he might have been home, but she must have dreamt it.

She rolled over, her back aching badly, and got out of bed. The tiny cabin bed was doing a number on her posture. The time on the clock read 12:05. *Gone midday!* Faye dressed as quickly as she could and fumbled her way out of the bedroom.

The front door was still locked, not that that mattered much. Mark could have come and gone while she was sleeping. She found her mobile phone lying on the counter where she had tossed it the night before. No new messages.

Mark had to have slept somewhere last night. Before she jumped to the wrong conclusion, Faye decided to call Mark's brother in case he had crashed at his place.

Jake answered on the third ring. 'Faye! To what do I owe the pleasure?'

'Have you seen Mark? He didn't come home last night.'

There was a pregnant pause, the silence of a man deciding if he should cover for a friend. Finally, Jake said, 'No. He wasn't out with us last night. I haven't seen him since we worked on the boat on Sunday. I'm sorry, Faye.'

Faye reached the same conclusion in a heartbeat. Mark must have been with another woman. 'Bastard.' She rang off without another word. She'd show him.

***

Berryman Financial Services were located just off Poultry, within spitting distance of the Bank of England. It was close enough for Faye to walk down from the City Road Basin. She arrived outside at quarter to three and pressed the buzzer above the green-and-gold signage.

Mark didn't strictly work in finance, as much as he liked to pretend otherwise. He was an IT nerd, project-managing IT software for those who actually did work in banking. But "logistics and sales management software" didn't sound quite as sexy as investment banking, and Faye was happy to play along with his little fantasy to help keep him happy.

She knew he should be in his office, pretending to send important emails but really just waiting for other employees to start leaving the office so he could leave too. Mark never did any more work than was strictly necessary.

The one thing he was good at was sales. As soon as the lift carrying Faye up to the floor housing Berryman Financial Services opened, she saw the leader board in the entranceway marked 'New Clients Signed This Month'. Mark's name was at the top of the list, with thirteen new clients in as many days. The next best, with twelve, was Pip Berryman.

Mark had told her all about Pip. The son of the owner, he was given every chance, but he still lagged behind Mark. He just didn't have the gift of the gab required for sales. No doubt if he was on the same low-pay, high-commission contract that Mark had, Pip would have been out on the streets years ago. Mark always said Pip only succeeded by riding the coat-tails of others, taking credit for the easy sales but never himself bagging a whale.

She saw Pip appear from the corner of her eye. She knew it was him from Mark's description. She'd thought Mark had been exaggerating about the three-piece suit, the silk pocket square, the foppish blond hair and the over-polished Italian leather shoes, but Mark's description had been spot on. Pip looked like he belonged in a courthouse more than he belonged in an IT services company.

'Hello, darling. Are you here to congratulate me?' he smirked.

'Is Mark here?'

'Sanders? Nah. That duffer didn't even turn up today. He lost himself a whale there. His free ride as the top dog is over. See his name at the top of that leader board? Do me a favour and stick him in second place. Right, lads, champers on me at The Green Man. Who's in?'

***

With no sign of Mark at the office, Faye roamed around the local bars looking for him. Nobody had seen him, though several bartenders admitted to knowing who he was. It seemed he was a regular in most of the pubs within a five-minute walk of his office.

After Faye returned to the boat, she found herself pacing up and down, five steps forwards, five back. With every length of their cramped sitting room, she could feel her heart rate rising. Mark might be a horn dog, but he would never miss the chance to bag a client. He'd spent all of Saturday and most of Sunday night talking about it. Why wouldn't he have gone to work?

His brother hadn't seen him, nor had Laura and Tim. His phone wasn't on. He hadn't been to the office. Where had he gone between Sunday night and now? For the first time since getting out of prison, Faye began to feel very much alone.

Should she go to the police? Would they take an ex-con seriously? She had to try.

***

Faye left the boat moored up, with a note on the dining table for Mark should he return while she was out.

The nearest police station was on Tolpuddle Street, a short walk along the canal, past the entrance to the Islington Canal Tunnel and through Chapel Market. A Victorian-style blue lamp hung above the doorway to denote the entrance. Beside the door a yellow CCTV sign glowed in the evening light, warning her that all comings and goings were being recorded.

The interior of the station was sparse and utilitarian. The walls were painted white, and the light grey countertop was made of plastic. It seemed as if the entire room had been designed to be wiped down and cleaned with bleach if the situation warranted it. The lobby was crowded with a queue running from the front door up to the main desk. Police officers were running back and forth behind the counter, escorting witnesses and victims to interview suites and scribbling down notes.

It took a few minutes for Faye to make it to the front of the queue. She overheard those in front complaining of petty theft and disorderly neighbours. When it was her turn, she averted her eyes and shuffled towards the counter without so much as glancing at the police constable behind the desk.

'I'm h-here to report a missing person.'

'Very well, ma'am. Please go through the door on your left,' the constable said in a slightly nasal voice, waving a pencil in the direction of a door which Faye hadn't initially noticed.

The door buzzed as the policeman remotely unlocked it, and Faye stepped into a small interview suite. There were two plastic chairs in the middle of the room, facing forwards.

The counter from the main reception continued along the back wall, and the nasal-voiced policeman reappeared. He pulled up a stool behind the counter and set his notebook down in front of him.

'Who is it that's missing, ma'am?' he asked.

'It's my boyfriend. Mark. Mark Sanders.'

'And your name is...?' the constable said.

'Faye Atkins.'

'Okay, Faye, I'm Police Constable Macklemore. Can you tell me what Mark looks like?'

'He's tall. About six foot, I guess.'

'Taller or shorter than I am?' The constable stood up and drew himself up to his full height.

'Maybe an inch or two shorter.'

'Okay. Is he slim? Fat?'

'Slim. He works out a lot. He's got curly brown hair, but no beard or moustache. His eyes are green, and his jawline is like a wide V.'

'Give me a second to write all that down,' PC Macklemore said. When he had scribbled down the description Faye had given him, Macklemore turned his attention back to Faye. 'Does he have any tattoos? Jewellery?'

She shook her head. 'Nothing like that.'

'Okay, Faye, you're doing really well. Does Mark have any medication he has to take?'

Faye chewed her lip and then said, 'No. Nothing like that.'

'And where did you see him last?'

'At home,' Faye said.

'Where is home for you?'

'We live on a narrowboat. *The Guilty Pleasure*. We're moored up a little east of here on the Islington Canal Basin.'

Macklemore rested his pencil behind his ear. 'I know it well. When was it you last saw him?'

'Sunday night. I went to bed first, and he wasn't there the next morning when I woke up.'

'Is that unusual?'

'I thought he had gone to work. I slept in late, you see.'

Macklemore popped the pencil from behind his ear and wrote that down. 'How late did you sleep in?'

'Til midday.'

'Don't you have a job to go to?' Macklemore looked at her disapprovingly.

Faye cast her gaze downwards and said through gritted teeth, 'I'm between jobs.'

She watched as he scribbled "Unemployed" next to her name. 'Right. Where does Mark work?'

'Berryman Financial Services. He sells IT services to other companies. But he never made it to work yesterday. I checked.'

'How does he get to work? Does the boat always stay in the Islington Canal Basin?'

'We move all the time–'

'You're continuous cruisers, then? We see a lot of them around here. Does Mark take the tube in to Bank?'

Faye thought for a moment. 'Tube. Bus. Boris Bikes. Whatever.'

Macklemore stroked his chin thoughtfully. 'Does he work in the same office all the time?'

'What do you mean? They've only got one office.'

'I mean, does Mark go out on sales calls? Could he have gone to visit a client?' Macklemore asked.

'They noticed he hadn't turned up. He was supposed to be pitching a new client, and he didn't show up,' Faye said. 'One of the other project managers got his commission.'

'So, it's not like him to miss being in the office? Has his routine always been the same?'

'I...'

'You what?'

'I don't know. We only moved in together a week ago.'

Macklemore arched his eyebrow in disbelief. 'A week ago? Hmm... Based on what you've told me, Mark is what we call low-risk. He's an adult, and we don't have any evidence of anything untoward. I'll take his mobile phone number and a recent photograph, and we'll get him on the system.'

'I don't have a photo. Is that really all you're going to do?'

'For now. Have you called 'round local hospitals? Beyond that, tell his family and friends, keep an eye out for him, and look after your boat.'

'And our cat.'

'Exactly. Here's my card. Call me if anything changes.'

An hour later, Faye was at home, turning over Macklemore's card, when a thought struck her. Whatever had happened to that nice lady from Sapphire Unit who had once given her a very similar-looking card?

Chapter 6: Home Sweet Home

Tuesday 14th June, 19:30

The flat was tastefully decorated, but so minimalist that it looked barely lived in, as if the owner worked long hours and barely had time to crash before going straight back to work. Ashley Rafferty had been fortunate in her timing. She'd bought the flat just before the students and the hipsters began to take over the Elephant. It had once been a family home, which was then subdivided into two apartments. It was in the heritage zone, a stone's throw from the Imperial War Museum, and still had the original single-pane windows.

Rafferty shivered as she hung her coat on the hook just inside the door, kicked the thermostat up to twenty, and pressed the big button on her landline phone.

'You have one new message. BEEP.'

Rafferty sighed, kicked off her sensible work flats, and hit play on her answerphone as she made a beeline for the kitchen. After the day she'd had in court, she needed a large glass of Malbec.

'Miss Rafferty? It's Faye Atkins. You gave me this number a long time ago and told me that if I ever needed someone, it would be okay to call you. Can you call me back on this number, please?'

Rafferty played the message again, jotted down the number from caller ID, and then wrote down the name Faye Atkins. Faye Atkins – where did she know that name from?

She paced up and down for a moment, desperate to recall where she had heard the name before. It was no use. She plonked down on her sofa, took a glug from her wine glass, and rubbed at her temples.

Atkins. Atkins. The surname rang a bell.

The image of a flat in Ilford flashed before her eyes. A woman with a black eye, an abusive thug with a history of being in and out of prison, and a girl of no more than fifteen cowering in the back room with panda eyes. That Faye. The same Faye who had called her once before when she got into trouble, the young girl who had gotten mixed up with the wrong crowd. If Faye had been born anywhere but the Pembarton Estate in Ilford, she might have stood a chance.

Rafferty picked up the phone, carefully dialled the number, and waited. It was answered almost immediately.

'Faye Atkins? This is Ashley Rafferty. I'm returning your call.'

The voice that answered was high-pitched, girlish, and hesitant. 'Miss Rafferty? I'm sorry to bother you. I didn't know who else to call. I've got nobody.'

And over the next fifteen minutes, Faye relayed the story of Mark's disappearance.

'I've called everyone I know, but nobody has seen him!'

'Keep calling the police station. They will be looking for him, I promise,' Rafferty said, though she didn't quite believe it herself. A grown man who disappeared for a day or two would never warrant a search party through central London.

'But I've tried that. Can't you help me? Please?'

'I'll see what I can do.'

Chapter 7: Anything but Paperwork

Wednesday 15th June, 09:45

Rafferty made it to work late that morning. The memory of that little girl had weighed heavily on her conscience, and sleep had not come easily. It wasn't any of her business, except for an off-hand promise she'd made several years earlier.

She found the boss in his office. Morton had obviously been there a while. There was a copy of the day's *The Impartial* newspaper discarded in his wastepaper bin, and a long-cold coffee sitting on his desk.

'Morning,' he said without looking up. 'How'd it go in court yesterday?'

'Dreadful.'

'At least it's over. Not that today's paperwork is going to be any more fun.'

'Damn! I'd forgotten about that.'

Morton looked up. He knew that was a lie. Rafferty never forgot the paperwork. He surveyed her carefully. 'Something tells me you think you've got something better to be doing.'

'It's this girl. I knew her from way back when–'

'When you were in Sapphire,' Morton finished for her. Rafferty had spent years working sexual abuse cases before becoming a parole officer and then finally being poached for Morton's Murder Investigation Team. 'One of the victims you dealt with?'

Rafferty nodded. 'We could never prove it. Her old man was a right piece of work, but we never nailed him for it. He went down for dealing, and then so did she.'

Morton took a sip of his cold coffee and pulled a face. 'Yuck. I'm not hearing a case, here. What's she got to do with us?'

'She got out of Holloway a week ago. Two days ago, her boyfriend of several years went missing. She needs help. The locals aren't giving it much cop. He's a grown man who's barely been gone for two days.'

'Sounds about normal,' Morton said. 'Any sign he's in danger?'

'No, but–'

'Then you know we can't deal with it. We're not Missing Persons. We've got no jurisdiction until such time as–'

This time it was Rafferty's turn to interrupt Morton. 'As there is substantive reason to suspect life has been taken or is under threat. Don't quote me the rulebook. I know the rules.'

Morton folded his arms. 'My hands are tied. If you want to spend time chasing down a missing boyfriend, you'll have to do it on your own time. You've got accrued leave. Use some of it.'

Rafferty brightened. 'Really? But what about my mountain of paperwork?'

Morton sighed. 'I'll do it.'

Chapter 8: Moving On

Wednesday 15th June, 11:00

Faye's stomach rumbled. With Mark gone, her prison release money wouldn't last more than a few days. She nibbled at an apple, desperate to make it last. She was standing out on the deck, leaning against the boat. It was a beautiful day, and the canal was crowded.

Another narrowboat owner waved at her as he approached. 'Oi! Did you hear anything last night?'

'N-no.'

'Bloody thieving bastards. Some git done in my window and made off with my laptop last night. You're lucky you ain't been done, nice boat like this and all. You'd best be moving on if you've got any sense about you. It's safer down Maida Vale way.'

'Thanks. I guess you're right.'

Faye headed inside to check the canal route Mark had planned out. It was all there on the table: a map, timings, bridge numbers, and his favourite spots to moor up circled in pen. He'd listed a few options to head towards next: Camden, Maida Vale, and Alperton. The latter had been circled in bold, as if it were somehow important to him.

Maybe it was time to move on. The thought of steering *The Guilty Pleasure* without Mark scared her. Up ahead was the Islington Tunnel, almost a thousand yards of pitch black darkness. Mark had only let her have the briefest of tries behind the tiller. She recalled his instructions.

'It's not like a car, babe. You move the tiller, the stern swings out. Keep her in the middle of the canal unless you need to pass another boat, and use the engine in reverse if you need to slow down. Keep her going very slowly when you're turning, because she moves from the middle, not the ends. Three miles an hour is more than enough.'

It couldn't be that hard, could it?

***

Faye finally psyched herself up enough to do it.

With surprisingly little ceremony, she unhitched the boat from the shore, brought aboard the mooring pins and rope, and kicked off from the towpath with one big push.

The boat began to arc away from the bank where she'd pushed, and Faye fired up the engine much too quickly. She felt the boat swinging behind her as the front and back, a whopping seventy feet apart, swung as if there were an invisible pivot located dead in the middle of the narrowboat. It was something like driving a really a big car in icy conditions without snow tyres.

She hit the reverse and dragged the boat towards the centre of the canal. So far, so good.

A horn rang out as another boat approached. Faye pulled left, trying to allow the other boat to pass. It seemed to be coming towards her in slow motion. In her mind, it was inevitable that they would crash into each other. And then the other boat passed on by, mere feet from the starboard side of *The Guilty Pleasure*. Faye breathed a sigh of relief.

The tunnel was upon her in no time. She glanced down it, checking, as Mark had told her to, for a light that would mean someone was coming the other way. When none could be seen, she lit up her own light and eased towards the tunnel.

The mouth of the tunnel soon approached, and the towpath ended. The darkness folded in around the boat. The farther in she got, the more distant the lights at either end of the tunnel seemed to be. What little light her own lamp offered was scant comfort. The walls began to close in. Faye's breathing became rapid, shallow. Her eyes slowly lost focus.

And then, before she knew it, it was all over. The boat was suddenly through the tunnel and farther along the canal than she had thought possible.

The next challenge was on her almost immediately. St Pancras Lock was one of the busiest in central London, with boats going up and down the Regent's Canal constantly. It should have been easy. It wasn't Faye's first, after all. But the first one had been quiet, and there hadn't been slack-jawed tourists staring at her.

The lock cottage, itself a tourist attraction, loomed large as *The Guilty Pleasure* drew closer to the lock. Faye slowed down. There was a queue ahead of her. She felt her heart pulse as she drew closer to the lock.

There were two gates: one going from high water to low water, and another going from the low water to the high water. The mechanics were simple, even if they looked intimidating. Faye had to drive *The Guilty Pleasure* into the lock, shut the gate behind her, fill up the lock with water, and wait.

The first problem was the lock gate itself. Faye moored up just in front of the gate and jumped off to check that the top paddles were shut. Once she had done that, she proceeded to hand crank by the bottom paddles. The handles would open the bottom panel of the gate and let out all the extra water that the previous narrowboater had used to climb to the higher water.

Faye strained against the handles. They were stiff by design to stop the gate accidentally opening, and Faye felt her hands begin to sweat. She lost purchase on the handles and practically tripped over her own feet as she struggled.

'Want a hand there, missy?' a gravelly voice said from behind her. Faye turned to see an elderly gent standing on the towpath. 'Only you're holding us up a bit.'

Faye glanced back to the east. The queue behind *The Guilty Pleasure* had begun to grow.

'Yes, please.'

'Okay. You go get on your boat, and I'll handle the gates for you. How's that sound?' He gave her a gap-toothed grin.

'Thank you.'

Faye quickly boarded *The Guilty Pleasure*. The gate opened quickly under the strength of the old hand, and Faye began to slowly guide the boat forward. It was a small space to slide such a large boat into. The stern swayed behind her as Faye fought to keep her straight. More than once, she clunked against the sides of the lock before finally coming to a stop inside the lower half of the lock.

She saw the old man arch an amused eyebrow at her mishandling of the boat. He waved her off as she turned to shut the lower gate. 'I've got it! Make sure you stay clear of the front lock gate, miss. You don't want to get snagged and sink that beauty, so back up a smidge.'

No sooner had Faye reversed a few feet than the lock gate closed behind her, and the old man turned on the taps to let the water in. It dribbled in slowly, and *The Guilty Pleasure* began to rise with Faye still standing at the helm. She kept a hand on the tiller to ensure she didn't slip forward, her confidence growing with every passing moment that she hadn't crashed.

The higher part of the canal to the west came into view. The water here was thick with a covering of algae, and green shrubbery grew along the banks. The frame of a Victorian water tower rose fifty feet in the air to the right. A handful of narrowboats were moored up to the left.

'Right, you're set, miss. I'll open the front gate for you, and then we can all be on our way.' He gave a small nod to the queue behind them, which was now several narrowboats long.

Faye made her way out of the lock, delighted to have made it through without incident. She set off at a heady clip, throttling up to three miles an hour. When she arrived in Alperton, she found a secluded spot to moor up and sighed in relief. Moving the boat was stressful. Mark had been right not to let loose too early. She hammered the mooring pins into the firm ground beside the canal, tied off the ropes, and headed inside to check her phone.

She had a dozen missed calls.

Chapter 9: Long Time, No See

Friday 17th June, 10:00

Faye finally returned Rafferty's phone calls on Friday morning. Rafferty had veered between worrying that something had happened to Faye and wondering if Faye was wasting her time. Two days of searching for Mark had yielded nothing. Without access to police resources, Rafferty was reduced to merely retracing Faye's footsteps to make sure she hadn't missed anything. She knew the brother was moored up in Maida Vale. She found the offices of Berryman Financial Services and confirmed Faye's information. She even called around the hospitals with his name and description.

They arranged to meet up at the boat, which Faye had moved since her original phone call. Faye told her to head to Alperton Underground Station and look for her between bridges sixteen and seventeen, just to the east of the tube.

She was easy enough to find. *The Guilty Pleasure* was larger than most of the narrowboats on the canal, and newer too. Her glossy olive-green hull and walnut colouring stood out amongst the boats moored up on the Paddington arm of the Grand Union.

Faye was waiting in a deck chair laid out on the bank. She had an old novel in her hands and looked as if she hadn't a care in the world.

'Faye?' The young woman seemed not to hear her. 'Faye? It's Detective Inspector Ashley Rafferty.'

Then, as if struck by a manic energy, Faye leapt up. 'Miss Rafferty!'

It was the same Faye that Rafferty remembered. Her deep blue eyes were unmistakeable.

'Thank you for coming, Miss Rafferty.'

Rafferty smiled. 'That's okay. Permission to come aboard?'

'Please.' Faye folded up her chair, placed it askew on the roof of the boat between two potted plants, and led Rafferty inside.

It was Rafferty's first time on a narrowboat. She ducked her head as she was led down the steps into the main cabin. She had expected it to be cramped, but she had not expected how much stuff had been crammed into every nook and cranny. The interior walls had been painted white, making the small space feel much roomier than it should, and long windows that had been covered by blinds were spaced along the length of the boat. A tiny sofa was in the first compartment. No cushions, Rafferty noted. It was quite obviously a man's space.

'Have you been here long?' Rafferty asked.

'In Alperton? Or on the boat?'

'Either. Both.'

'I had to move the boat because of break-ins up on the Islington Basin. This was the next stop on Mark's plan. I thought he'd come find me here.'

'I heard about the break-ins,' Rafferty said. 'Is there anything worth stealing on board?'

'Not really. The boat itself is expensive. I suppose someone could steal the engine or something.'

'No phones? Laptops?'

'Just this,' Faye said as she pulled an old Nokia from her pocket.

It was a seriously out-of-date model, the kind parents might entrust to a preteen too young for a smartphone. Rafferty quickly dismissed robbery. 'Nobody's going to want to steal that,' she said. 'Perhaps I could have a quick tour?'

'Sure. We've got the living room here. There's a fold-out table for Mark to work on hidden to your left,' Faye said.

Rafferty turned, and sure enough, there was a small table bolted to the left of the sofa that could be flipped up to work on. It seemed as if even the gap under the sofa had been well-used.

Beyond the living room was a tiny bathroom with just enough space to turn on the spot. The basin was bolted into one corner, and the shower was angled away from the loo roll. His and hers toothbrushes were on a tiny shelf underneath the window. There were no luxuries, no beauty products, none of the myriad potions and lotions that Rafferty had in her own bathroom.

The next room along was the kitchenette. It was well kitted out, with high-end appliances that contrasted sharply with the empty cupboards.

'And the bedroom is at the back. It's a bit of a mess. Would you like a cup of tea, Miss Rafferty?' Faye asked politely.

'Please. Milk, two sugars.'

The kettle was boiled, two cups fetched from a tiny cupboard that Faye could barely reach, and the last two teabags retrieved from the tea caddy. The fridge was barren. When Faye retrieved from within its depths a tiny one-pint carton of milk, there was only enough for a dribble of milk in each cup.

Rafferty politely sipped her tea and then put it down again immediately.

'What's it like living on a boat?'

'I'll let you know,' Faye said. 'I'm still noticing the vibration underneath me every time we have to move the boat. It's cold, and it's cramped. But it beats prison.'

'For what it's worth, I believed you were innocent,' Rafferty said.

Faye gave her a wry smile. 'That makes two of us.' She looked away as if embarrassed by the subject of her conviction. When she looked back, her face was blank. She quickly changed the subject. 'I'll tell you one thing boat owners won't tell you.'

'What's that?'

'You've got to empty out the toilet cartridges.' Faye pulled a face. 'Disgusting.'

'That sounds horrific.'

'Between that and topping up the water and diesel, it's pretty high maintenance. Mark used to do all of it. He knew the boat inside out. He was so good at taking care of me. I don't know how I'm going to cope without h-him.' Faye began to well up, and a tear streaked down her cheek.

Rafferty instinctively reached out to hug her, but Faye recoiled. She looked Faye in the eye and said, 'We'll find him, I promise.'

They concluded their tour with a view of the tiny bedroom, which was little more than a sideways bed, a shelf full of knick-knacks, and a pile of dirty clothing on the floor. There was another door at the rear of the bedroom.

Rafferty departed determined to do everything she could for the young woman. Poor Faye needed a friend now more than ever.

Before she headed for the tube, Rafferty nipped into the local Sainsbury's, bought a bag of essential goods, and trekked them back down to *The Guilty Pleasure*. She left them on the bow without a word and quietly made her escape into the night.

Chapter 10: The Search Begins

Friday 17th June, 15:00

Rafferty returned to the office that Friday afternoon. Morton was long gone, off liaising with Kieran O'Connor at the CPS about another case. She found DI Ayala and DS Mayberry in the break room, arguing over the last slice of cake.

'H-how about we s-split it?' Mayberry said.

Ayala shrugged. 'Fine, but I get the bigger half.'

'N-no way. It's my t-turn to choose.'

Rafferty sighed. Men! 'Did your parents never teach you anything? One of you cut it in half, the other gets to pick.' She watched them as their brains slowly ticked over and they realised that her method was right. Neither could out-do the other. 'And when you've done that, I need a favour.'

Ayala smiled over a mouthful of cake. 'Anyt'ing.'

'I need one of you to look up the financials of a man called Mark Sanders. Here, I've written down everything I've got on him. Whoever isn't doing that, I want his mobile phone data. Whom he's called, when, and where his phone has been,' Rafferty said. 'And one more thing: keep it on the down-low.'

'E-even from Morton?' Mayberry said.

'Especially from Morton.' She looked between them, half-expecting to have to referee who would do each task. 'Call me when you know anything.'

***

From Rafferty's chat with Faye, she knew that Mark was one of two siblings. Less than two years ago, they'd been living at home in Ilford. When their Dad died, they each came into a small fortune. Much like their dad in his youth, both chose to make their homes on the waterways.

Jake Sanders was two years Mark's junior, and baby-faced along with it. From his website, Rafferty had found out that Jake described himself as an accountant of sorts, but really was little more than an outsourced payroll processing service. It seemed Mark wasn't the only brother with a habit of using a misleading job title. Jake's unique selling point was that he offered a 'floating office' service, moving his boat back and forth to meet up with wealthy clients all over London. Rafferty found him at his home mooring in Limehouse Basin.

His boat was much smaller than Mark's, with no dedicated kitchen. The lounge had been laid out like an office, forgoing a sofa in favour of a small partner desk and two chairs.

'Mark has always been a free spirit,' Jake said. 'I wouldn't be surprised if he was off partying somewhere. It wouldn't be the first time.'

'When was the last time he disappeared?'

'He had a business trip a few years back, State-side. He disappeared for a week in Vegas. He came back a week late, wearing the biggest shit-eating grin you've ever seen. He thought it was hilarious. Mum and Dad were worried sick, of course,' Jake said. 'Not that they're around anymore.'

'Would he ever blow off a business meeting?' Rafferty said.

Jake frowned. 'No. Never. Mark has a "work hard, play harder" philosophy. He'll get wrecked, but only after he's made the cash to pay for it.'

'Is he good with money?'

Jake snorted. 'He's good at spending it. We both got a load when Dad died. Mine was invested in my business. Mark blew his on women and fancy holidays.'

Rafferty looked around the boat. It wasn't much of a business. 'He's a womaniser, then?'

'I didn't say that.'

'No, but you said he blew his inheritance on women. Your dad died after Faye went to prison, didn't he?'

'Yes, but–'

'So, it follows that he spent money on other women behind Faye's back.' Rafferty jabbed a finger towards him accusingly.

'Fine. Mark likes to have a woman on his arm. Is that so wrong? Faye was in prison. Can you really expect a man to go four years without so much as looking at another woman?'

'I expect a man to be honest about how he feels.'

'I'm guessing you're single, then,' Jake said. 'Not that it's any of my business. Is there anything else I can do for you today?'

'Don't leave London without telling me. Call if you hear anything.'

Rafferty placed a business card on his desk and let herself out. *I'm guessing you're single, then. Cheeky bastard.*

Chapter 11: The Note

Saturday 18th June, 06:00

There was a creak on the deck that morning. Faye awoke with a start, wondering if Mark was finally home. She leapt from their shared bed, threw on her dressing gown, and stumbled out of the bedroom.

The sun blinded her as she headed for the door. A quick glance at the clock on the sitting room wall said it was five past six in the morning. She expected Mark to walk through the door any minute and give her some half-arsed excuse about why he had been gone all week.

Faye unlocked the front door and squinted into the sunshine. Her eyes sought out the source of the creak.

'Meow!' Fabby the cat was sitting outside. She ambled over and wrapped herself around Faye's legs.

'How on earth did you get out here?' Faye said. Then she caught sight of the newspaper that the cat had been curled up on. It was a copy of Friday's *The Impartial* newspaper. Black ink was splashed across the front in a bold, masculine font. It read:

BRING £100,000 IN CASH TO THE DUELLING GROUNDS AT HAMPSTEAD HEATH AT MIDNIGHT TONIGHT. COME ALONE. DO NOT INVOLVE THE POLICE, OR MARK WILL BE DEAD.

Faye's heart sank as she read the note. She quickly dialled Rafferty. 'Come on, come on! Wake up!'

Despite the early hour, Rafferty answered. 'I'll be right there. Stay put. Put the note down and do not touch it again.'

***

Saturday 18th June, 07:25

Rafferty had to call it in. A man's life hung in the balance. She hit the hands-free button on her phone as she leapt into her car and sped towards Alperton.

'Come on, Morton. Pick up. Pick up. Pick up!'

He did. 'Rafferty, aren't you supposed to be on leave?'

'He's been kidnapped,' Rafferty said. 'She's got a ransom demand. What do we do?'

'Slow down a second,' Morton replied. His voice was infuriatingly calm. 'What does the note say?'

Rafferty put her foot down as the lights ahead turned from red to green. 'I'll text you a picture when I get there. The kidnapper wants a hundred grand, tonight, or Mark Sanders is dead.'

'A hundred thousand pounds? Is Sanders rich?'

'Not as far as I know.'

'Then, why does the kidnapper think your girl can come up with a hundred thousand pounds at a few hours' notice?' Morton asked.

The question hung in the air. The kidnapper knew enough to take Mark from his own boat and to find the boat again to leave the ransom note. That spoke to a personal connection. But, apart from the life insurance money that Mark had used to purchase *The Guilty Pleasure*, neither Mark nor Faye had ever had money. She had nothing at all, and Mark wasn't doing much better. Mayberry's enquiries into his finances had shown his bank balance swinging above and below zero on a monthly basis. Mark Sanders was living a strictly pay-cheque-to-pay-cheque existence.

'What should I do?' Rafferty demanded.

'Go to her,' Morton said, still infuriatingly calm. 'Plain clothes. Don't park too near. If the kidnappers are watching, and we should assume they are, then we need to keep our involvement to the minimum. I'll get hold of SCD7. They've got specialists in this sort of thing. Until then, we're assuming jurisdiction. Can you handle babysitting Miss Atkins until then?'

'On it.'

***

The Guilty Pleasure was exactly where she'd been when Rafferty had visited earlier in the week. Another boat had moored up a few hundred yards farther along, just about far enough away for privacy, but close enough to be near the footbridge for easy access to either side of the canal.

She found Faye sitting in the living room. Her eyes were bloodshot, and her mascara had streaked.

'A-Ashley!' Faye sobbed, and threw her arms around the police officer. She was clutching the note in her fist. She hadn't put it down since Rafferty's phone call. Rafferty broke away, donned a pair of plastic gloves, and gently coaxed the ransom note from Faye.

She put the note straight into an evidence bag while a quivering Faye sobbed uncontrollably. Rafferty examined the writing through the plastic to confirm that Faye had relayed the message correctly, and then placed the bag down on the sofa so she could complete the chain of custody seal. The note was crumpled, dirty, and looked as if it had been trampled upon. *Forensic countermeasure?* Rafferty wondered.

'I've lost him, haven't I?'

'We'll do what we can.' Rafferty held up the evidence bag containing the note. 'Where exactly did you find it?'

'On the well deck at the bow. The cat was sitting on it.'

Rafferty looked around the small sitting room. There was no sign of Fabby. 'Where is she now?'

'I don't know. She'll be here somewhere. She likes to hide under tables and attack the legs of anyone who walks by.'

'Mine's like that too,' Rafferty said. 'Sweetest thing in the world, and then she's trying to kill you. Shall we go find Fabby?'

It wasn't really about the cat. Rafferty wanted to snoop around the boat, and this seemed like an inconspicuous way to distract Faye and look for any clues.

She took Faye's silence as consent and made a beeline for the stern. The last time she'd been on the boat, Rafferty had made it as far as the small kitchenette. Through the undersized doorway at the back, she found the bedroom.

It struck Rafferty as remarkably cosy. There was a double cross bed folded down from one wall, with thick blankets in a topsy-turvy pile. The space underneath the bed seemed to have been stuffed with dirty clothes, mostly Mark's, and it was there that Rafferty found Fabby the cat. Big eyes looked up at her dolefully, and then a tiny paw swiped at her left boot.

'Easy, little one. I'm not going to hurt you.'

Rafferty crouched down and held out a perfectly-manicured hand. The cat sniffed it cautiously and then edged out from under the bed. Her fur was matted, and she was thinner than Rafferty would have liked, but Faye did seem to be looking after her.

'Faye! Do you have any of the cat food I bought for you left in the cupboard?'

She hollered back from the little lounge. 'Yes, Miss Rafferty. It's in the top cupboard!'

Rafferty paused. It was a moment of normality amid the stress. For a moment, it felt like Rafferty was simply visiting an old friend. She made her way back into the kitchen, found the cat food in the cupboard, and promptly broke the pull-ring on the cap.

'Bugger.' Rafferty quickly opened the drawers in front of her. There had to be a can opener around somewhere.

'What have we here?' Rafferty whispered to herself. In the back of the cutlery drawer, she found a mobile phone.

Faye appeared in the doorway. 'I'm sorry. Did you say something, Miss Rafferty?'

'Is this Mark's phone?'

Faye nodded. 'That's it. Wherever did you find it?'

'It was in the cutlery drawer.' Rafferty eyed Faye, watching her body language.

'Ohh. He always puts his phone in odd places like that. If you leave anything on a table around here, it's liable to end up on the floor.'

'Right...' Rafferty said.

Faye seemed to have an answer for everything. For now, she wasn't distraught, either. The boat had yielded no real clues, and the note was wholly generic. To Rafferty's untrained eye, the note seemed masculine, uncompromising, and direct.

'Faye, I've got to show the note to my colleagues. Let me take it back to them, and then we can work out what to do.'

'Please! We can't involve the police. It's got to be just you.'

'At least let me send them a photograph.'

Faye acquiesced, the note was photographed, and then the photograph was promptly emailed to Morton and the team.

Chapter 12: Jurisdiction

BRING £100,000 IN CASH TO THE DUELLING GROUNDS AT HAMPSTEAD HEATH AT MIDNIGHT TONIGHT. COME ALONE. DO NOT INVOLVE THE POLICE, OR MARK WILL BE DEAD.

The photograph was displayed at one hundred times magnification on the big screen in Morton's Incident Room. A specialist from the Kidnap Unit, part of SCD7, was on the way. Morton, Ayala, and Mayberry were waiting for them.

'It's short and to the point. It sets out the demand without giving away any extra information. What do we think of the handwriting?' Morton asked, turning to Ayala and Mayberry.

Ayala held five fingers aloft and began counting off the details. 'One: all caps. Two: they've used a broad, fibre-tipped black pen, so there's not much final detail. Three: the penmanship is bold, confident, and unstyled. Four: the writer applied even pressure and shading. Five: there is no hint of hesitation marks. It's a professionally put-together note.'

Morton stroked his chin. 'You think so? The grammar is off: "or Mark will be dead." That doesn't throw up any red flags for you? Why not "or Mark will die"? Why not "or I will kill Mark"? It's a weird turn of phrase.'

'M-maybe they're trying to hide how many kidnappers there are?' Mayberry said.

'Could be. The use of "I" or "we" would indicate whether we're looking for one kidnapper or multiple kidnappers. Any other theories?'

'I have one.' The voice that came from the back of the room belonged to a woman who had once fired Morton. Morton's mind flashed back to his time working for her as an undercover officer. That hadn't ended well.

Morton turned to see that his kidnapping expert had slipped in without them noticing. She was tall for a woman, almost edging out Ayala in height, with long silver hair and a face that had aged gracefully despite the ravages of the two decades since Morton had last seen her.

'Anna Silverman, as I live and breathe! You're with the Kidnap Unit these days?'

'I am,' Silverman said simply, and turned to focus on the screen. 'This note isn't just neutral. It's impersonal. The author isn't taking responsibility for what's going on. Look at the final clause. The author doesn't *threaten* to kill Mark. They're simply stating, dispassionately, that he will die if they don't get what they want. It's like they're distancing themselves from the consequences that they're threatening.'

'Is the threat credible?' Morton asked.

Silverman stared intently at the note. 'Yes. It is. The writer has gone to great lengths to avoid errors. Writing a note like this during or after a kidnap is difficult. It's a high-pressure situation, and every second counts.'

'Could the kidnappers have written the note beforehand?' Morton asked.

'Certainly. If they did, then it suggests planning, forethought, and premeditation. That would add to the credibility of the threat.'

'So, what do we do? The victim's girlfriend is adamant that she wants to avoid police involvement,' Ayala said.

'What choice does she have? Presumably, she doesn't have a hundred grand.' Silverman looked over to Morton for confirmation.

'She hasn't got ten pounds.'

'Interesting.' Silverman pulled her iPhone from her pocket and began to peck away.

'I'm s-sorry,' Mayberry said, 'but w-what's interesting?'

'The demand is outrageous. It's a huge amount of money. Either it's serious, in which case our kidnappers are woefully misinformed, or the kidnappers never expected anyone to come through with the money.'

'T-then w-why the ruse?'

Silverman smirked. 'Why, indeed. There's only one course of action. Somebody has to appear to make the drop. And, unless we can find Faye's doppelgänger in the next few hours, Faye's going to have to be it.'

'You can't be serious!' Morton protested. 'She's barely a child. She's had no training. If we send her in unprepared, she could be facing a violent murderer in the dark. There's no way we can provide adequate cover in Hampstead Heath. That place is huge!'

'Then we had better prepare her. You've got one of your officers with her now, don't you?' Silverman said. 'She's going to have to do what she can with the time we've got.'

Chapter 13: Money, Money, Money

The logistics of sending Faye in were complicated. They couldn't be seen to whisk her away for a briefing at Scotland Yard lest the kidnappers notice and kill Mark in revenge.

After a heated debate, Silverman assumed control while Morton ran interference with the chief. If the brass caught wind of them using a civilian as a lure in a kidnapping case, there would be hell to pay.

It was down to Rafferty to brief Faye on what needed to be done. Rafferty was already on-scene. That damage had been done. If Rafferty had been made, then it was all over before it began.

The team needed help to make sure the kidnappers didn't escape. The drop-off point at the Duelling Ground in Hampstead Heath was an odd choice. The Duelling Ground itself was totally flat and exactly forty paces wide. It had been designed that way so that gentlemen in the eighteenth century could duel fairly.

It also meant there was nowhere to hide immediately before the drop-off point.

There were several approach pathways. To the south was the South Meadow, thick with trees and lots of places to hide. If the kidnapper was lying in wait, this treeline was the most likely place for them.

To the north, water cut off the entrances, with the Stone and Sham bridges acting as choke points which the police could fence in. To the east was Highgate, and to the west was the rest of the heath.

With so many ways in and out, Hampstead Heath was an excellent choice for the kidnappers. Morton knew they'd need to haul in the local constabulary. Without on-the-ground local knowledge, it would be much too easy for the kidnapper to slip away in the dark.

Air Support was a given. The latest Eurocopter EC145 would be tasked to be in the area, but not directly over Hampstead until it was time. They needed to be near enough to respond, but not near enough for the kidnapper to notice.

Everything was a balancing act. If the kidnappers were spooked, they'd flee, and Mark Sanders would die.

If Morton didn't have enough units in the area, then the kidnapper would get away with a bag of fake money. And Mark Sanders would die.

The only acceptable outcome would be to capture the kidnappers in the act and leverage their arrests to get Mark home safe.

Chapter 14: The Duelling Grounds

Saturday 18th June, 23:45

Faye had been extensively briefed. She had gone, with Rafferty following her at a distance, to the local branch of her own bank. It was there that Silverman had passed her a briefcase full of prop money. Faye's eyes had widened at the sight of what appeared to be one hundred thousand pounds in unmarked, non-sequential, twenty-pound notes. It was obvious that Faye had assumed the banknotes were real, and Silverman had no cause to correct her misunderstanding.

The case itself had a GPS tracker within it as a fall-back, though Silverman didn't share this with anyone. Not even Morton. Especially not Morton.

Silverman still didn't trust his instincts. The last time they'd worked together might have been twenty years ago, and she knew he was competent enough, but leopards rarely changed their spots. As far as Silverman was concerned, Morton was damaged goods. His conduct back then had irrevocably destroyed her trust. But he was the ranking officer, and it was his sergeant who had become the go-between, so she had no choice but to work alongside the man. It was down to Silverman to make sure that Faye did exactly as she had been instructed and that nothing went wrong. If something did go awry, it would be her neck in a vice, and it would be small comfort that Morton would be right there alongside her.

***

At a quarter to midnight, Rafferty left Faye on Merton Lane to the east of Hampstead Heath. Silverman wanted plenty of space between Faye and the police so they wouldn't spook the kidnapper.

The Air Support Unit was on standby. Morton had asked them to keep far enough away to be out of earshot, but close enough to respond in less than five minutes. They had a chopper in the air circling nearby Golders Green, ready to swoop in when they were called.

Hampstead Heath Constabulary were on hand, too. They had six men and two dogs on the ground. Four were wearing plain clothes, and two uniforms were on their regular beat circling the main pathways.

Faye knew they were out there. She'd been reassured that the police would be all around her. But she couldn't see any of them, and she assumed in turn that they could not see her. The trees loomed overhead, cutting out what little moonlight there was, and a chill ran through the summer air. Faye felt the hairs on her arms stand on end.

'I'm scared,' she whispered into the tiny microphone pinned to her lapel.

'Just keep going,' Rafferty's voice said comfortingly in her ear. 'We've got you covered. Just keep on the path going around the outside of the park until you're past the bathing pond, and then take a sharp left.'

Faye did as she was told. She clutched the briefcase she had been given close to her, her knuckles turning white, so tight was her grip. The money was the only way to get Mark back, and there was no way she was going to lose it.

The foliage overhead grew thicker as she approached the Highgate Gate. 'Do I turn here?'

'No,' Rafferty replied. 'Straight ahead, and right at the next gate.'

Faye could hear her own breathing looping through the microphone to her earpiece. Her heart thundered in her chest. For a fleeting moment, she thought she saw movement ahead of her.

'Is... is that you?' she asked.

'Keep going, Faye. You're only a few hundred feet out. You'll be there in a few minutes. We've got eyes on you. Just trust us.'

***

Morton and Ayala were wearing plain clothes, each spaced a few hundred feet from Faye. Ayala was to her right, near Sham Bridge, while Morton was by Hampstead Gate. The night seemed unnaturally still. Morton had caught no sight of anyone but Faye since she had entered the park.

'Air Support,' Morton whispered into his microphone. 'How far out are you?'

'Ninety seconds.'

'Good. Get us thermal imaging,' Morton said. 'Co-ordinate it with Silverman, but loop me in on any audio. We've got boots on the ground, but if there are any heat signatures that don't belong to one of us, I want to be the first to know.'

***

The next two minutes were the longest of Faye's short life. She struggled to maintain her composure. There, again, in the bushes – something, or someone, was moving.

The shadow appeared to be keeping pace with her as she headed north on the short path towards the Duelling Ground. It appeared to be a man. Tall, dark, and imposing. She couldn't see his face.

'It's him,' she whispered. 'He's watching me.'

'Where?' Rafferty said.

'To my left, in the bushes.'

Rafferty flicked a button on her microphone. 'Have we got anyone in the bushes to the west of Faye's location?' When nobody responded, indicating it wasn't one of them, she switched to an open all-units broadcast. 'All units are GO!'

***

Morton was closest. He legged it through the bushes towards Faye's location. As he closed in on the location where Faye had seen the man, the roar of the helicopter's engine grew louder and louder. Twenty feet out, the helicopter floodlights switched on. Three beams jolted from the sky. One fixed on the man Faye had seen, static and unmoving. The other two roamed around, seeking out Faye and Morton.

The lights were blindingly bright. Morton squinted through half-closed eyes. Not one man. Two men. One was standing and the other was... on his knees. The man standing up looked at Morton in astonishment.

'Have you got him?' Rafferty asked over the radio.

'Negative,' Morton said. 'All units, fall back. They're not our kidnappers.'

***

The two men were arrested, not for kidnapping, but for public indecency. Operation Rabbit was dead in the water. Any kidnappers would have long since been scared off by the lights and the roar of the helicopter's blades.

The officers descended on the Duelling Ground. Faye was seated on one of the two benches, a silver thermal blanket wrapped around her.

Morton gave her a half-smile as he approached. 'Take her home, Rafferty. There's nothing more she can do tonight. And stay with her, if you don't mind.'

Silverman was livid. 'Wait a minute, Inspector Rafferty. Where do you think you're going? How dare you give the order to go?'

Morton glared. 'She's taking Faye home. The last time I checked, DI Rafferty was under my command, not yours. And she was acting on my orders. If you've got a problem, you can take it up with me. Privately.'

Rafferty arched an eyebrow, silently asking Morton if he wanted her to stay, to back him up. He gave her a slight shake of the head as if to say 'get out of here', then watched her scarper with Faye under her arm.

Chapter 15: Sofa

Sunday 19th June, 02:00

Rafferty had agreed to sleep aboard *The Guilty Pleasure* "just this once" in order to reassure Faye. The poor girl hadn't heard the blackmailers come and go, and feared they could return without her knowing.

'I'm dreadfully sorry the sofa is so tiny,' Faye said. She stretched and stifled a yawn.

The sofa, while small, was just about enough to envelop Rafferty's petite frame.

'It's okay. Go get some sleep. I promise nobody is going to come aboard while I'm here, and in the morning, I'll fit new locks to the front door that only you have the keys to. How does that sound?'

Faye smiled wearily, as if she thought she could finally let her guard down long enough to go to sleep. She disappeared into the bedroom with a small wave. Snoring soon echoed from the bedroom, nasal and squeaky.

Rafferty felt her own eyes beginning to close, despite the guilt. It'd been gone one o'clock by the time they escaped the fiasco at the Duelling Ground, and Silverman's voice had echoed in her brain the entire way. It was Rafferty's fault the kidnappers had escaped. She should have known there'd be civilians in the park.

Rafferty let those thoughts slip away as she pulled an old blanket up over her. As she was falling asleep, she felt the cat jump up on her legs and find a space in the crook behind her knees. The warmth and weight of the cat was somehow homely and comforting, and soon, Rafferty drifted off to sleep.

***

Rafferty slept like a log. The sun was streaming through the window by the time she awoke a little after eight o'clock. Faye was still snoring loudly, and it took Rafferty a moment to catch her bearings.

She glanced down to make sure the cat was not still sleeping on her legs, stood, and stretched languidly.

From the corner of her eye, she saw a small piece of paper fluttering in the breeze underneath the door. It was half-in and half-out of the boat. Rafferty knelt to retrieve it and saw that it was a clipping from *The Impartial* newspaper, like the ransom note. It was crumpled and wet, and once she had laid it out flat on the dining table, Rafferty gave a gasp. In the same bold black penmanship was a second message from the kidnappers:

I SAW THE POLICE. SAME TIME TONIGHT, BURNHAM BEECHES. DROP THE MONEY AND LEAVE. THIS IS YOUR LAST CHANCE.

***

'There's got to be something, boss!' Ayala cried.

It was Sunday morning in the Incident Room and Mayberry was operating the projector screen to show the stills from the CCTV cameras around Hampstead Heath.

'I wouldn't count on it,' Morton said darkly. His face was ashen, his eyes sunken. He had not slept. 'The Heath is just too porous. The kidnappers could have entered and exited in virtually any direction. We don't know when or how they made us. They could have been watching from a distance, using innocent third parties to recce the area, or even have flown a drone over us. We wouldn't have noticed in the dark, especially with the helicopter noise in the background.'

'So, w-what do we do?' Mayberry said.

'We assume he's dead and treat this as a murder inquiry. That lets us assume jurisdiction. I can't work while I'm under Silverman's feet.'

Ayala smirked. 'What's with you and her, boss?'

'Never you mind, Bertram.' Morton took a sip from his coffee and then continued as if he had never been interrupted. 'We've got no corpse to work with. What do we know?'

'We know he's a continuous cruiser. He's in IT, but he pretends he's in finance. His brother, also a narrowboat man, thinks he's a womaniser. That's it,' Ayala said.

'That's not everything. What's changed in his life? Her. She's out of prison–'

'For a drugs offence! A non-violent one, at that.'

Morton shrugged. 'I'm not accusing her. Yet. But it's awfully suspicious that she comes back into his life, and he disappears.'

'Why?'

'Another w-woman?' Mayberry suggested.

'Another woman killed him? Or he was killed because he was seeing another woman?' Morton asked. 'Interesting theory. If he was cheating, it would give both the girlfriend and the mistress reason to be upset with him.'

Morton's phone rang as he spoke. He glanced at the caller ID. 'It's Rafferty,' he said to the others.

He set the phone down on the table, cleared his throat, and then said, 'Hello, Ashley. You're on speaker.'

'David, there's another note.'

Chapter 16: Here We Go Again

Much like the first, the second note was quickly photographed, and the picture was displayed on the big screen for Morton, Ayala, and Mayberry to analyse.

Morton read it aloud: 'I saw the police. Same time tonight, Burnham Beeches. Drop the money and leave. This is your last chance.'

'Nothing about Mark this time. But they've let slip that it's just one person,' Ayala said.

'Or they w-want us to t-think that,' Mayberry said.

'Why Burnham Beeches?' Morton wondered aloud. Burnham Beeches was a small woodland, way out in Slough, twenty-seven miles along the M40.

'They could be a local,' Ayala suggested.

'Maybe. It does suggest they've got their own transport. Burnham Beeches is miles away from any tube stations. How much land does it cover?'

Mayberry tapped away at his laptop. 'Three h-hundred and seventy-five hectares, b-boss.'

'And yet, our kidnappers haven't actually suggested a spot to drop the money. What are they expecting to happen? Faye can't just wander around looking for any old spot to throw a hundred thousand pounds on the ground. Something isn't right here,' Morton said.

'You think they're not serious about the hundred grand?' Ayala said.

'I thought it was fishy the first time. Nobody has seen any evidence that Mark would be worth that much. He's a poor guy with an even poorer girlfriend. Everything about this seems mixed up. The neat penmanship, the careful preparation, the lack of any forensic clues, all of which points to a professional. The inept note without a specific drop location points to an amateur,' Morton said.

'Two kidnappers, then.'

'I don't know. The note says "I". Everything about this is inconsistent.'

Chapter 17: The Frogwoman

Sunday 19th June, 09:45

Amber Baldwin prided herself on her little business card. It announced that she was a Police Diver, a member of the Met's Underwater & Confined Space Search Team, but she preferred to call herself "The Frogwoman". They wouldn't let her print that nickname on her card no matter how nicely she asked.

And she was the only woman on the team. The other divers were all men.

Usually, she was assigned to work on the Thames. The variety of things she'd found in the river was astounding. There'd been baggies that had once been filled with drugs. There'd been guns, knives, and stolen goods. Anything and everything could be dumped in the river's murky depths.

Today, she was on the Paddington arm of the Grand Union Canal. In many ways, the canals were the easiest part of the job. They were shallow enough to stand up in, for the most part. They were a lot warmer than the Thames, and cleaner, too. The biggest challenge was the algae. Every summer, it bloomed thick and furry across the surface of the canal. The combination of warmer water and direct sunlight seemed to help it thrive. There was duckweed, too, oodles of it. It clung to the propellers of the narrowboats and tied itself around the divers and their equipment. Finally, there were the overhanging branches. Trees lined many of the canals. Pretty, yes, but for Amber, they were another hazard to work around.

She was near Kensal Green, a popular part of town for continuous cruisers thanks to a generous fourteen-day stay policy and easy access to Kensington and Chelsea. There were permanent moorings too, with tethered electricity, waste disposal, and water on tap. Amber didn't really see the point in living on a boat if it meant being in one place all the time, but she could see the appeal in the location. Her own salary barely covered a studio in zone four.

The waters had been quiet all morning. There were a few narrowboats dotted along the towpath just past the cemetery, with the space between each boat growing greater the farther she got from Kensal Green tube station.

She could hear the sounds of the incarcerated to the south, where Wormwood Scrubs dominated the landscape. The southern wall of the prison backed onto scrub adjoining the canal. Occasionally, a jogger or a dog walker passed by, many of them pausing to glance at the woman in the water. In the distance, another member of the team was taking a break. How the man could drink coffee when it was this warm, Amber didn't know.

Behind her, the water moved in her wake. She was looking for a knife. One of the gangs that operated in the area had been linked to an open stabbing investigation, and it wouldn't be the first time they'd tried to use the canal to hide the murder weapon.

There were a few good spots to dump things. The centre of the canals was the deepest part, but many narrowboat owners had barge poles which they used to keep detritus off the propellers, and these were liable to snag on anything under the water there. The edges were shallower, but things could be concealed among the tree roots.

Today's discovery was underneath one of the boats. *The Common Touch* was a smaller narrowboat, and it appeared to have been moored up for a long time. The windows were shuttered, and one of them was broken. She was listing towards the bank, and the exposed portion of the underside of the boat was cracked. If Amber had been looking for somewhere to dump something, it would be under here.

Somebody else had had the same idea. Three feet under the boat, bobbing against the anodes on the underside of the hull, was a body.

The deceased was male, looked to be in his late twenties, and was beginning to bloat from decomposition. Amber prodded him and then recoiled. It wasn't her job to get him out from underneath there. At least, she hoped it wasn't.

It was time to call it in.

Chapter 18: The Pathologist

Sunday 19th June, 11:30

'Yep, he's definitely dead,' Doctor Larry Chiswick smirked.

The pathologist was an aging man with hippy-length grey hair and a personality that veered between much too serious and far too mirthful. He'd been summoned from his Sunday morning lie-in to attend to the body in Kensal Green canal, and he was taking great pleasure in making everyone else working know it. If he had to be miserable, so did they.

'Gee, thanks. Am I good to go?' Amber asked.

'Sure. As soon as you've fished our boy out of the water.'

'Me?' She'd never had to handle a dead body before.

'You think I'm getting in there with you? Slide him out from underneath the boat and give him a shove from underneath. He won't hurt you.'

Amber reluctantly did as she was told. The body felt swollen, slightly soft, and a ripe, sweet smell hit her the moment he had been freed from the confines of *The Common Touch*.

'On three. One, two, three!'

Soon, the dead man was on the towpath.

'What's the current like in there?' Chiswick asked.

'Weak. It's non-tidal, so the eddies trail whatever boats come past.'

'That explains the abrasions. I can't see any other signs of injury. I'll have to get him back to the morgue for autopsy. Can you bag me a water sample?' Chiswick said.

Amber nodded and took the proffered sample vial.

Chiswick smiled curtly. 'Thank you.'

***

It didn't take long to identify the body. As soon as Chiswick entered 'canal' as a keyword, the system flagged up a missing person. The descriptions were a match, and the face looked similar enough, though it was impossible to be sure with the adipocere.

'Mark Sanders. Who put you in a watery grave?' Chiswick mused. He clicked through to look for an open investigation. He needed to know whom to inform that he had Sanders in the morgue.

The name DCI Morton was listed under 'Senior Investigating Officer'.

'Trust you to open a murder enquiry before you've even got a body.' This time, Chiswick's smile was genuine. He picked up his phone and debated which call to make first: let Morton know, or get next of kin to identify the body.

'Sod it. Formalities first. Morton can wait.'

***

Jake Sanders arrived a little after lunchtime with a local constabulary officer who had been dispatched to perform the next-of-kin notification. He looked a lot like how Chiswick imagined Mark would have looked before he died: he had a strong, chiselled jawline, grey-blue eyes, and sandy ash-blond hair. Even Chiswick had to admit he was handsome.

His jaw was set, and he was desperately trying not to cry. There was a quiver to his lip that Chiswick knew no man could fake.

Chiswick led him through to where Mark's body was lying underneath a sheet.

'I have to warn you, Mr Sanders, that your brother may not look as you remember him due to his time in the water. Are you sure you're ready?'

Jake Sanders gave the slightest nod.

Chiswick pulled back the sheet just enough to reveal the head, and Jake Sanders swore.

Though he knew from Jake's reaction what the answer would be, Chiswick still had to ask. 'Is this your brother?'

'That's him. Cover him up, for God's sake, please!'

Then Jake turned and dashed out of the room.

'Third door on the left!' Chiswick called after him. They never did make it to the bathroom.

Chapter 19: Stakeout

Sunday 19th June, 12:00

Morton was in the middle of preparing for a trip out to Burnham Beeches when he got the call from the pathologist. He relayed the news to the waiting Incident Room.

Ayala was standing by the coffee machine, mainlining as much coffee as he could. He'd been up for thirty-six hours and no longer looked his usually impeccable self. Mayberry was sitting at the conference table snoring, his head laid on his right arm, while Silverman hovered nearby, glaring disapprovingly.

'Sanders is dead. The doc's got him on ice downstairs. Mrs Silverman, your role here is done. Thank you so much for your assistance. We'll take it from here.'

Morton gestured for Ayala to escort her out of their Incident Room. She began to protest, and Morton smiled sweetly. He said nothing until she was gone.

'Does this mean we can go get some shut-eye, boss?' Ayala asked.

'Nope. We're going to the drop point at Burnham Beeches.'

'What?' Ayala exclaimed.

'The kidnapper is the killer. We know where the kidnapper will be tonight. Wake Mayberry up, go change into your civvies, and make up a tent somewhere in the Beeches. I want you to look like you've been there all day so you blend in. And yes,' Morton added, 'you do have time for a nap.'

'On it,' Ayala said. 'Mayberry! Wake up!'

***

Sunday 19th June, 22:00

Burnham Beeches was an hour out. Morton drove, with Rafferty and Faye in the back seat of his car. He used the time to watch Faye in the mirror. She seemed withdrawn, mistrustful. She barely said a word to him, and only when she was spoken to directly.

Rafferty had a little more luck. The one topic Faye seemed to enjoy talking about was her cat. That, she had in common with Rafferty.

Faye seemed less stressed than Morton would have been if it had been Sarah who had been "kidnapped". He understood her mistrust of men and of the police. She had been through much in her short years, and yet, somehow, her lack of visible emotion was concerning. Was it simply that Faye had learned to bottle up her emotions? Prison could do that.

'So, Faye, it'll be like last night. At midnight, you'll get out of my car and walk fifty feet ahead. You'll drop the bag, turn around, and get straight back in the car.'

Faye brightened as if relieved she would not have to go through the trauma she had endured in Hampstead Heath. 'That's it?'

'That's it,' Morton confirmed. 'I'll leave my headlights on full beam the whole time so we'll be able to see you. If you get into any trouble, scream. Got it?'

'Got it... Mr Morton?'

'Yes?'

'Won't the kidnappers know you're the police?' Faye asked.

Kidnappers, plural. Morton made a mental note. 'I'm sure they will. They'll see us drive up, drop the money, and then they'll see us leave.'

'Oh... okay. When will we get Mark back? Tonight?'

The question seemed earnest, innocent, and even childlike. Morton knew he couldn't give her an answer without lying to her, so he said nothing.

The rest of the journey was silent. Eventually, Morton turned onto the pretentiously named Lord Mayor's Drive. He pulled past the visitor centre and parked up just beyond a small picnic table. It was gone eleven at night, and nobody was to be seen.

He thumbed his encrypted radio. 'Ayala, Mayberry, you there?'

'We're here. We saw you pull in.'

'Seen anything this afternoon?'

'Nothing of note,' Ayala's voice crackled over the radio. 'It's been pretty quiet since suppertime. I've got thermal imaging cameras pointed in all directions. When they get here, we'll know it.'

'Good work, Ayala,' Morton said. There was a moment of silence, and he could practically imagine the junior officer blushing. Compliments weren't Morton's style, but this one was deserved. He squinted into the darkness, trying to find their tent. 'Where are you guys?'

'About four hundred feet ahead and to your left. Our tent is dark green, so you won't be able to spot us.'

Just as long as the kidnappers don't stumble over you in the dark, Morton thought.

Morton's watch eventually beeped for midnight. He turned to Faye. 'Go.'

He flicked his headlights to max as Faye stepped out of the car, and a long stretch of grass was illuminated them. He heard the door slam shut as Faye stomped off with the briefcase in hand. She set it down as instructed and leapt back into the car a minute later. She appeared to be shivering, so Morton casually flicked the heating up.

'Ayala, we've made the drop.'

'Got it, boss. We're watching. No sign of any heat signatures so far. You off?'

'We'd better be. I want to make a show of leaving in case someone's watching from a distance. Happy camping, boys.'

***

Ayala and Mayberry took turns napping. One a.m., two a.m., three a.m., four. Nothing was showing on the thermal imaging cameras. Twice, Ayala got out to check that they were tracking properly, though he dared not venture over to the briefcase, just in case.

At six a.m., joggers began to appear. One wandered over to the case, looked around, and then backed away. Ayala held his breath. Could this be it?

He watched as the jogger pulled out their mobile. Who could they be calling?

A few minutes later, he had his answer. Dispatch called out for units in the area. A jogger had called in a bomb threat. The stakeout was over.

Chapter 20: The Autopsy

Monday 20th June, 10:30

Dr Larry Chiswick hummed cheerfully as he cut open Mark Sanders. Until the lab phone rang, anyway.

'Dr Chiswick? This is Forensic Services. I'm calling about the blood sample you sent over yesterday for analysis.'

'The Sanders sample?' Chiswick asked. He had drawn it the first time he looked at the body, and had sent it off in the hopes of being the first in the queue come Monday morning. To get a call so quickly was unusual.

'Yes, sir. I'm calling to warn you that Mr Sanders was HIV positive.'

Chiswick looked around Autopsy Room 1. Sanders' blood was all over the place.

'Shit.'

***

Two hours of clean-up and one course of post-exposure prophylaxis later, Chiswick was back at work. He was doubly careful this time, wearing thicker-than-usual gloves that made his hands feel clumsy and numb.

He had his trusty voice recorder set up on a side table to record his thoughts as he examined the body. The tape would be taken down by his diener to be transcribed and entered into the record.

'Mark Sanders, age twenty-eight. The body was discovered trapped beneath a narrowboat in warm water, rendering a precise post-mortem interval impossible to calculate. From the adipocere, I would estimate that Mr Sanders died approximately a week ago. The police notes record him as having been seen alive by several witnesses on the night of Sunday 12th June, and as such, this is the earliest possible and most likely date of death according to the best evidence available.'

Adipocere was a soap-like material. Many of the police officers that Chiswick worked with thought it was a covering, something that formed over the skin. In fact, it was the body itself. The process of saponification converted the fatty acid esters under the skin into soap. It made the body look almost as if it had been mummified. For Chiswick and his colleagues, it was a godsend because it stabilised the body, preventing further decay.

'At first inspection, I assessed there to be no visible peri-mortem injuries. Closer inspection on the body confirms this. There are numerous cuts and abrasions, all of which appear to have occurred after the body was placed in the water. In particular, I note a breakage to the twelfth rib on the right-hand side. There is no localised bleeding in this area, which indicates the injury was post-mortem. At the time of recovery, the body was found floating face-up, with the right side pointing towards the centre of the canal. It is possible that this injury occurred as a result of the body being nudged underneath the narrowboat known as *The Common Touch*. It would have taken considerable force from a blunt object to create the impact impression I see before me. The impact impression appears to be triangular, with radiating breaks approximately two inches long.'

Chiswick paused. It was easy to rule out things that hadn't killed Mark Sanders. But there was no sign of an injury which would have proven fatal.

Chapter 21: Team Meeting

Monday 20th June, 13:00

'Doc says we've got nothing,' Ayala relayed. 'He says there's no visible sign that Mark was struck, shot, stabbed, or otherwise injured.'

'Then that leaves us with the less visible,' Morton said. 'Poison, drowning, etc.'

'Doc says the water is making things difficult. He's still working on it. The lab has a rush on toxicology. Even with top priority, we're looking at a day or two there.'

'Then we start with the basics. Mayberry, the board, if you please.'

Detective Sergeant Mayberry had been sitting quietly at the back of the room. He wasn't one to talk much, but he was always listening. His notes were impeccable, and his handwriting bordered on calligraphy. Morton watched as he picked up a pen and wheeled a whiteboard in front of the projector screen.

'Let's start with the victim,' Morton said. 'What do we know?'

Ayala began to reel off facts about the victim as if he was reading from Wikipedia. 'We know he's twenty-eight. He's got a brother, but his parents are long gone. He owns a seventy-foot narrowboat called *The Guilty Pleasure* which he lives aboard. He and his girlfriend Faye continuously cruise the canals, moving up and down the waterways so they don't have to pay mooring fees.'

'Good. We know he's physically fit. He works in IT, but on the sales side. You getting this down?'

Morton looked over to Mayberry, who hastily began scribbling on the board. A spider's nest of information began to appear, each fact an arm arcing away from the name Mark Sanders, which was writ bold in the middle of the board.

'What about the people in his life?' Morton asked. 'Rafferty?'

Rafferty stirred. She looked tired. Another night of babysitting was beginning to take its toll. Ayala thrust a mug of coffee into her hands. She smiled and took a sip. 'There's Faye, obviously. She moved on board *The Guilty Pleasure* a little over a fortnight ago.'

'How long have they been together?' Morton said.

'Four and a half years, including her four-year stint inside. I checked the visitor logs, and he visited her once a week without fail.'

'Nice guy. What was she in for?'

'Possession.'

Morton whistled. 'Four years for possession? Somebody needed a better lawyer.'

'Faye has had a very unlucky life.'

'I'm sorry to have to ask, but what exactly is your relationship with her?' Morton said.

'It was way back, at least ten years ago, now, and I was with Sapphire,' Rafferty said, referring to the team responsible for investigating rape and serious sexual assault. 'I was investigating Norman Atkins, Faye's stepdad. The case fell through. Norman was a business owner, a pillar of the community, and the CPS dropped the prosecution like a hot potato.'

'Didn't they get Faye removed from his custody?' Ayala asked.

'They tried. Child Protective Services got involved. I don't know what happened after that. I gave Faye my number and told her to call me if she ever needed anything, even if she just wanted to talk,' Rafferty said.

'Did she ever call?'

'Twice. Once was when she was arrested. She'd fallen in with a gang, though I don't think she realised it. One of them asked her to take a backpack over to another friend. Faye had no idea what was in it. She ended up going down for possession.'

Morton rolled his eyes. He'd heard a lot of sob stories in his day. 'And the second call?'

'That was last week, when Mark went missing.'

'You mean when Mark was murdered,' Morton retorted.

'We don't know that for sure. The doc hasn't determined cause of death. It could be an accident.'

'An accidental kidnapping plot. That's a new one to me.'

'She wasn't the only person in his life. You're jumping to the conclusion that she did it because all you see is a criminal,' Rafferty protested.

'But we can't rule her out,' Morton said.

'I saw her, David. Her grief, her anguish. That was genuine. What if we can prove it?'

'How?'

'Her handwriting. I had her write down everything she could think of about his usual routine.' Rafferty produced the note from her handbag. 'This handwriting is looping, girly, feminine.'

'And?'

'And the kidnap note isn't.'

Morton thought for a moment and then raised his hands in surrender. 'We'll have to get a handwriting expert to confirm that. But it still doesn't prove she didn't kill him.'

'So, what's your case theory? She killed him, and someone else faked a kidnapping? You think we're looking for a team of two?' Rafferty looked from Morton over to Ayala, and then to Mayberry, searching out an alternative idea.

'It could be the brother,' Ayala said. 'What was he like?'

'Quick to sell Mark out. He practically yelled that Mark was a womaniser. If Mark was cheating, then that could point back at Faye,' Rafferty said.

'We're into wheels-within-wheels logic territory here,' Morton said. 'Jake could be pointing the finger to distract us from looking at him. We could be looking at the spurned lover, annoyed that Faye is back in Mark's life.'

'Or his lover's partner, angry at her for cheating,' Ayala said, throwing another possibility into the mix.

'Ignore the love angle for a moment. We've got no evidence either way,' Morton ordered. 'Who else is there?'

Rafferty's hand shot up. 'Pip Berryman. He worked with Mark and landed Mark's whale client when Mark didn't show.'

Morton turned to Mayberry. 'Write him on the board. Anyone else?'

'The other woman,' Ayala said. 'The one he's been cheating on Faye with.'

'We've discussed that. Unless you've got some sort of evidence, it's pure speculation,' Morton said.

'I t-think I c-can prove it,' Mayberry said. He pointed at Mark's phone, which Rafferty had bagged and brought back to examine. 'L-look at h-his messages.'

Morton picked up the phone. 'You had IT crack this?'

'Y-yes. It's p-pay as you go.'

'Good lad.'

The phone unlocked with a single swipe, and Morton went straight for Mark's messages. Auntie Ethel, boring. Brother, nothing interesting. Faye, already on record from looking at her phone.

'Aha!'

There, listed without a name, was a number which Mark had texted almost daily for over a year. The messages were prolific, at all times of the day and night, and many were graphic in nature.

'H-he's b-been sexting her.'

'Or him,' Ayala chipped in. 'What? We don't know.'

'Let's find out.' Morton put the phone on speaker, placed it in the centre of the conference room table, and dialled the number.

It rang eight times, and then went to voicemail.

'Hi, you've reached Laura. I can't take your call right now, so leave me a message!'

***

'That's odd,' Chiswick mused.

Each of the victim's organs had been weighed and the result compared with the normal weight established over tens of thousands of historical autopsies. Mark Sanders' lungs were almost bang-on average weight. He hadn't drowned.

If, as Chiswick had hypothesised, Mark Sanders had been drowned in the canal, then his lungs would show signs of emphysema aquosum, more commonly known as waterlogged lungs. It was a neat explanation for Mark's death. He hadn't been shot, stabbed, or physically assaulted. Toxicology wasn't back yet, but there were no signs of poison in his system, either.

Drowning just seemed to fit. The most obvious signs – petechial haemorrhaging, Paltauf's spots, the presence of pulmonary surfactant, etc – were missing, but that could easily be explained by the time Mark had been submerged in the canal.

But, alas, no water on the lungs meant no drowning.

Back to the drawing board once more.

Chapter 22: It's Never Lupus

Monday 20th June, 15:00

Rafferty's judgement was usually sound, but Morton had to know for sure. They searched the boat quickly and quietly, and found nothing of note.

One thing Morton did snag was a shopping list in Faye's handwriting.

'Why do you want that? I've already got a handwriting sample,' Rafferty said.

'Because she knew you'd be taking that note. If she wanted to fake her handwriting, it would have been child's play to plant the note on you, and thus fool us as to who had written the ransom notes. She'd have no reason to conceal her handwriting when she was doing a shopping list.'

The shopping list, Rafferty's note, and the two ransom notes were quickly taken down to forensics for analysis. The handwriting analyst was a Frenchwoman, a newcomer to the Met by the name of Gabrielle Boileau. Around her neck, she was wearing a Huguenot cross on a gold chain which offset her piercing blue eyes and the perfectly white teeth that could have come from a magazine.

She started talking as soon as Morton arrived, without pomp or ceremony.

'You've got two authors. No ifs, no buts. One person wrote this sample and this sample.' Gabrielle Boileau indicated the shopping list and the note Rafferty had supplied. 'Another person wrote these two.' Boileau indicated the ransom notes.

'How sure are you?'

'I'm always sure, *cher*. I don't make mistakes, and I don't take to policemen questioning my work, either.' Her accent made it sound like she was saying "please-men", and Morton had to slyly suppress a smile.

'Could you walk me through how you know that? Pretend I'm a simpleton who doesn't know anything about this.'

Morton could have sworn he heard her mutter: 'Pretend?' but she turned briskly back towards the notes.

'Look at the ransom notes. Strong, even pressure, no hesitation. There is a slight lean to the left. The letters are perfectly formed,' Gabrielle said.

'I can see that.'

'A blind man could see that. On the other hand, these' – she pointed to the shopping list and note – 'are scratchy, hesitant, flowery, and uneven. The writing slopes to the right. The samples are wholly inconsistent.'

'Could someone fake this difference?'

'Is it possible? *Oui*. Likely? *Non*. *Cher*, this woman is not your kidnapper.'

Morton cursed. He hated being wrong.

The first suspect was always the lover. Faye had motive if she knew Mark had been cheating. She was the new thing in Mark's life. She had access to the boat. Except for the pesky note, Morton would have sworn he had Faye Atkins bang to rights.

God, he hated being wrong.

Worse still, he'd have to apologise to Rafferty.

Chapter 23: Love, Life, and Betrayal

Monday 20th June, 16:45

Faye arrived shortly before teatime on Monday. Yet again, it had meant Rafferty physically going to fetch her for Faye to agree to an interview, and only then on the condition that it was informal.

They made a space in the visitors' room on the ground floor. It was brightly lit, with colourful walls, and a small collection of kids' toys had been placed in a basket beneath the window.

Morton took the seat beside the basket, leaving Rafferty and Faye to sit opposite him.

'Hi, Faye. How are you holding up?' he asked once they were all seated.

At Morton's suggestion, Rafferty had broken the news in private before they left the boat. He wanted to know how she'd react away from the station, and would then benchmark that response against her emotions during the interview. While the note ruled her out as the faux-kidnapper, Morton had learned the hard way never to trust a witness.

'I'm okay. It still hasn't sunk in that Mark is... gone. I don't know how I'll cope without him.'

'I'm sorry for your loss. Can you tell me a bit about Mark?' Morton said.

'What do you want to know?'

'Tell me about his work,' Morton said, starting with the less controversial of the two topics he needed to bring up.

'He's a Project Manager for Berryman Financial Services. They're actually an IT company; the financial part refers to their clients,' Faye said. She seemed to almost be reeling it off by rote, despite the note of pride in her voice.

Morton scribbled in his notepad. She was still using the present tense when she referred to Mark, as if he were still alive. 'It sounds competitive. What were his colleagues like?'

'Awful. They kept trying to poach his sales. He's been there for a couple of years, and every week he'd tell me a new story about someone trying to take credit for what he'd done. There was one guy, Pip, who just wouldn't give up.'

Morton arched an eyebrow disbelievingly. Pip Berryman was the owner's son and was heir to a large fortune. He didn't seem the type to need to get competitive with an unqualified school leaver like Mark.

It was time to segue into relationships. 'Was he outgoing? Did he have a large group of friends?'

'It's always been the three of us, really. Mark, Laura, and I.'

Laura. Morton's eyes danced. 'Who's Laura?'

'Our best friend,' Faye said. 'We've known each other since preschool. We've been inseparable ever since.'

Morton cut to the chase, hoping to surprise her. 'Did you know Mark's been sending sexually explicit messages to Laura?'

Faye looked shocked. 'She's my best friend! She'd never do that. You're wrong. Dead wrong.'

Morton held up Mark's phone with one of the less-explicit messages on display. 'Is this Laura's number?'

As if in slow motion, Faye thrust a hand into her bag to retrieve her phone and then opened her own contacts list. She scrolled down to Laura's number and mouthed each digit as she compared.

'That bitch.'

Chapter 24: Can't Stop Loving You

Tuesday 21st June, 10:45

Laura Keaton had long since moved on from Ilford. Gone was the accent, and gone were the mannerisms of the council estate. She had long since traded the London Borough of Ilford for the shining steel and glass of a luxury penthouse flat thirty seconds from the centre of Canary Wharf.

It didn't take a genius to realise she was trading on her looks. She had three GCSEs, and not one above a grade D, hardly cause for sudden wealth. Nor would the six months she'd spent working in an Ilford nail salon stand her in good stead for her dizzying ascent into London's middle class.

The flat, and the money, belonged to Tim Fowler. Unlike Mark, Tim really did work in finance. He worked for one of the old firms, the market makers, and made a much more consistent margin than many bankers. He was older, wiser, and probably should have known better. Like many a man, he was a fool for a pretty face.

'She is really pretty,' Rafferty said grudgingly.

She was standing with Morton outside the interview suite at the Met. Laura had come in voluntarily, ostensibly to help with enquiries.

'Is she?' Morton said. He cast a sly glance at Laura. She was pretty attractive.

'Don't play that game with me. You're telling me you didn't notice the pearly white teeth, the enormous boobs, and the porcelain-perfect skin? Not to mention all the diamonds dripping from her fingers. I've seen less bling in the Tower of London.' Rafferty put her hands on her hips and sighed enviously.

'All I see is a murder suspect.'

Rafferty smirked. 'Liar.'

Morton ignored her. 'You can watch from here. I think if we both interview her, she'll shut down.'

'Going on the Morton charm offensive, are you? Isn't she a bit young for you?' Rafferty chided him as he headed into the interview suite.

Morton sat down, produced a blank tape to record the interview, and unwrapped it in front of Laura.

'What's that for?'

'Standard procedure, I'm afraid. You don't mind, do you?' Morton said.

'Not at all.'

The tape was begun, the formalities completed, and Morton quickly settled into the rapport-building stage of the interview. 'You've known Mark and Faye for a long time, haven't you?'

'Since we were kids. Faye's like my sister.'

'She said exactly the same thing,' Morton said.

He watched as Laura began to open up to the interview. She leant forward more, and her hands became more animated. She didn't even know she was doing it. Morton mirrored her posture, closing the gap between them.

'She did? That's so sweet of her.'

'Was Mark always part of your group?'

Laura leant back a tiny bit, apparently uncomfortable with the sudden shift to Mark. 'Not always. I mean, we knew him back then. Ilford's a small place, and he lived one street over when we were little, but it wasn't until we were teenagers that we really hung out.'

'Isn't he older than you?'

'Yeah, he is. Like five years. That's probably why we didn't hang out so much. He was always the cool kid, and then, when his dad got their first boat, he was always throwing parties on it.'

'That sounds exciting. I'm... old, and I've still never been to a boat party.'

'You should! They're amazing,' Laura said. 'Like, the first one I ever went to – I was, like, fifteen–'

And Mark was twenty, Morton thought.

'– And we had this bottle of vodka, and then...' her voice trailed off as she realised that she was confessing, on tape, to underage drinking.

Morton waved her off. 'I'm not going to arrest you for underage drinking.'

'Right. Well, like I said, it was one hell of a party.'

'When did Faye and Mark start dating?' Morton said.

'It was a while after that. They flirted for ages. Mark thought of himself as a bit of a player. They started dating properly, like, six months before she went to prison. I'm not sure when it became Facebook-official. I can check?'

'Thank you, but no. Were they happy together?'

'Absolutely. He was her whole world.'

'Was she his?' Morton said craftily backing her into the corner.

She hesitated, and then said, 'Yes. He loved her.'

'Hmm,' Morton said. He let the silence build between them and then produced a folder of printouts of messages Laura and Mark had exchanged. 'Perhaps, then, you might know why Mark was texting another woman?'

'He can't have been. He wouldn't.' Laura's voice had an edge to it, a tremor that hadn't been there before.

'He did. We have his mobile.'

'Who is she?' Laura said with a butter-wouldn't-melt expression. She knew it was her number and should have owned up to it straight away.

'Let's find out.' Morton nodded towards the observation window. Out of sight, Rafferty dialled Laura's number. Her phone began to ring.

'Fuck.' She blushed fuchsia.

'You were the other woman.'

'Please don't tell Tim. It was just... I like the attention. I liked a man my own age wanting me that way.'

'Was it physical?' Morton said.

'We kissed. Once. It was a mistake.'

'You never slept with him?'

'Never.'

'You're sure?' Morton eyed the tape recording. If she said yes, he would have to tell her about Mark's HIV status. If she continued to deny it, his status was confidential – and none of her business.

'Of course I'm sure!'

'Okay. Thank you for coming in. If anything changes, please give me a call. Interview terminated at eleven twenty-two.'

***

Faye's attention seemed to come and go. Her eyes were glazed over, and she seemed not to notice Rafferty watching her intently. She wouldn't answer Rafferty's questions except to insist that she and Mark had not slept together since she was released from prison.

Visiting a genito-urinary medicine clinic was always a stressful situation, and more so than ever when it was such a serious test. If Mark was HIV positive, then Faye had to get tested. They had no way of knowing if Mark had been positive before Faye was incarcerated, and the risk was too great.

'Are you sure you don't want me to come in with you? Faye? Hello?' Rafferty reached forward and gently touched Faye on the arm.

'What're you doing? Don't touch me!' Her expression contorted into one of anger.

Rafferty was taken aback. 'Sorry! I just wanted to check you were sure you don't need me to come in with you.'

'Come in where?' Faye demanded, as if she had suddenly awakened to find herself in a medical waiting room.

This time, it was Rafferty's turn to look bewildered. 'In the exam room?'

'Oh... no. I'll be fine.'

A nurse came to call for Faye a few minutes later. Rafferty decided to wait. Faye would no doubt need a lift home.

Rafferty's thoughts turned to the other woman, Laura. It was obvious that she too had slept with Mark, but until Laura admitted that, Rafferty's hands were tied. The boss' orders were strict: Mark's status was confidential, and they could only tell someone who was, by their own admission, at risk of exposure from his activity.

Rafferty could only hope that Faye would pass along the information.

Chapter 25: Jealousy

Wednesday 22nd June, 08:45

It was easy to find Tim Fowler, but much harder to get in to see him. His office was on the twenty-second floor of a tightly guarded skyscraper in the square mile, no doubt located there solely for its proximity to the London Stock Exchange. Morton had to threaten the front desk with the inconvenience of having police loitering outside while he sent someone for a search warrant. They caved when Morton refused to leave, and he was escorted up to Tim's office accompanied by a security guard.

Tim was a tall man. He was greying, balding, and had what Sarah would have called "a dad bod". At Morton's appearance, he waved off the security guard and invited Morton to sit down.

The office was sparse, with a huge oak table and six computer monitors dominating the room. Behind Tim's desk, floor-to-ceiling windows showed off a panoramic view of the London skyline.

Unlike Mark, who pretended to work in finance, Tim really was a trader. But like Mark, he was in software too. Tim was a small margin trader, making tens of thousands of trades per minute, nickel and diming buyers and sellers at minimal risk.

'It's called front-running,' Tim explained. 'I watch for market movements – that is to say, people buying or selling any given stock. If someone is buying up a company, I buy the cheapest shares before they do and then sell them on to them for a tiny profit.'

'And how do you get in before them?' Morton asked.

'Two ways,' Tim said, holding up two fingers as if lecturing a child. 'First, our trades are all automated. Nobody can work faster than a computer, and we have the best system money can buy.'

'And second?'

'Physical proximity. When you're trying to make a trade a thousandth of a second faster than the next guy, being within a hundred yards of the London Stock Exchange means you can beat the guy who's half a mile away. Ordinary traders who don't operate out of the city never get a chance.'

'I bet you'd hate a Tobin tax, then,' Morton said, referring to the recurring idea that trades should be taxed to prevent exactly this kind of behaviour.

Tim laughed. 'You're not wrong. I'd either go bust or relocate to another jurisdiction, along with everyone else. It'll never happen.'

'And if it did?'

'Que sera, sera. I'm making hay while the sun is shining. If the gravy train stops, I've got enough stashed away to ride out the storm.'

I bet you have, Morton thought.

'And what about Mark? Does some of this lucre trickle down to the companies providing ancillary services?'

'Mark was small-time,' Tim said with a dismissive wave of his hand. 'Berryman are behind the curve on the tech.'

'Aren't you one of their clients?' Morton asked.

'Sort of. I threw Mark a bone and hired him to work on a prototype system for us. It's all in a sandbox that we'll never use. He's just not up to running our systems. I can get better guys for less money by outsourcing. And the best quants and programmers are never going to be found somewhere like Berryman.'

'Where would they be, then?'

'I've got them locked up downstairs,' Tim joked. His face creased up as a he cracked a smile. There were well-worn crow's feet around his eyes and equally deep furrows on his forehead. 'Two hundred grand a year golden handcuffs, all the tech they could ever want, and stock options for those smart enough to push me for more. It sounds like a lot, but we'd pay ten times that to keep them around. Do me a favour, don't tell them that.'

'How did you and Mark meet?'

'Work. He was in his first week with Berryman when he came knocking. He was old-school. No bullshit phone calls, email proposals, or calling my people. Nope, he pretended to be delivering my lunch and barged right into this office. That took balls of steel.'

'So, you hired him?'

'Nah. I threw him out. Security tossed his ass in less than two minutes. He stood outside until close of business, just waiting for me. I thought I was in for a fight. Some guys just can't handle rejection. I took a couple of our security team down with me, just in case.'

'And?'

'And he pitched me again. Begged for five minutes. Poor bastard was soaking wet. It was December, and he was standing there in a cheap polyester suit, so desperate to land a client that he'd freeze half to death just to try one more time. I had to respect that. Any man willing to work that hard is worth taking a chance on.'

'It sounds like he owed you a lot,' Morton said.

'He didn't owe me shit. He introduced me to the love of my life. Without him, I'd still be doing coke off a pocket-money prostitute every night. Now, I get to spend my days with Laura.'

He sounded sincere. Morton bit his lip. Sometimes, part of the job meant shattering a happy illusion. 'Then, you didn't know they were cheating on you? Mark and Laura, that is.'

Tim's eyes widened. His face reddened, and then, before Morton could duck, Tim lobbed his mug of coffee in his direction. 'Get out! Get out, get out, get out!'

Morton stood up, calmly removed his jacket, and pulled a tissue from the inside pocket to dab up the coffee. 'Mr Fowler, you're upset, so I'll give you one chance to apologise and offer to pay for my dry cleaning. If you're not smart enough to take that chance, I will arrest you for assaulting a police officer in the course of his duty. Do you understand me?'

Tim slumped in his chair. 'I'm sorry. I just... I love her. She's all I ever wanted. I gave her everything: a home, nice clothes, holidays to exotic places. Who am I kidding? It was never me she wanted. It was just my money. It's always the goddamned same!' Tim thumped his desk, causing everything on it to leap half an inch in the air.

'This isn't the first time for you, is it?'

'No. Every goddamned time. Every woman.'

Morton almost felt sorry for him, until he remembered that Tim Fowler was a banker. He wanted to ask, 'Have you thought about dating a woman your own age?'

Instead, he said, 'What was your relationship with Faye like?'

'Non-existent. Laura mentioned her a few times, but I only met her the once.'

'When was that?'

'Sunday before last.'

'The twelfth?'

'That's it. We all had dinner on Mark's boat. It was a double date, or it was supposed to be. I can't believe they sat next to me all night, lying to me the whole time.'

'And when did you leave the boat that night?'

'About nine, I think. I was the first to leave. I had to be up early on Monday for a conference call with our investors. I left just after Faye said she was heading to bed. She claimed she was tired and not used to being out of prison just yet, but I think she found all the banking talk a bit boring, to be honest.'

'What about the others?'

'Mark and Laura were going to finish off the open bottles of wine, then call it a night.'

'Do you know what time Laura came home that night?' Morton asked.

'Sorry, no. She was there when I woke up. I guess she came in after I turned in for the night. That was about eleven.'

'Thank you for your time, Mr Fowler.' Morton paused. He couldn't leave without giving the man some sort of heads-up. 'Mr Fowler? One bit of unsolicited general advice. Whenever you find out a partner has cheated on you, get tested. Just to be safe.'

Chapter 26: The Doppelgänger

Wednesday 22nd June, 13:00

Four suspects, four possible killers.

There was Faye, the butter-wouldn't-melt girlfriend. There was Laura, the mistress spurned. And there was Tim, the friend betrayed. Each had their name and photograph plastered on the wall in the Incident Room. Mayberry had scrawled motives next to each.

Finally, there was the brother who didn't appear to have a motive.

'But why would the brother kill Mark?' Ayala asked.

Rafferty slapped a handful of photocopies on the table. 'I think I can answer that.'

Morton leant forward in his chair and snatched up the set of photocopies. The first was marked 'Life Insurance'. Morton whistled.

'That's right, a hundred and fifty thousand. The brother gets the lot,' Rafferty said.

'And, presumably, the boat?' Morton said.

'We've got no sign of a will yet. It's a good bet that Jake gets everything, and he needs it, too. Look at the second printout.'

The second printout was a credit report on Jake Sanders. 'Four hundred? I've seen bankrupts with better scores than that. What did he do, crash a bank?'

'Close,' Rafferty said. 'He took out a payday loan. Just one. A measly hundred quid at that. Then he borrowed from some-one else to pay the first loan. And again. And again. Before he knew it, he was up to his eyeballs in debt.'

'Rollovers. That explains it. Not a lavish lifestyle then?'

'He certainly wanted to keep up appearances. He's got one nice suit, one nice tie, and one nice pair of cufflinks, all to show off to potential clients. But no money. Jake Sanders was in dire straits, and Mark's death solves all of his money worries.'

'Nice work, Rafferty. Before we bring him in, does anyone else have anything to add?'

Mayberry silently raised a hand. 'W-what if they k-killed the wrong M-Mark?'

'What do you mean?' Morton said.

'H-here.' Mayberry turned to his laptop and plugged it back into the projector screen. He showed the team a Facebook profile.

'Mark Sanders. Another Mark?'

'Y-yes.'

'Is this Mark rich?' Morton asked, thinking of the ransom demand for one hundred thousand pounds.

'Y-yes. He's a b-banker who l-lives on a yacht.'

Another Mark, one who also lived on a boat, and also worked in banking. That couldn't be a coincidence.

'How far is this Mark's yacht from the nearest place our Mark moored up *The Guilty Pleasure*?'

'J-just over a mile.' Mayberry pointed at Google maps, showing the short skip between Limehouse Basin and St Katherine Docks.

It was plausible. Kidnapping a rich banker with a yacht could feasibly yield a ransom of that size. But what kind of moron would confuse a private yacht with a narrowboat?

Chapter 27: The Brother

Thursday 23rd June, 10:00

'How often it comes down to money,' Ayala lamented.

He and Rafferty had been dispatched to bring Jake Sanders in for questioning. The boss had procured a search warrant for Jake's boat. Anything and everything financial was theirs for the taking. Technically they weren't yet ready to arrest Jake Sanders, so they'd have to rely on him coming in for an interview voluntarily.

His boat wasn't at his home mooring.

'Odd,' Rafferty said. 'He's not a continuous cruiser.'

'Then how do we find him?'

'I've got a friend at the Canal and River Trust. They keep track of which boat numbers are where. Let me give him a call. What was his boat called, again? Something stupid, wasn't it?'

'Yeah. *The Mobile Office.*'

***

A short phone call later, Rafferty and Ayala were on their way to find *The Mobile Office* in Uxbridge.

'Where did your friend say he was?' Ayala asked as Rafferty drove down the A40.

'Just past Bridge 185, whatever that means.'

'Stick it in the Sat Nav.'

They did, and were soon turning onto the A4020. By the time they found somewhere to park, it had begun to rain cats and dogs. The towpaths were deserted, the embankments muddy, and soon Ayala and Rafferty were drenched.

The boat looked much as Morton had described her: a little over half the size of *The Guilty Pleasure*, with the ramshackle appearance of an old boat that had been repaired one too many times.

Rafferty rapped smartly on the window and then called out: 'Jake Sanders! This is the police. We have a warrant to search your boat. Please exit the boat immediately.'

Her call was met with silence. 'Open her up,' she said, nodding to Ayala.

Ayala looked at her in disbelief. 'With what?'

'The tyre iron that's in my boot. Catch.' She threw her keys at him so fast, he nearly fumbled them. Thankfully, the keys didn't end up in the canal.

Ayala disappeared at a jog and reappeared a few minutes later with sweat on his brow and a tyre iron under his arm.

They smashed the door open in one swing, splintering it terribly. Inside was musty, like an old library in which the roof had leaked.

'Crack open that window, Bertie boy.' Rafferty nodded towards the window to his left, behind Jake's desk.

'So, what are we looking for?' Ayala looked around the cabin.

'Correspondence, mostly. We know he's borrowed money, and he still owes it. If his financials are as bad as they seem, he's got motive. We just need the paper trail to prove it.'

There was paperwork everywhere.

'How was Jake struggling so much? He's got loads of clients, this boat is cheaper than living in a flat, and he must be making a killing selling low-cost services to London clients.

Something doesn't add up here,' Ayala said. 'What does a payroll processor do, anyway?'

Rafferty looked up from rifling through a filing cabinet. She had been boxing up everything and labelling it neatly. 'Process payroll, I presume. Why don't you Google it?'

He did. 'Huh. I never knew that was a thing. It sounds like his job is to process the wages for a company and disburse them to the employees.'

Rafferty looked at him, bewildered. 'Why don't they just pay their employees directly?'

'So the internal accounts department don't know what everyone earns. All they see is a single line item for staff wages rather than all the individual numbers. Jake must be earning a fair cop from that, so where is it?'

'People blow money in all sorts of ways,' she said sagely.

'True. But can you see anything valuable here? That TV is a decade old. His laptop isn't much newer. This boat is ready for the scrap heap. Where's the money gone?'

'Could be he was on drugs. Or maybe he loves the company of women he can't afford. Hey, turn on the TV. It's dead quiet in here, and we'll be a while.'

Ayala did as instructed, and a spotty picture flared to life. Static hissed over the audio.

'On second thoughts, maybe not,' Rafferty said. 'I'll put something on my phone. What're you in the mood for?'

'Something upbeat. I'm going to go search the bedroom.'

Ayala's nose wrinkled as he headed back towards the single berth. If the office/sitting room at the front of the boat was a little musty, it was overwhelming in the back. There was mould visible in the eaves, and the carpet looked as if it had been pulled from a skip. How Jake lived like this, Ayala didn't know.

The bed was unmade, with clothes strewn across the top of it. Jake seemed to favour white shirts, for he had six identical garments hanging on a small rail that had been nailed above the bed. There were few personal possessions, and those that Jake did own were stuffed inside a tiny bedside unit. Ayala left those alone.

In the bottom drawer of the unit, Ayala hit pay dirt. Betting slips.

'Rafferty! Come take a look at this.'

He showed her. There were fistfuls of receipts, all of which were recently dated.

'He likes a flutter, then. Here, lay them out on the bed,' Rafferty ordered.

'Why?'

'We need to know how much he was spending. There have to be a few hundred here. If we group up just those from the last two weeks and then add up how much he's spent, we can guestimate how much money Jake has been throwing down the toilet.'

In silence, they uncrumpled each betting slip, smoothing them out and either laying them face up on the bed or adding them to the growing pile of older slips. Jake seemed to be betting about a hundred quid each time, thirty or forty times a day.

'How often do you think he won?' Ayala said.

Rafferty used her phone to check the results of each slip in turn. 'I don't know. All those I've checked so far are winners. That doesn't mean he hasn't lost money and gotten rid of the slips. If he's gambling three and a half grand a day, then he's got to be losing at least a tenth of that on average. There's no way he's beating the house.'

'Then he's losing two grand-ish a week,' Ayala said.

'For a payroll processor turning over about sixty thou a year, that's a huge shortfall. Where's the extra coming from? He can't have borrowed all that money. Nobody would lend him that much, would they?'

They bagged up the slips and then started to package up Jake's desktop computer. It was password-protected, and they'd need IT to unlock it for them.

'Rafferty, over here,' Ayala called out. He was holding a shredder in his hands, the heavy-duty kind. It was filled to the brim with cross-cut strips of paper. 'Does this look like the same paper the betting slips are printed on?'

'Yep. Bag 'em.'

Jake returned home while they were searching through the shredder. They heard the door swing on its hinges as he boarded *The Mobile Office*.

'Oi!' he yelled. 'What're you doing? I'm calling the police!'

Rafferty flashed her ID. 'We are the police. I have a search warrant for this boat. We're going to need you to come down to the station to answer a few questions.'

'But... but... my door!'

***

Jake started out co-operative enough. He provided his PC password "so they wouldn't break it open". It turned out to be "SportOfQueens", which, Rafferty thought, IT would have guessed in about ten minutes.

His accounts were digitised and neatly organised. Over the past year, Jake had turned over a little over sixty thousand pounds gross, and, after allowing for expenses and his extortionate mooring fees, was left with somewhere around fifteen thousand. Hardly a fortune for a professional living in the centre of London.

It didn't explain the gambling, either. Ayala had been dispatched to talk to the betting shop to try to size up Jake's losses. The exact amount wasn't important. What was important was where the money he was losing had been coming from.

'R-Rafferty?' Mayberry stammered. He was sitting at Jake's desktop, hammering away at the keyboard.

'What is it?'

'The n-numbers don't add up.'

'We know that. A child could spot that,' Rafferty said.

'N-not his. H-his clients.'

That got her attention. 'Show me.'

***

Morton was waiting for Jake's lawyer to arrive. He had requested one immediately, which was the sign of either a very guilty man or a very smart man. Jake didn't strike Morton as a smart man.

The question was, what was Jake guilty of? It was obvious he had been pilfering money from his clients. None of them had lost much – fifty pounds here, a hundred there. A blip on the radar for a large corporation. Jake had stolen a little from a lot of people rather than a lot from a few. That was smart.

What wasn't smart was his total failure to hide it. The fraud was unbelievably straightforward. Each payroll cycle, Jake added a little extra to the total he paid out in wages on behalf of each client, and then sent the client a summary. Jake was abusing the system to hide in plain sight. The businesses that employed him were hiding the employee salaries from their own employees by outsourcing payroll, giving Jake ample opportunity to fudge the numbers, with the accounts staff none the wiser. As long as the amounts weren't egregious, nobody noticed, and Jake made out like a bandit by stealing little and often.

The lawyer arrived, late as usual, and began strutting his stuff. 'Darren Passek. I represent Jake Sanders. Where is he?'

'Waiting in interview suite three for you. Please knock on the door when you're ready to begin,' Morton said.

The lawyer walked off, his lanky arms swinging beside him. After a short consultation, he knocked on the door, and Morton could finally begin questioning Jake.

'Mr Sanders, thank you for coming in,' Morton said.

'Like I had any choice.'

'You're not under arrest. You're free to go at any time, but I would appreciate your co-operation,' Morton said.

Jake seemed to relax, leaning back a little in his chair. His lawyer nodded in assent, and Jake said, 'Okay. Fire away.'

'Where were you on the evening of Sunday June 12th?'

'I was on my boat for most of the day, but I also went over to help Mark out with a bit of maintenance work on *The Guilty Pleasure*. It wasn't anything complicated. We made sure the bilges were clear of oil and water, swapped out his fan belt because it was starting to crack, double-checked the couplings, and topped off the battery with fresh deionised water. Nothing too difficult, really, but Mark didn't like doing it. He always needed me for that sort of stuff. Dad used to do it for him until he...' Jake dabbed at his eye with an imaginary tissue.

Morton scribbled as if making notes, though he didn't need them. He watched Jake out of the corner of his eye. Jake still appeared fairly relaxed. 'When were you aboard the boat?'

'Late afternoon? Early evening? I can't remember.'

'And, who did you see?'

'Mark. Obviously.'

'Did you see Faye?'

'No,' Jake said. 'I think she was inside, getting ready for their dinner party. After we were done with the engine, we took a look at the outside of the boat, checked for any cracking, re-spooled up the ropes and the like. Nothing too strenuous. It was an excuse to sit up top and have a beer, really.'

'Okay. How did Mark seem to you that afternoon?'

'Normal. Well, stressed, actually. He was itching to get some work done before dinner, so we didn't spend all that long working on the boat.'

'What was Mark stressed about? The sales pitch you told me about last time we spoke?' Morton asked.

Jake squirmed in his seat. 'That... and Faye. He was having second thoughts about them living together. She was getting clingy, and he hated that. He's always been a free spirit, my Mark.'

He's quick to point the finger at someone else, Morton thought. 'You said that last time. You thought he was seeing another woman. Do you know who?'

'No.'

'Would it surprise you to learn he's been sending explicit messages to Laura Keaton?' Morton asked.

'No way! That old dog. She's an absolute fox. I'd kill for one night with that woman.' Jake beamed a smile, and then realised what he'd said.

The lawyer, Darren Passek, cut in, 'My client didn't mean that literally.'

'Noted. Mr Sanders, did you know about Mark's life insurance policy?' Morton said.

'He had life insurance? But he was twenty-seven!'

Morton showed him the paperwork. 'It looks like it was through his work for Berryman. A hundred and fifty thousand pounds. Can you read the line at the bottom, there, marked "beneficiary", please?'

'Jacob Luke Sanders. Holy shit. You don't think I...?' Jake's voice trailed off.

'Did you?'

'No!'

Darren Passek's arm shot out again. 'I think I need a few minutes with my client.'

It wasn't a request.

'You've got it,' Morton said. 'Interview suspended at 15:32.'

Chapter 28: Moving On

Friday 24th June, 15:00

Dreary Alperton was beginning to wear thin. The smell of biscuits from a nearby factory had been a draw at first, but it soon became sickly. The towpaths were littered with rubbish, and the noise from Wormwood Scrubs Prison to the south rang out every hour, on the hour, throughout the day.

There was only one thing for it. Faye would have to move the boat once more. She'd done it before, so she knew she could do it again. She didn't know exactly how she had managed it, especially with the tunnels, nor did she know where she'd be moving on to, but move, she would.

Faye debated texting Rafferty first. Rafferty had been great. She had come around as often as she could, and it almost felt like the two of them belonged on the boat together. Faye had come to think of her as a big sister. However, with the investigation into Mark's death, it struck Faye that Rafferty was far too busy to ask her to help move *The Guilty Pleasure*.

There was a map on the dining table. The Grand Union stretched for miles in both directions. The farther out Faye took the boat, the more open space there was to moor up.

Mark's plan didn't list an exact location for each stop. He'd mentioned some of the farther-out places, and they all looked to be within an afternoon's travel, even at a sedate three miles an hour. Faye read them aloud: 'Sudbury, Uxbridge, Denham, Rickmansworth.'

It seemed the only way on was to head west.

The radio blared cheerfully as Faye studied the map. 'Folks, it may be summer, but be sure to wrap up tight and lock your windows and doors. There's warm air coming in off the Atlantic, and it's blowing up a gale.'

Out of the window, the clouds were grey, and the towpath was pooling with water. A light wind whipped across the surface of the canal, rocking *The Guilty Pleasure*. So much for the great British summer.

***

Jake Sanders and his lawyer found themselves in the interrogation suite once more. The lawyer looked browbeaten, worn down, and tired. The fire in his belly, the need to defend an innocent man, seemed to have atrophied. Still, Passek puffed up his chest self-importantly, straightened his tie, and leant forward with his elbows on the desk.

'What's on the table?' Passek demanded.

Morton met his icy glare and smiled politely. Lawyers were so predictable. 'Plead guilty, and you can probably save on your legal fees,' Morton said with a twinkle in his eyes.

'What if my client has information relevant to your investigation?'

Morton spread his hands as if in mock surrender. 'Then he can either divulge it, or we can add perverting the course of justice to the charge sheet.'

'Throw us a bone, here. Any deal has got to involve a bit of give and take,' Passek said.

'Give me the information, and I'll take it to the prosecutor. If it's worthwhile, I'll plead your client's case,' Morton said. 'I'm not in the business of guarantees, but Mr O'Connor is usually lenient when we've been given good information.' Morton was referring to Kieran O'Connor, one of the brightest Crown Prosecution Service lawyers of his generation. He and Morton usually saw eye to eye, though they'd had their fair share of disagreements.

Passek laughed haughtily. 'You want us to just trust you?'

'No. I don't want anything. You're the one asking me for a favour, here. Give me the information if you want me on your side. Or say nothing, and I'll ensure that Mr O'Connor throws the book at your client. No doubt you're aware of his reputation as a prosecutor.'

Jake sat forward. 'I want to talk. I want Mark's killer brought to justice as much as anyone. His killer deserves to die for what they did, but I'll settle for life behind bars.'

'I'm listening,' Morton said.

'Tim Fowler knew Mark was sleeping with his girlfriend. They fought about it a while back. Tim punched Mark in the face.'

'When was this?'

'Two weeks before he died. Tim invited Mark up for an after-work beer. When Mark got there, Tim floored him.'

'And?'

'And what? Tim has a motive!'

'You all have a motive. What makes Tim's more plausible than anyone else's?' Morton said.

'He's proven to be violent. He can't stand anyone taking his precious Laura away. You know he keeps her around like a showpiece? He can't stand to be out of her company, not even for a few minutes. She's not human to him, she's a plaything.'

'And Faye was being cheated on. Laura was the lover Mark didn't choose. You have financial difficulties. From where I'm sitting, any of you could be plausible. Did you or did you not lose money gambling?'

'I... Yes, I have a problem. There, I've said it. I'm an addict. I can't help it.'

'And, where did you get this money? We know you don't earn enough to gamble the way you do.' Morton produced the bag of winning gambling slips from under the table.

Passek cleared his throat. 'And, just how do you know that? Those are his winning slips. All you have proven is that my client lawfully won quite a lot of money. Besides, those slips only speak to the volume of betting that my client undertook, and not the net outcome.'

This time, Morton's smile was a sad one. 'Anybody who gambles this often ends up losing money overall. The house always wins.'

***

The shredded betting slips had been piled up on a table in the forensics department. Mayberry had begun to sort through the tiny pieces to try to reassemble as many slips as he could.

At first, Mayberry thought it would be an impossible task, a gigantic collection of puzzle pieces for hundreds of tiny puzzles, but then Brodie came to the rescue.

'Feed 'em in here, laddie,' Brodie said, indicating a huge scanner. He watched as Mayberry began to lay the shredded slips face-down on the scanner.

Mayberry filled all of the available space on the scanner. He had barely made a dent in the main pile. 'D-done.'

'One batch, laddie, one batch. We'll have to do every piece.'

'Then what?'

'Then we see what we can or cannae do. We've got slips from a few dozen betting shops. Each shop has their own font, their own colour, and their own paper. That'll let us group the pieces by shop. From there, we'll try to match the text.' Brodie turned away to start running the software required for the task.

'W-will it work?'

'Mebbe. It's a big ask. Come back to me on Monday, and I'll let you know.'

'You mean I'm d-done?' Mayberry smiled.

'After you finish scanning that lot, laddie.' Brodie grinned as he pointed at the big pile of shredded paper still to scan.

***

It seemed harder this time around. Moving the boat in the sunshine with no wind had been a challenge, and yet it didn't measure up to doing the same in the pouring rain. The wind whipped up droplets of water all around Faye as she stood up top to steer. The movement of the boat felt sluggish against the wind. Turning took more time and effort than ever before, and, more than once, Faye bumped up against the towpath while trying to keep clear of oncoming boats.

Faye went farther and farther west, crawling along at less than walking speed. The spaces that were available were miles from civilisation. The best spots were near the footbridges, and the only empty spaces Faye could see were miles away from any of the convenient crossings. Boats were clustered three abreast where the canal network passed a London Underground station, and there was barely room to get by.

Eventually, Faye found a space she liked. It was almost out of sight of the next narrowboat. She sidled *The Guilty Pleasure* alongside the towpath and quickly jumped off to secure the mooring pins.

The rain was pelting down harder than before, and the bank had begun to turn muddy. She hurriedly drove in each pin, then looped the mooring rope through, just as Mark had shown her. As soon as the boat was secure, she dove back inside, desperate for cover. Mud tracked her footprints.

She kicked off her trainers by the door and sat on the sofa to peel her sodden socks off her feet. The cat plodded over, pawed at her leg, and then sat by the front door as if asking permission to go out.

'Not today, Fabby.'

Chapter 29: Denied

Morton personally filled out the application for a search warrant.

As usual, he had to go through the rigmarole of an appearance before the Magistrates' Court. It seemed redundant to follow their inane procedure every time. Morton knew he could attend via live-link now, but it seemed weird to mix the formalities of a court appearance with what was tantamount to a fancy version of Skype.

Morton quickly found himself before the bench, a single magistrate looming above him, peering down over his glasses as if Morton were an ant to be studied. A bailiff approached with a Bible and pressed it into Morton's hand.

'I know what to say.' Morton waved him off. He recited, by rote, the oath. 'I swear by Almighty God that the evidence I shall give shall be the truth, the whole truth and nothing but the truth. To the best of my knowledge and belief, this application discloses all the information that is material to what the court must decide, including anything that might reasonably be considered capable of undermining any of the grounds of the application.'

'Thank you, Mr Morton.'

'Detective Chief Inspector Morton, actually.'

'DCI Morton, I have your application before me. This is a search warrant for a narrowboat. You've listed it as a residential premises.'

'Yes. It is used full-time as a permanent residence. It belongs to the estate of a murder victim and is currently occupied by his girlfriend.'

'It is a vehicle, is it not? Should this not be an application to search a vehicle?' The magistrate looked over to his clerk for confirmation.

'That is an irrelevant question,' Morton said flatly. He'd come prepared with notes, just in case. He turned to the section defining premises and read aloud: 'Premises as defined in s23 of the Police and Criminal Evidence Act include any vehicle, vessel, aircraft, or hovercraft. If I can deal with the reason why we need to search *The Guilty Pleasure*, I'm sure you'll agree that a search warrant is in order here.'

'Hmm. Is a boat really a vehicle after all? I'm going to need guidance on what a vehicle legally is.'

This guy would be fun at a party, Morton thought. 'While your clerk researches that point, can I outline why I'd like to search the boat?'

The magistrate gave Morton a thin-lipped smile. 'Please.'

'Simply put, it was the last place the victim was seen alive. We know he was there on the night of Sunday 12th June, and nobody has seen evidence of him being alive since. It is perfectly possible that the boat is our primary crime scene.'

'Then you must have a suspect in mind.'

'Faye Atkins.'

'The same Miss Atkins who lives on the boat and was the partner of the deceased?'

'Yes. She was on the boat on the last night he was alive,' Morton said.

'Is there any exculpatory evidence that might undermine your suspicion?'

Morton hesitated. He was oath-bound to give them all the facts. 'We performed handwriting analysis on a ransom note left at the scene. It did not match Miss Atkins' handwriting.'

'Presumably you agree that Mr Sanders' murderer is the most likely suspect to have written the ransom note?'

'It's possible.'

'Then it would appear you've disproved your own theory, wouldn't it?' The magistrate pushed his glasses up his nose with a spindly index finger and glared down at Morton.

Morton met the magistrate's glare with one of his own. 'It's possible the ransom note was opportunistic. It's also possible that someone wrote the note on her behalf. Regardless of the odds of a conviction based on current evidence, I believe it is readily apparent that there could be material on board which could be of beneficial importance at trial. That is the legal test you must apply here.'

There was a pregnant pause. The air seemed to weigh heavily in the courtroom. The magistrate leaned down to whisper to his clerk. The clerk flipped through a legal textbook and seemed to be arguing with the magistrate.

Finally, the magistrate nodded firmly, as if he had made up his mind.

'Your request is denied.'

Morton wanted to swear. 'I must protest. This is a murder investigation. How can you expect me not to visit the deceased's home?'

'Next!'

The next thing Morton knew, a bailiff was politely tugging at his elbow. When he was by the door and out of earshot of the magistrate, the bailiff whispered, 'Sorry about him. He's a cranky one.'

Morton left the court empty-handed. There was one option left. He could arrest Faye and use the power under section eighteen of the Police and Criminal Evidence Act to conduct a warrantless search of *The Guilty Pleasure*.

Chapter 30: The Other Man

With the boss off trying for a search warrant, it was down to Rafferty to winnow down the other suspects. The main four were indistinguishable: Jake, Laura, Tim, and Faye all had had the same access to the victim, and each had a plausible motive.

That left the two peripheral suspects, neither of whom Rafferty could take seriously. First, there was Pip Berryman, the guy who had stolen Mark's new client when he didn't show up for work. Secondly, there was the other Mark. This Mark also worked in finance and lived aboard a boat. Mayberry had theorised that the kidnappers had erroneously targeted the wrong Mark Sanders.

'Really?' Ayala had said disbelievingly. 'If a killer can't tell the difference between a yacht and a narrowboat, there's no way they'd be clever enough to leave so little evidence.'

'Then, it won't take us long to rule it out,' Rafferty said. 'It'll shut Mayberry up, at least. Speaking of Mayberry, where'd he go?'

'No idea. Last I saw, he had his nose buried in the records we found on Jake Sanders' desktop computer. He's probably down in IT, talking to that guy with the ridiculous name,' Ayala said.

'Zane? Yeah. That isn't actually his real name. He just thinks it's cool. It's probably something boring like Jim or Luke or Bertram.' Rafferty watched as the vein in Ayala's temple began to throb. He hated his name so much that the mere mention of it would send him off on one. Then she continued as if nothing had happened. 'Well, if Mayberry's on that, then let's go work the doppelgänger angle.'

***

Doppelgänger Mark Sanders could not have lived a more different life from the 'real' Mark. *The Guilty Pleasure* was a beautiful boat in her own right, and certainly one of the more beautiful narrowboats on the canal network, but no narrowboat could compare to the superyacht that awaited Rafferty and Ayala at West India Dock on the South Quay.

The *Gaeltacht* was an impressive sight, with sleek lines that seemed to effortlessly traverse the 150-foot length of the boat and a shiny white finish that no doubt took many staff to maintain. *Gaeltacht* was printed subtly in a silver font that caught Rafferty's eye as it sparkled in the sunshine. There were three decks visible above the prow, with sheets of tinted glass hiding the occupants within. Rafferty knew nothing of the lives of the ultra-rich and had never set foot aboard a private yacht before. Now, more than ever, she cursed her bad luck being born on a council estate in Hackney.

Ayala whistled. 'That is a sexy boat.'

'Let's take a closer look.'

Rafferty led the way, dodging through the crowds as she threaded towards the water's edge. Uniformed security appeared from the boat to block her way.

'Ma'am, we can't allow you to go any farther,' the tallest of the grunts said.

Ma'am? Rafferty thought. Her eyes narrowed. 'Detective Inspector Ashley Rafferty, Metropolitan Police. I'm here to speak to Mark Sanders.'

'Is Mr Sanders expecting you?' The guard's tone implied he already knew the answer.

'It's a matter of life and death.'

'Wait here.' He sounded bored, but he snapped his fingers to beckon another grunt. He whispered instructions and sent the junior security officer sprinting onto the deck.

They waited in silence. Rafferty kept looking over to the gangway for the junior to return.

The boss goon put a finger to his ear. 'Uh-uh. Right away,' he muttered into his earpiece. 'Follow me,' he said, beckoning with a gnarled finger.

He led them down towards the gangway and then bowed as Ayala and Rafferty passed him to board. They were met on board the boat by another man who bowed and showed them through to the main lounge.

'How many staff did you spot?' Ayala asked.

'A dozen. There've got to be more about,' Rafferty said under her breath.

When they were seated on plush couches, the staff member turned to them. 'Can I offer you refreshments?'

'Tea, please, for us both.'

'Very well, ma'am. Please wait here.'

Ma'am again? Rafferty pulled out her phone, turned on the front camera, and double-checked her make-up. She did look more tired than normal. Dealing with Faye was exhausting. While her camera app was open, she snapped a few pictures of the cabin to show Morton. The whole room reeked of money. Above her was a chandelier with dozens of tiny crystals refracting rainbows onto the carpet. The carpet was remarkably plush, with a red and gold pattern. Towards the back of the main cabin, there was a spiral staircase going up to the top deck.

'You hear that?' Ayala said, nudging Rafferty as he spoke. 'Footsteps.'

'I don't hear anything.'

Ayala was right. A man in his early thirties descended the spiral staircase at a clip, skipping every other step. He bounded towards them, full of energy.

'Hello! I'm Mark Sanders. To what do I owe the intrusion?' he said with a snarky attitude. 'I'm just kidding. Has anyone got you a drink yet? Dear me, you can't get the staff these days. Ezra!'

The elderly valet who had greeted them reappeared. 'Yes, sir?'

'Drinks, Ezra, drinks. Make mine a Sazerac.'

'Very well, sir.' Ezra bowed as he retreated. He returned barely a minute later with the drinks, almost as if he had predicted the request for a Sazerac before it was made.

A Sazerac? Rafferty glanced at her watch. It was barely ten o'clock in the morning.

Sanders sat down on an Eames chair opposite them. No doubt it was an original. 'Don't mind Ez. Poor chap's been with the family forever. He worked for my father until he passed. I can't bear to let him go, even if he's got a bit slow in his old age.'

'Okay,' Rafferty said, nonplussed. 'Mr Sanders, we're with the Murder Investigation Team. I'm Detective Inspector Rafferty, and this is Detective Inspector Ayala.'

'Murder? Good lord, who's dead?'

'Mark Sanders,' Rafferty said.

'Is this some kind of a joke?' Doppelgänger-Sanders said. 'Plainly, I'm not.'

'Another man by the name of Mark Sanders was murdered two weeks ago. His family was asked for a ransom demand that was far beyond his means. We believe the kidnappers may have targeted the wrong Mark Sanders by mistake.'

'You think they were after me? Dear lord. It's got to be the Russians. Or the Armenians. Hang on. Ezra!'

Ezra appeared again as if by magic. Rafferty had the sneaky suspicion that the old man had been loitering just outside so he could eavesdrop.

'Ezra, be a dear and go fetch Carlton. I need his latest security threat assessment report too, please.'

Rafferty took a sip from her tea. 'Who's Carlton?'

'My head of security. Aha, here he comes.' Doppelgänger-Sanders pointed at the doorway as the bald gentleman who'd stopped them on the quayside entered.

He kicked off his shoes at the door. 'Sir!'

'Mr Carlton, these police officers seem to think I could be in danger.'

Carlton laughed. 'Sir, we've had no more threats than usual this month. Would you like me to increase the number of guards on patrol?'

'Absolutely.'

'Mr Sanders,' Rafferty said. 'If I may, I'd like to offer you police protection while we investigate.'

'Nonsense! Mr Carlton here will ensure my safety, won't you, Carlton?'

'Absolutely, sir!'

Ezra reappeared with a stack of binders. 'Sir, this the report you asked for.'

'Excellent,' Doppelgänger-Sanders said, leaping to his feet. 'Give a copy to these officers, would you?' He turned to Rafferty and Ayala and said, 'Thanks for stopping by. If there's anything else you need, please have a word with Mr Carlton.'

He bounded from the room, leaving Ezra to escort them back to the quay.

The pile of folders teetered as Ayala carried them. When they were back on solid ground, he put them down and glanced at the folder on top. 'There have got to be thousands of threats in here!'

Chapter 31: Amateur

It had been raining for days, seemingly without stopping. The wind was howling, and lightning flashed across the sky. Faye was sitting in bed, her arm tucked around one of Mark's jumpers. The bed was the last place that she could still feel his presence. Fabby was curled up beside her, shaking every time the clouds rumbled.

'I wish Mark was here,' Faye whispered to the cat. She wanted nothing more than to have his arms wrapped around her, and for his deep, soothing voice to tell her everything was going to be alright. She hadn't got used to sleeping alone yet. In prison, there'd been someone near her every waking moment for four years straight. The last two weeks were the loneliest that Faye had ever endured.

The boat rocked as Faye clutched Mark's jumper closer against her. Though the canal was non-tidal, the water was rising. The flood valves, built to drain the canals when the water level surged, seemed unable to cope. Though Faye couldn't see it, the banks had been submerged. The grass of the towpath into which she had sunk her mooring pins was turning into a slurry of mud and canal water.

A flash of lightning flitted across the sky as the boat lurched again. The water seemed to be churning as the wind whipped it back and forth. *The Guilty Pleasure* strained against her mooring ropes, her tonnage rendering the ropes taut. She rocked and she rocked, and, slowly but surely, the mooring pins began to rise.

All of a sudden, one mooring pin pinged free of the grass by the towpath. As soon as one went, the others began to rise up out of the bed, the slurry no longer able to contain the boat. The last mooring pin gave way, and the boat lurched suddenly forward, throwing Faye around in her berth.

Faye screamed. The boat was out of her control. She swept up the cat in one arm and ran for the helm. Furiously, she unlocked the front door. More haste proved to mean less speed. Faye panicked. She needed to get the engine running, and quickly. The boat was picking up speed. The wind and the water were jostling her towards the middle of the canal.

In the distance, Faye could see another narrowboat. It grew larger as she tried to bring *The Guilty Pleasure* under her control. She yanked the throttle into neutral and flicked the ignition. The yellow preheat light flickered to life. The diesel needed to warm up before the engine would turn over.

Closer and closer *The Guilty Pleasure* came to the boat in front of her. There wasn't time. The starter motor wouldn't engage.

'Noo!' Faye screamed. A collision was imminent. At the last moment, she clutched tighter at the cat, ignored the yelping and the scratches, and leapt into the water.

An almighty crunch sounded as *The Guilty Pleasure* collided with the narrowboat in front of it.

Chapter 32: Too Much Attention

Friday 24th June, 17:30

The Cheshire Cheese was rammed. Lawyers, students, journalists, and tourists packed out every nook and cranny of the historic Fleet Street pub.

At a worn-out table in the rear bar, Morton sat nursing a pint of Sam Smith's. It was his third since he'd met up with Kieran O'Connor half an hour earlier, and he was beginning to feel a mild buzz. The bar staff knew them by name, and Kieran had tipped generously to make sure there was always a pint in his hand.

If Morton had to hear Jenny the barmaid patiently explaining to a tourist that the tables in the nearby dining room were only for those dining one more time, he thought he might rip his hair out. God only knew how she didn't go insane.

'So, I turned up for court, and there she was, the woman from the other night. I had to go through an entire bail application without looking at her,' Kieran said. 'I can't believe my luck.'

'It's your own fault, O'Connor. You will drink in lawyer bars all over Holborn every night. Is it any surprise that you end up chatting up other lawyers?'

Kieran glared. His eyes were red, and there were bags under his eyes. It'd been a long week. 'Feck off, Morton.'

'You should go meet a nice girl,' Morton said. 'If you date other lawyers, you'll be competing over everything. You'll never find time for each other, because you're both workaholics, and it'll end badly. Remember that doctor you dated last year? You barely saw each other. With another lawyer, it'll be worse, because you'll have to see each other afterwards.'

Kieran drained his glass. 'Easier said than done, my friend. London in your thirties is like going fishing in a pond that's already been overfished. Most of what's available has been thrown back for good reason.'

Morton gestured at Kieran's almost-empty pint glass. 'Sounds like you need another one.'

'Go on then, one more, and then I've got to get going.'

The bar was crowded. Students, many of them looking barely old enough to drink, were swarming the overworked barmaid. 'Jenny, two pints of bitter when you get a sec. We're in no hurry.'

She poured them immediately, taking a tenner in return.

Morton took one in each hand, took a sip from the pint in his right hand, and smiled. 'Keep the change.'

Kieran's head was on the table when Morton returned. 'You alright?'

'No. Look.' Kieran showed Morton his phone. The press had found out about Jake's gambling, and Kieran's phone was lighting up with text messages letting him know.

'Shit.'

'You've got to arrest him,' Kieran said. 'Soon. If you don't, we'll get a media storm, our witnesses will hole up away from the press, and any evidence left will be completely destroyed by our suspects.'

'I need more time. We don't have enough to convict.'

'Then let him out on police bail. Seize his passport and make sure he reports to a station daily. Put an ankle tag on him if he'll agree to wear one.'

Chapter 33: Wham!

Friday 24th June, 17:25

Joanna Marsden's evening had started much like any other. At five o'clock on the dot, her collie had appeared in the sitting room with his lead held between his teeth and had set the lead down on her lap. Vic was such a clever dog, perhaps cleverer than her first husband after whom he had been named.

The canals were the perfect place for dog-walking. There weren't too many people around, and the greenery made a change from the usual drab grey of the surrounding skyscrapers.

Rain wasn't a problem, either. Vic loved to jump in every puddle he could. Torrential rain, on the other hand, soon proved problematic. On the way back from their Friday evening walk, the muddy towpath seemed to be one long puddle. Thank God for wellington boots.

The boats seemed to be rocking back and forth in the water almost as if they were at sea. Joanna couldn't live aboard a narrowboat. It would be much too cold, too cramped, and the movement would nauseate her. She watched the boats as they walked, wondering who lived aboard them and why they had chosen a life on the canals rather than a regular flat.

She was most of the way home when she spotted one boat rocking much more violently than the others. In distance, Joanna could see that a girl was standing atop the boat, wrestling with the tiller.

'Good lord, is that boat moving? In this weather? Miss! Miss! Look out!'

Joanna's screams were lost in the wind. Vic began to bark. The girl on the boat was heading for a collision. Joanna watched helplessly from a distance, her fingers crossed, pleading for a last-minute course correction.

It seemed to happen in slow motion.

The boat crashed into a moored-up narrowboat. Joanna didn't hear it happen; the rolls of thunder drowned out the noise. She ran forward, Vic snapping at her heels, just in time to see that the girl had leapt into the water. Joanna kept running, cursing the arthritis in her knees. Vic shot forward and jumped into the canal, paddling after the girl as if his life depended on it.

By the time Joanna got to the girl, a couple of minutes had passed. She jumped into the water, recoiling at the sudden temperature shock. Her limbs felt heavy as the wind whipped the water around her face. At least the water wasn't too deep.

She reached Vic and the girl. The dog was nudging from underneath, trying to keep her afloat. Joanna seized the girl's arm and dragged her to the water's edge, then heaved to hoist her up onto the bank. The girl was unconscious and barely breathing. Her right arm was locked in place as she clutched a tiny cat tight to her chest. It escaped with a long meow as soon as they were out of the water. Joanna clambered up after the girl and felt for a pulse. It was weak, and the girl's breathing was shallow.

'Breathe, damn it!' Joanna swore. She placed her hands over the girl's chest with her palms flat and began chest compressions. What was it the TV advert had said? Push to the beat of "Staying Alive". Joanna hummed it aloud as she pressed on the girl's chest.

The girl sputtered, rolled over onto her side, and chucked up water.

'W-where am I?' she muttered.

'Your boat crashed. You're okay,' Joanna said. 'I'm going to call you an ambulance.'

She reached into her pocket and pulled out a sodden mobile phone. It wouldn't turn on.

'I'm going to get help. Stay here, okay? I'll be back in no time.'

Chapter 34: Emergency Contact

Friday 24th June, 19:00

The Northwick Park Hospital was the nearest A&E for Faye. The paramedic who assessed her on the towpath dropped her off in the Accident & Emergency department but was unable to bump her straight through, as there were more urgent cases waiting. The storm had done a number on the local community. Trees had fallen, storm drains had overflowed, and those reckless enough to risk driving had caused a spike in traffic accidents. The hospital was slammed.

Faye was kept in the waiting room for several hours as more urgent cases kept getting bumped above her by the triage nurses.

Eventually, she was seen by an admissions nurse in a tiny room off the busy A&E corridor.

The nurse was brisk and to the point, as if the patients were on a conveyor belt of human misery that she needed to get through before her shift was over. 'What happened to you then, love? Another car crash?'

'They told me my boat crashed,' Faye said. 'The mooring pins came loose in the storm. I almost drowned. H-have you seen my cat?'

'Your cat?' The nurse's expression softened. 'I'm sure she's fine. Let's focus on you for now. What happened when the boat crashed?'

'I was trying to stop it. The engine wouldn't start. It happened so fast.'

'It's okay, dear. You're okay. Did you lose consciousness at all?'

Faye bit her lip. 'I... I think so. One moment, I was heading for the boat, and then I was on the towpath. Someone was standing over me. And then... then I was here.'

'Right. We'd better get you admitted. Can you roll up your sleeve? I need to take your vitals.'

***

The Medical Assessment Unit was full to bursting. Faye's trolley was parked in a corridor, as there were no beds available inside the ward. The hospital, like so many in London, was groaning under the weight of an ageing population. Patients who should have long since been sent home were waiting on appropriate homes to go to and the social care needed to get them there.

As Faye waited, people streamed past every few seconds: nurses, patients, distraught visitors. More than one bumped into her, and few of them did more than mumble an apology as they did so. One guy had the gall to tell her to get out of the way.

It was nice to be out of the wet clothes she'd emerged from the boat in, though a hospital gown was not a great improvement.

Eventually, a nurse came over and told her she could go home.

'Go where? I don't have a home any more,' Faye said. She thought briefly of her mum's. No, she couldn't go back, not as long as her stepfather remained there.

'Don't you have a friend or emergency contact you could call?'

Faye paused. She could call Laura. Or her mum.

Then it hit her. There was one person who had looked out for her every time she needed somebody. 'Yes. I don't have her number, though. I think I lost my phone with the boat.'

'What's her name?' the nurse asked. 'I can look her up for you.'

'Ashley Rafferty.'

***

'Thanks again for doing this, Miss Rafferty,' Faye said. She had asked the nurses to call Rafferty to plead her case. She needed to go somewhere, and she couldn't be released unless she had somewhere to go. 'It'll just be for one night, I promise.'

Rafferty sighed inwardly. She knew better. Faye was as helpless as a newborn lamb. She had no money, no clothes, no job, and nowhere to go. As if it was ever going to be just one night.

'And thank you for bringing these clothes for me.'

'You're welcome,' Rafferty said. The less said about the clothes, the better. Faye was markedly smaller than Rafferty, so Rafferty had resorted to the old standby of pilfering whatever was available in the Met's lost and found box. 'We'll go shopping this weekend.'

'But, Miss Rafferty, I don't have any money.'

'It's my treat. And, if you're moving in with me, please call me Ashley instead of Miss Rafferty. You make me sound so old!'

'Okay, Miss Ashley.'

Chapter 35: Home Sweet Home

Saturday 25th June, 03:00

It didn't take Faye long to make herself right at home.

Rafferty had cleared her junk out of the living room and unfolded a sofa bed which now dominated the room. She introduced Faye to her cat, Mr Snuffles, who took an immediate liking to her. Like Faye, Mr Snuffles was a stray. He'd been a little ball of white fluff when Rafferty rescued him. Like Faye, Rafferty hadn't planned to open her home to another living being, but it had worked out for the best.

Rafferty quickly fetched extra blankets and pillows from her storage unit in the apartment building's basement, and then they planned a quick trip to the local supermarket to see to all of Faye's basic needs.

'Thank you,' Faye said for the hundredth time as Rafferty picked up a cheap toothbrush for her. She had the same reaction to every item Rafferty picked up: new socks, underwear, and even a stack of easy ready-meals for Faye to microwave. By the time they made it to the checkout, Faye was holding back tears of gratitude.

When they got home, Rafferty uncorked a bottle of red wine and poured two generous glasses. Faye's eyes lit up.

'I've never had red wine.'

Rafferty was stunned. Faye was twenty-two years old, and yet still a child in so many ways. 'Then, I hope you like it.'

She did. Faye gulped down the wine much too fast and immediately asked for another glass. Between the two of them, the Châteauneuf-du-Pape didn't last half an hour, and they had to move on to a six-pack of beers. Faye seemed much more at home after a few drinks.

'I miss him,' she said. The mood in the room quickly shifted from jovial to melancholy.

'I'm so sorry, sweetie,' Rafferty said, putting an arm around Faye and hugging her close.

Faye recoiled visibly, pulling herself away. For just a second, her expression was one of unbridled rage. Her nostrils flared, and her arm muscles tensed up.

Rafferty pulled back. 'I'm sorry. I'll leave you to get some sleep. If you need anything, you know where I am.'

'Miss Ashley? There is one thing. What happened to Fabby?'

Shit, Rafferty thought. *I'd forgotten about the cat.*

'I'll go look for her tomorrow,' Rafferty promised. 'I'm sure someone's taking good care of her.'

Chapter 36: The Wreckage

Saturday 25th June, 09:30

The Guilty Pleasure was a write-off. Rafferty and Ayala met on the canal early on Saturday morning to see if there was any chance of recovering latent evidence from the boat. They arrived to find a circus on the canal. Men in vests marked Canal and River Trust were running around, and one was barking orders through a megaphone.

The water had subsided, leaving the towpath covered in mud. Rafferty trod carefully as she made a beeline for the man with the megaphone.

'Detective Inspector Rafferty,' she introduced herself. 'What's going on?'

The man lowered his megaphone and shook Rafferty's hand. 'Mike Barnham, Canal and River Trust. We've got two boats to recover. Why are the police involved in a simple canal crash?'

'One of the boats, *The Guilty Pleasure*, may be a crime scene.'

Barnham arched an eyebrow. 'I take it you're talking about more than being drunk while in charge of a narrowboat.'

'The owner of *The Guilty Pleasure* was murdered two weeks ago.'

'I guess we won't be billing him for removing her from the water, then. Do you think the crash was deliberate? We figured it was just an accident, what with the storm we had last night. We've got half a dozen wreckages to deal with today. Every boat that can't move under her own steam needs to be craned out of the water to make way. And we've got downed trees all over the place, too.'

The scene looked like something out of a tornado movie. Fencing had collapsed on parts of the towpath, shrubbery had fallen into the water, and the two boats were barely visible above the waterline.

'Was anyone hurt?' Rafferty said.

'Aye. There was a young lass taken to hospital last night. Mr and Mrs Macullum – they own the other boat that sank, the *Arcadian* – were alright, though they're mighty shook up. That's them over there.' Barnham pointed to an elderly couple sitting in plastic chairs. They were watching their boat with tears in their eyes.

'What will happen to the boats?'

'Normally, I'd just haul them up out of the water, winch 'em onto a lorry and tow 'em, but I'm guessing you'll want to see the inside of *The Guilty Pleasure* if it's murder you're investigating. Let me put her on the towpath, check she's structurally sound, and then you can investigate all you want. That sound fair to you? There's a bit of extra grass just down the bend, there, so if we pop her there, she won't be in anyone's way.'

Rafferty looked towards the space Barnham was indicating. It didn't look big enough for a boat, but she trusted his expertise. 'It sounds good to me. I'll leave my colleague, here, Detective Inspector Ayala, to chat with the Macullums and then see to some crime scene tape.'

She turned away from Barnham to speak with Ayala, and the megaphone-barked orders resumed.

'Where are you going, then?' Ayala asked.

'I've got to see a man about a cat.'

***

Battersea Dogs and Cats Home was on Battersea Park Road, just opposite one of Rafferty's favourite Irish pubs. Virtually every Londoner knew of it, and it was Rafferty's best bet for finding Fabby.

The cat was microchipped, so she should be relatively easy to find. Unfortunately, the contact details on that microchip were Mark's, and the address on record was one he'd long since moved out of.

If it were not for the three-storey high picture of a dog above the door, Rafferty would have dismissed Battersea as just another glass-fronted office building in a city full of them. A quick Google said they were due to open at half ten, and Rafferty made it with five minutes to spare. When the doors opened, she paid her £2 admission fee without bothering to get a receipt for expenses and made her way to the enquiries desk.

'Morning. I'm looking to find a cat that may have been brought in during last night's storm,' Rafferty said to the receptionist.

There was a sharp intake of breath. 'We had a lot of animals come in last night. We're still processing them. Could you come back later today?'

'I'm afraid not. My name is Detective Inspector Rafferty. The cat in question belongs to a murder victim, and I'm hoping to reunite his next of kin with the cat as soon as possible.'

The receptionist seemed satisfied that it wasn't a run of the mill request. 'Let me go speak to one of our team members and see if they can help you out.'

Rafferty checked her phone as she waited for the receptionist to return and found another four messages from Faye. She almost regretted giving the poor girl her old mobile to replace the one that had sunk with *The Guilty Pleasure*. Faye was texting almost constantly. None of it was important. Most of it was inane questions about where something might be in the flat, followed by another text two minutes later announcing that Faye had found it.

The receptionist returned with another woman in tow. 'Inspector Rafferty? I'm Michelle. Sandra told me you're looking for a cat. Can you describe it?'

'She's a tabby, female, about five years old. She's been microchipped and responds when called.'

'Phew. That ought to make things a bit easier. Follow me through to the back, and we'll see if she's among the cats at intake.'

Intake was all the way across the other side of the building, near the Sopwith Way entrance. It took a few minutes to get there, but when they did, Fabby was easy to find. The lady who had helped Faye, one Joanna Marsden, had dropped her off after Faye had been taken away from the boat by the paramedic. Half an hour of paperwork and a small donation later, Rafferty walked out with Fabby tucked up in a transport box under her arm. She'd be home before lunchtime.

***

Ayala was left to deal with the crime scene alone. He'd been asking for more responsibility for a long time, ever since becoming an Inspector. Now that he had it, he wondered if he hadn't been better off doing the grunt work after all.

He had three tasks. One, talk to the Macullums about their boat, the *Arcadian*. Two, oversee the Canal and River Trust as they pulled both boats out of the canal. Three, secure and search *The Guilty Pleasure*. Ayala took the jobs in that order.

The old couple were shivering as he approached. It was still raining, and they were much too old to sit in the rain while their boat was pulled from the water.

'Mr and Mrs Macullum? I'm Detective Inspector Ayala. I'd like to ask you what happened last night. It might take a little while, and it's a little cold out here. There's a small café just around the corner, if you're able to make it up the steps off the towpath.'

They agreed without demurring. Soon, the trio were the oddest-looking brunch party in London. They found a table in the back of the café, and Ayala ordered three mugs of hot tea and three full British breakfasts.

When the waitress was gone, Ayala asked what had happened.

'I've never seen anything like it,' Mr Macullum began. 'Ethel and I have been on the canals for... how long, dear?'

'Forty-four years, dear.'

'Forty-four years, and not once have we had a collision. We've seen them. Everybody has. It's usually a novice who misjudges a lock gate. Why on earth did she plough into the *Arcadian*?'

'I'm afraid it was an accident. Our information is that the boat came untethered in the storm,' Ayala said, relaying the story Faye had given to Rafferty.

Mrs Macullum slammed her mug down, spilling tea all over the table. 'It was not! We saw her. She was at the helm the entire time. She could have avoided us easily.'

Ayala set down his own mug and mopped up the spilled tea with a napkin. 'You think it was deliberate?'

Mrs Macullum spoke for them again. 'If it wasn't deliberate, she was wholly inept. Even the most novice of narrowboaters could have managed to avoid us. We didn't come adrift, nor did anyone else.'

Mr Macullum was sitting quietly. Ayala turned to him. 'What do you think, Mr Macullum?'

He shrugged his shoulders with a click. 'I don't know. It certainly could have been an accident. She didn't look like she knew what she was doing. I know I bumped the canal side a few times when I was a new hand. Why would anyone deliberately crash a narrowboat?'

'It's possible that her boat is in fact a crime scene,' Ayala said.

He realised as soon as he'd said it that he should have kept his mouth shut.

'She destroyed my boat to cover up a crime!' Mrs Macullum declared. 'I want her arrested. Criminal damage, drunk in charge, whatever it takes. That floozy deserves to be in jail.'

And for the next twenty minutes, she ranted and ranted while she chewed over her breakfast. Ayala paid the bill after brunch and made a hasty retreat back towards the canal.

When he made it back, the crane was in position. It was parked on the road up above the canal, with the hook dangling down from above. He found Barnham directing his team. They were putting winch straps underneath the boat.

'How long 'til you're ready to lift her out of the water?'

'Should be less than thirty minutes,' Barnham said. 'We want her to come out in one piece, so we've got to put straps every few feet.'

Ayala watched them work. They were methodical, deliberate, and surprisingly quick. Two teams of two men were looping the straps around the boat. They started at opposite ends, putting one loop around and then moving ten feet closer to the middle. In no time at all, there were seven sets of straps along the length of *The Guilty Pleasure*. The team then joined up each loop and attached steel rings for the crane to latch on to. One of the men was calling directions into a radio to let the crane operator know which way to go. They latched on after a bit of to-ing and fro-ing, and the crane began to strain against the weight of the boat.

As *The Guilty Pleasure* was raised up, the water poured out of her. At first, the run-off came through the windows, great rivers of dirty canal water pouring down the side of the boat. Duckweed seemed to sprout from the sides of her, great knots of long green stems flooding out of the windows.

The Guilty Pleasure rose slowly through the water and into the air. Ayala could see an enormous crack along the bow below the water line, which had to be the point where she had collided with the *Arcadian*. The crane held her above the waterline until she was no longer dripping, and then slowly swung to the left. The Canal and River Trust staff scurried out of the way as the crane operator placed her upon the bank ever so gently.

After she was landed, the straps were quickly removed.

'She's all yours, Inspector Ayala,' Barnham said after they had performed a structural inspection. 'Be careful if you go in.

She looks alright from here, but I'd wear a hard hat all the same, if I were you.'

'Cheers.'

Ayala quickly fenced off the portion of the canal with blue-and-white crime scene tape. Then he took Barnham's advice and borrowed a hard hat. It didn't exactly match his carefully tailored suit, but, on this occasion, Ayala was happy to trade off looks for safety. There didn't seem much point in putting on evidence booties when the possible crime scene was already thoroughly contaminated, but it was procedure, so Ayala covered up, donned plastic gloves, and boarded *The Guilty Pleasure,* ready to collect any evidence he could find.

She looked like a shipwreck, which Ayala supposed she was. The interior, which had been decked out in solid wood, had absorbed a great deal of canal water, and it dripped from the ceiling. Ayala had to duck to avoid scraping his hard hat on the ceiling as he entered. The floor was slimy with green canal water, and there was a tiny bream flip-flopping on the counter. Ayala tried to scoop up the fish with his hands, failing miserably as it slipped from his fingers. He tried again, this time using a wastepaper bin to catch it. He took it outside and returned it to the canal.

Upon his return, he proceeded quickly through the boat. There was little of value to be seen. Any forensic evidence would have been washed away. Ayala wasn't sure what he was supposed to be looking for, anyway. The cause of death was unknown, so there was no murder weapon lying around to discover.

Paperwork had congealed into a messy lump on the counter. Whatever information Mark Sanders' correspondence had once contained, it was now garbled beyond comprehension. The textiles had fared even worse. The sofa was a giant lump of algae, and the bedding at the rear of the boat was as sodden as everything else. The pillow alone seemed to have soaked up several litres of the Grand Union. There were tiny insects everywhere. Ayala didn't have the time or inclination to try to return those to the water.

The storm had broken many of the panels in the boat, which revealed that the electronics, the water tank, and several parts of what Ayala presumed were the engine had all been hidden away neatly. There was also a lot of empty space concealed behind the woodwork. *Could there have been enough space to stash a body?* Ayala wondered.

The worst part was the split cartridges in the bathroom. Two or three weeks' worth of human excrement had flooded from the storage and pooled over the shower.

Ayala sprinted off the boat and dashed for the cover of the nearest boat. He heaved, retched, and deposited his overpriced brunch on the towpath.

Ayala cursed his back luck. He always got given the shit jobs.

Chapter 37: Not My Job

Saturday 25th June, 12:01

Auger and Co were by far Jake's most lucrative client. They were a temp agency, one of the largest in the City of London. On any given day, they would have a thousand temporary employees allocated to almost as many locations, and every single one of them would be logging their hours so they could get paid.

Most of the paperwork they had was in-house. Their hours were logged electronically, and payments including taxes, liens, and the like were dealt with by the computer. Then there were the adjustments – extra hours, travel and other expenses, holiday and sick pay for those not on zero hours contracts.

It was a complex system, and only Jake Sanders had oversight of everything going on. It was his job to reconcile the costs, authorise the payments, and ensure that Auger and Co stayed within the law while paying minimal National Insurance. The total salary bill then left their bank account as a single payment via BACS. All of which gave Jake Sanders the access he needed to pilfer thousands of pounds a month to pay non-existent employees.

It wasn't a complicated fraud. He included dummy employees on the BACS transfer and routed them through dummy accounts that he'd opened with a variety of different banks, and ultimately paid himself for non-existent work. Morton had dispatched Mayberry to the Fraud Squad to find out just how extensive the theft was.

In the meantime, Morton wanted to find out what the clients knew. He didn't want to get involved with a fraud case.

They were boring, and they involved far more paperwork than Morton cared to read, but if it was the underlying factor in a murder, then he had to take his investigation as he found it.

Auger and Co were based just north of Moorgate Underground Station in a fashionable office by Finsbury Square Garden. It took forever to find somewhere to park, as all the roads were double-yellows, and Morton refused to get caught out again.

He'd called ahead to make an appointment with Monsieur Jacque Auger. The boss didn't usually work Saturdays, and had only reluctantly agreed when Morton said the magic words "murder enquiry".

Auger was waiting for Morton in the lobby. 'You are late.'

Morton almost laughed. 'Good thing I'm not here for a job, then. Mr Auger, I presume.'

'My time is valuable, Monsieur Morton. I allotted you half an hour.' Auger made a show of checking his watch. 'You have six minutes remaining of that time.'

The apology for his tardiness that had been on Morton's lips disappeared. 'This will take as long as it takes. As part of my murder enquiry, I am investigating a number of financial irregularities. This meeting is a courtesy, one which I do not have to extend to you. If you'd prefer that I return on Monday morning with a search warrant and a team of forensic accountants, then I can.'

Auger's haughty demeanour dissipated. 'Financial irregularities? What financial irregularities? Shall we sit?'

Auger motioned for Morton to sit in the lobby. There was nobody else there except for the receptionist on the front desk, who made herself scarce when Auger motioned for her to scoot.

'Can I confirm that your firm uses Jake Sanders as payroll processor?'

'Yes, that's correct.'

'Have you been happy with his service?' Morton asked.

'Until thirty seconds ago, absolutely. His payroll-processor-on-a-boat service was charming.'

'How long have you been using him?'

'Three years.'

Morton whistled. In three years, Jake would have handled hundreds of thousands of transactions on behalf of Auger and Co. 'I believe Mr Sanders has been skimming from your accounts with fraudulent transactions. Our investigation is underway, and we would like to get a complete copy of your records to reconcile with those recovered from Mr Sanders.'

'You'll have them by five o'clock,' Auger promised. 'I shall deliver them to you personally. Do you know how much he might have stolen?'

'I really can't say, Monsieur Auger. Were there no red flags that money might have been going missing?'

'*Non*. We have been profitable, very profitable. If he was stealing, he was subtle. Our payroll bill hasn't changed much since we hired him, though I can't say I've been keeping a close eye on it.'

'That chimes with our assessment of the situation,' Morton said. 'From what we can tell so far, he stole inconsequential amounts. He was well-versed to hide the fraud by only giving you the total spend for each payroll cycle. Only Jake himself had a copy of the breakdown of that total, so he knew he could hide the theft. I have a team investigating as we speak.'

'Very well. I am afraid our six minutes are up. I have a meeting to get to. Will you keep me apprised?' Auger said.

'Of course.'

Chapter 38: By the Numbers

Mayberry had always loved numbers. Numbers weren't like people. They never lied.

The Fraud Squad was divided into four teams, one of which was tasked with the sort of generic theft Jake Sanders had orchestrated.

Jake Sanders' numbers were telling a very different story from the one Jake had told. The theft could not have been more straightforward. Fake transactions, tiny payments. He stole little and often, never trying to score big in any one hit. The methodology struck Mayberry as being at odds with murder. Jake had been careful enough to steal a little at a time, and killing to claim life insurance seemed to be on the other end of the scale. Murder was messy, bloody, and cold, and Jake didn't seem the type of man capable of murder. Everything Mayberry had seen said Jake was more at home with an Excel spreadsheet and a pile of old receipts than anything involving people.

Nor was Jake particularly clever. He hadn't done much to hide his fraud. There was a paper trail that led nowhere, and only he could have ordered the payments. He seemed to be relying on his clients assuming that any missing funds had to be nothing more than a rounding error.

'H-how much d-did he steal?' Mayberry asked of DCI Manuel de Granados, the head of the team.

Granados was an older gentleman, virtually bald, with a handlebar moustache that Einstein would have envied. He squinted up at the projector screen, where all of Jake's Excel files were open.

'Twenty clients, and six or seven hundred pounds' worth of fraudulent transactions per payroll cycle per client, by the looks of the last few months. Let's call that an even fourteen thousand a month on the low end. Most of the fraudulent transactions are very low value. Look at line 134.' He pointed to the screen. 'Travel reimbursement, employee 1345. There is no employee 1345 in the list for that client.'

'It's only eight p-pounds!'

'Eight quid is small enough that you'd never bother to question it. And that's one of the smallest transactions. He's got some that are low three figures and a handful of payments in the four-figure range. That's as greedy as he got. It doesn't take many of those to add up. I haven't averaged out the fraud yet – can't until we identify all the dodgy transactions – but it's going to be low- to mid-six figures a year in total.'

'H-half a m-million pounds?' Mayberry said, dumbstruck.

'At the top end. It could be a lot less.'

Suddenly, a hundred and fifty thousand pounds in life insurance didn't seem like it was worth killing for.

**

'Fabby!' Faye screamed as Rafferty walked through the front door. She was smiling from ear to ear, and leapt off the sofa to let the cat out of the carry basket. She swept the cat up in her arms and clutched her tight, as if she'd never expected to see her again. 'Where did you find her?'

'She was at Battersea Dogs and Cats Home,' Rafferty said. 'The lady who pulled you both from the canal dropped her off there after you were taken to hospital.'

'Thank you! Thank you, thank you, thank you,' Faye gushed.

And then she hugged Rafferty. Voluntarily. The girl who hated to be touched, who recoiled from physical contact, who seemed to be away in her own little world, voluntarily hugged Rafferty.

Rafferty smiled, hugged her back, and said, 'You're welcome.'

Chapter 39: Return to Normal

Monday 27th June, 07:30

'Faye! Wake up.' Rafferty nudged her sleeping house guest gently.

'W-what day is it?' Faye stammered.

'It's Monday morning. I've got to go to work. There's breakfast on the kitchen counter for you. I've left my spare keys there for you, too. Why don't you go down to the Job Centre today and sign on?'

Faye looked confused. 'Sign on for what?'

'Jobseekers allowance,' Rafferty said, exasperated. 'You need to get back on your feet, and you need a job to do that. I'm not chucking you out or anything, so don't worry too much. Just go and see them, okay? You know where it is?'

Faye waved her off. 'I'll find it.'

Rafferty watched as Faye sank back down under the covers and out of sight. Sometimes, Faye seemed so mature, so normal, and at others, she was just an overgrown teenager with no sense of responsibility. Four years inside had really done a number on her. She didn't cook, clean, or contribute, and yet didn't seem to feel at all ashamed about eating Rafferty's food, sleeping on Rafferty's sofa, and watching Rafferty's TV.

It wasn't like Rafferty hadn't dealt with living with someone like that before. Her big brother had been just the same – when he was fifteen. With a bit of luck, Faye would adjust, and fast. She couldn't stay forever, no matter how little Rafferty wanted to turf her out onto the street. If only she'd start pulling her weight while she was there.

Chapter 40: Get on with It

The Monday morning fry-up in The Feathers was a time-honoured tradition. Whenever Morton didn't have an urgent enquiry to make – and the investigation into Mark's death could certainly wait an hour – he liked to start the day right: with bacon, sausages, eggs, beans, and toast, but no black pudding. It was all the stuff that Sarah had long-since emptied from their cupboards in favour of wheatgrass and spirulina. Sometimes his wife just couldn't appreciate how delicious cholesterol could be.

The man sitting opposite him had no such encumbrance. Kieran O'Connor was a free man – at least, as free as any man who worked ninety hours a week could be. Lawyers often joked they were married to the law, and for Kieran, it was true. He was a workaholic with a penchant for fine suits. Even now, with baked beans and buttered mushrooms to contend with, he was wearing a three-piece suit. It was bespoke, of course, probably Savile Row or Italian. The man was a walking contradiction: working class Dublin lad, barrister, fry-up before work, three-piece suit, friends with the boys in blue, Notting Hill mansion.

As long as he carried on buying the breakfasts, Morton would always consider him a friend.

'So, anyway,' Kieran said as he chewed over a mouthful of bacon, 'if you don't pick him up now, I'll look like an eejit. His clients know, we know, and the press knows. Sooner or later, when he thinks the heat is off, he'll hide any remaining evidence, and we need to be seen to be doing something.'

Morton held up his hands in surrender. 'You win. Can I at least finish my breakfast first?'

'You're the boss.'

***

Brodie was looking smug when Mayberry found him in his office on Monday morning.

'H-how'd it g-go?'

'It was hell. You owe me, laddie.'

Brodie shoved a folder in his direction. Mayberry opened it to find printouts of thirty-odd slips.

'T-that's all?'

Brodie glared at him. 'What do you mean, "That's all"? I worked all weekend to get you those, laddie. You had cross-cut shredded paper, and I gave you meaningful data. The proper response is "thank you", laddie.'

'T-thank you.'

'You don't need more, anyway. I think it's enough. Look at them – they're all losers. I compared the slips we could recover from the shredding pile with the winning slips from the same time frame. He made the same bet every time.'

'W-what bet?'

'He bet on the favourite. His system was to go for the most popular option, no matter whether it was first to score in a footie match or the three-thirty at Kempton. I ran the numbers. He was losing money hand over fist. The bookies always price in a healthy margin on the odds-on favourite. He must have been losing ten to twenty percent a day.'

'How m-much do you think he was g-gambling?'

'Two grand a day. He had to have been losing a few hundred of that.'

'Almost e-exactly what he'd been stealing?'

'Quite.'

'So, some of it was left?'

'I think so. He stole two thousand a day from his clients, gambled it, and got about eighteen hundred back in winnings.'

'W-why?'

'I've got a theory. Let me do some digging, and then I want to talk to your boss.'

Mayberry looked at him blankly.

***

Morton arrived at the aptly-named *The Mobile Office* a little after nine o'clock. He was alone. It wasn't like he needed backup to arrest an accountant, of all people. What was he going to do? Make a three-mile-an-hour getaway along the canal?

It was moored right where it should be, at Jake's home mooring. There were power cables running from the quayside to the boat, and it looked much like every other boat in sight: quiet, cramped, and isolated. It was a little less impressive than *The Guilty Pleasure* both in size and in appearance, with cracking paintwork around the windows and a much more dishevelled look to her.

Morton banged on the door loudly. 'Jake Sanders, open up!'

No answer. Morton had come prepared, after the same had happened to Rafferty and Ayala.

'Last chance, or I'll bust open what's left of this door,' Morton called out.

The door was in tatters, with boarding across it that had been roughly nailed in place. Evidently, Jake hadn't replaced it since Ayala and Rafferty had been forced to let themselves in the last time.

'One. Two. Three!' Morton kicked at the door right above the lock, and it broke easily inwards. Splinters shot everywhere as the door fell apart.

The living room was quiet. Too quiet.

'Mr Sanders, if you're there, then come out with your hands up. This is the police.'

No reply.

Morton edged towards the back of the living room. It wasn't a big boat. He paused at the door to the bedroom and listened. He couldn't hear anything inside. Morton slowly reached for the doorknob, expecting Jake to try to jump him at any moment.

The door was locked from the inside. Jake was home.

'Mr Sanders!' Morton yelled. 'Unlock this door!'

Again, no reply.

'One. Two. Three!' Morton kicked the bedroom door the same way he'd taken out the front door, hitting it just above the lock, but it didn't budge. He tried again, and the lock broke. The door swung inwards, revealing the tiny bedroom.

There, on the bed, was Jake Sanders. Asleep.

'Oi!' Morton said, nudging him. 'Wake up.'

Jake Sanders was cold, too cold. Morton reflexively felt for a pulse but found nothing.

Jake Sanders was dead.

***

The pathologist took forever to arrive. He saw Morton loitering outside the boat.

'Gone and killed another one, have you?' Chiswick laughed. 'What happened this time?'

'Suicide. I found this.' Morton handed Chiswick an evidence bag in which he'd placed the suicide note that he'd found clutched in the dead man's hands.

Chiswick read it.

I cannot live with the guilt of what I did any longer. I brought shame upon my family and upon myself. Please know that I go to the grave knowing that I will never be unburdened. My conscience weighs heavily upon my chest. To my friends and remaining family, I apologise for all the pain and suffering that I have caused you. I do not ask for your forgiveness, only your understanding. I was in a dark place, as if a fog had descended over the world. Nothing mattered. I drifted from day to day, desperate to escape, to be free. I hope the next world will be more kind to me, and to Mark, than this world ever was. Yours truly, with what love I have left to give, Jake.

'So, not murder, then. I'll go take a look at the body.' Chiswick bounded off in search of Jake's corpse, whistling cheerfully as he did so.

Chapter 41: One Down

Monday 27th June, 13:00

The bodies were piling up. First, there was Mark Sanders, and now his brother Jake. The media was having a field day speculating about a potential serial killer. One death on the canals would have been unusual. Two was a spectacle.

The team gathered in the Incident Room where a second board had been set up with a picture of Jake, a photocopy of the suicide note, and a report from the Fraud Squad outlining the extent of the fraud.

'Suicide,' Morton said firmly. 'Preliminary analysis of the note confirms Jake killed himself. The note was written in his handwriting, using his pen, on his own headed notepaper. Not only that, I had to break down two doors, both locked from the inside, before I could get to him. We aren't looking at a second murder, which means we have to focus on Mark.'

Mayberry raised a hand. 'B-but what if J-Jake was the killer?'

'Maybe he was,' Morton said. 'We need to prove it, either way. I personally think Jake was just a fraudster. He stole money. There is no evidence he ever committed a violent crime, and the amount of money he was set to receive from Mark's life insurance is far less than he successfully stole from his clients. If Mark hadn't died, we'd never have known about the fraud.'

'Then who killed Mark?' Rafferty said.

Morton tapped the whiteboard. 'We've still got four suspects, even without Jake.'

'Four?'

'Laura, Tim, Faye, and Pip Berryman.' The mistress, her boyfriend, the lover betrayed, and the rival. Any of the four could have killed Mark on the canal side and thrown his body into the water.

Rafferty stood up. 'I think Jake did it. He had the best access to the waterways. Look at the canal map. *The Guilty Pleasure* has been travelling east to west along the Grand Union. Mark's body was dumped in the middle of that journey. Jake had access to a boat and could easily have used that to dump the body.'

'And Faye was on the victim's boat,' Morton countered. 'As you said, she was on the boat he owned, she definitely went past the point where we found Mark's body, and she has motive, to boot. If she knew about the affair, she could easily have offed him.'

Ayala coughed loudly to interrupt the impending argument and then nudged the conversation back into safer waters. 'How far could the body have drifted?'

'Forensics aren't sure,' Morton said. 'Chances are, Mark's body was dumped at night. There isn't much natural movement in the water, but if he was dragged in the wake of another boat – and the abrasions on the body are consistent with that – then he could have gone in anywhere along either branch of the Union.'

'Isn't it most likely he was dumped near the discovery site?' Ayala asked. 'The odds have to favour the dump site being proximate to the discovery site.'

'Yes,' Morton said. 'And it all comes back the one person we absolutely know had to have gone past that part of the canal while they were aboard *The Guilty Pleasure*: Faye. She had access to the boat, she clearly had the opportunity to commit murder, and she has the strongest motive. He cheated on her. I think she killed him, and now she's playing us for fools.'

'Oh, come off it, David!' Rafferty exclaimed. 'Faye's handwriting doesn't match. She was asleep when I found the second note, or are you forgetting that? I was there. She would have had to walk past me to plant the note.'

'She could have had someone else write the note,' Morton reasoned. 'It's not impossible to change your handwriting, either. And, as to access, she could have exited from the window at the back of the boat, popped the ransom note under the front door, and been back in bed long before you woke up.'

Rafferty looked offended. 'What more do you want the poor girl to do? Take a polygraph?'

'That would be a start.'

'Then, I'll make sure she does. Will that shut you up?'

Morton half-shrugged and turned his attention to the remaining suspects. 'Pip Berryman seems an unlikely possibility. While he had motive, he seems affluent enough without needing to kill for a single client meeting. Physically, he had no better access to the boat than you or I. Does anyone seriously think Pip could be our killer?'

His question was met with silence.

'Then, let's look at Laura and Tim. They had access. They were on the boat the last time Mark was seen alive. Laura was having an affair with Mark, which would have been difficult to sustain once Faye was released. We know from Jake's interview that Tim knew about the affair, and it doesn't take a genius to see why he might be angry at Mark. Add in Mark's HIV status and the potential for Tim or Laura to have been infected as a result of the affair, and we've got two strongly motivated suspects. Of the two of them, Laura appears to have had better access as, by all accounts, Tim left the boat before she did that night. We need to confirm that timeline.'

Rafferty pouted. 'We're going on hearsay now? Jake would have said anything to plead down the fraud charges to simple theft. What happened to real evidence?'

'Find me some, and we'll run with it,' Morton said.

'Fine. I'll take the suicide note down to the handwriting specialist.'

'You do that. Take Mayberry with you. Ayala, you're with me. We're going to visit the coroner to make sure this is suicide.'

***

Gabrielle Boileau was quick to answer Rafferty's summons. She arrived in the Incident Room, panting, ten minutes after getting the call.

'*Mes apologies, chére.* I was held up by the superintendent. He is a friendly man, *non?*'

Rafferty smirked. It was the first time she'd ever heard anyone say something nice about the superintendent. The man was crass, talentless, and quick to blame his inferiors for his own shortcomings. No doubt he was making an effort to impress the young Frenchwoman.

'I suppose,' Rafferty said tactfully. 'I need you to look at a suicide note and confirm whether the handwriting is consistent with a prior handwriting sample.'

There were plenty of samples to choose from. While Jake's accounts were all computerised, his own notes were not. He had opted not to entrust the details of his gambling to the computer, instead scribbling shorthand notes that were indecipherable. The paperwork had been seized for the fraud investigation against him, giving them pages upon pages of his spider-like scrawl to use as a comparison.

'Very well.' Boileau rifled through the box of samples Rafferty had placed on the desk. 'Hmm.'

She seemed to be searching for something, but Rafferty didn't know what. Eventually, Rafferty's curiosity got the better of her.

'What are you looking for in there?'

'*Les mêmes lettres*, Madam Rafferty. Most of the samples are, pardon my English, bollocks. They are numbers, initials, and Monsieur Sanders' signature. For my comparison to be meaningful, I need to see complete prose.'

Rafferty leapt into action. Somewhere in the boxes, she'd found letters that Jake had once written to a woman. They had never been sent, which was probably just as well, because their sheer cheesiness had made Rafferty want to barf. 'What about this?'

Boileau took the letter, read it, and burst into a fit of giggles. 'Your English men... they really write like this? *C'est parfait.*'

The letter, which included an awful rhyming poem, was soon displayed on the big screen alongside the suicide note.

'Interesting,' Boileau mused. 'Look at the letter. The Ls are elongated, curved slightly to the right. There are linking strokes between every letter, which shows that the writer's hand rarely left the page. Projecting pen strokes interact with the lines above and below them. Punctuation is brief, sloppy. The shading is strong, indicating lots of pressure.'

'Okay. And what about the note?'

'It is consistent. There are some hesitation marks, of course–'

'Of course?'

'It is a suicide note,' Boileau said. 'One does not simply write such a thing from start to finish. Did you find, perchance, any failed drafts?'

Rafferty shook her head. 'This was all Morton found.'

'Then, it is no surprise that his handwriting is imperfect. The love letter could have been written a dozen times so that 'e might impress the woman. The suicide note was written but once. Hesitation marks are normal under such stress.'

'I don't want to argue with an expert, but aren't hesitation marks also the hallmark of a forgery?'

'*Oui*, in certain circumstances. It would take an expert to forge such a note as this. Everything else is consistent. And was the note not found behind two locked doors?'

'It was.'

'Then, I am afraid, we must conclude that this is suicide.'

***

The pathologist was whistling when Morton arrived at the morgue. He was a strange fellow. Forty hours a week cutting up bodies never seemed to dull his world view. He also had a penchant for biting sarcasm that confused many new recruits.

He was leaning over a corpse with a transparent plastic mask over his face, wearing a grin that made him look socio-pathic.

'Morning, David. Want to give me a hand?' Chiswick grabbed the corpse's wrist and gave Morton a wave.

'Cut it out, Larry,' Morton said. 'That wasn't funny the first time you did it, and it's not funny now.' Actually, it had been quite funny the first time, if only for being so unexpected. But Morton would never tell the pathologist that.

The pathologist turned his attention back to the body on the slab.

Morton coughed loudly. 'You said you had the results back for Jake Sanders' blood tests.'

'Oh. Those. Yes. Suicide. Off you go. I'm a busy man, David.'

This again? Morton thought. He ought to know better than to question the pathologist's sense of humour by now. 'Okay. It was funny. Now, can I have your attention?'

Chiswick's smile returned. He waved again with the corpse.

'Larry. Please.'

'He killed himself, David. You found him behind two locked doors. You can't possibly think it was anything other than suicide.'

Morton was beginning to get impatient. 'Tell me some-thing I don't know.'

'Corpses have unique tongue prints, just like fingerprints.'

'Really?' Morton said. 'Please tell me you weren't playing around with dead people when you found that out.'

'Nah. I read it in a magazine.' Chiswick took off his blood-stained gloves and began to rummage through his filing cabinet. 'Here.' He handed Morton a report.

'Amitriptyline and oxazepam,' Morton read aloud.

'Yep. He had a prescription for the former. It's used as an antidepressant.'

Jake had been on antidepressants. Could his gambling have been an offshoot of that depression? 'How long has he been on those?'

'Since his father died. Four years.'

Exactly when the gambling began. Morton felt a sinking feeling. Jake wasn't their man. He was a broken, depressed gambling addict. He wasn't a murderer. 'And the oxazepam?'

'It's an over-the-counter sleeping med. The combination is popular among the suicidal. They drift off to sleep and are gone in about twelve hours.'

'Is it painful?'

'I wouldn't know,' Chiswick said. 'I haven't died.'

Chapter 42: The Truth, the Whole Truth, and Nothing But

Monday 27th June, 15:30

The polygraph test was a relic of a bygone era. It was against Morton's better judgement to use one at all, and he had only acquiesced at Rafferty's insistence. The problem was inaccuracy. Polygraphs, despite commonly being referred to as "lie detectors", could only measure three variables: sweat, heart rate, and breathing.

The premise was simple enough: the three variables would be recorded and plotted by needle onto paper. The patterns would show spikes that, in theory, could indicate lies.

In practice, Morton thought, they were little more than stress tests. The courts would never admit polygraph test results as being probative of guilt.

Faye was seated in an empty incident room on the third floor. It belonged to another team and had been cleared out that Monday morning. Her chair was in front of the desk where the machine had been set up so she could not see the man questioning her. His name was Gerald Parks, formerly of New Scotland Yard. These days, he was retired, and he only consulted on an occasional basis. Morton wasn't looking forward to the next budget meeting, when he'd have to justify hiring Parks to go through with this farce.

Morton and Rafferty were sitting in the back of the room as observers. They had set up a camera aimed at Faye which relayed her expressions without their being able to influence her at all. It would be down to Parks to conduct the interview.

There was an arm cuff looped around Faye's wrist to measure her heart rate and blood pressure. Electrodes ran from the polygraph machine to her fingers to measure sweat levels. Her chest was bound with straps to measure the slightest change in her breathing patterns.

Almost as soon as the equipment was in place, her readings were all over the place.

'Miss Atkins, please try to relax. Take a deep breath,' Parks said.

Faye's eyes were wide with fear. She strained in the chair, trying to turn around to face her questioner. 'Do we have to do this?'

'Miss Atkins, you don't have to do anything you don't want to do. If you're up to it, I'd like to ask you a few simple questions with yes or no answers. If you're uncomfortable at any time, we can stop. Do you understand?'

The needles stopped jerking almost immediately, as if someone had turned off a switch. Morton saw Parks frown as if this was most unusual.

'I understand,' Faye said.

'Just yes or no, please. I'll start with some control questions. These don't matter at all, so just say the first answer that pops into your head. Is your name Faye Atkins?'

The needle began to leap again. 'Y-yes.'

'Please relax, Miss Atkins. I'm not here to trip you up. You are twenty-two years old. Is that correct?'

The needle moved more smoothly. 'Yes.'

Parks turned to give Morton a quick thumbs-up. 'Miss Atkins, have you ever stolen supplies from work?'

'No... I've never had a real job.'

Parks scribbled out that control question. 'Have you ever lied to get out of trouble?'

'No... Wait, yes.' Faye seemed to screw up her face, morphing from a persona hiding her foibles to a childlike innocence.

The interviewer arched an eyebrow. It wasn't normal for his subjects to so easily admit to dishonest albeit harmless behaviour. He asked a few more standard control questions from his prepared list, and then he moved on to the meat of the interview.

'On Sunday, 12th June, you were on board *The Guilty Pleasure*, weren't you?' Parks asked.

'Yes.' No sudden movement.

'And your boyfriend, Mark Sanders, was there too?'

'Yes.' Still no movement.

'It was the last time you saw him, wasn't it?'

'Yes.' The needle stayed within the same range.

'You killed him, didn't you?'

'No!'

There was a small jump. It wasn't enough to alarm Parks. He seemed to shrug, as if her reaction was simply anger. His questions were intended to be stimuli, and it was natural for her to become stressed in response to an accusation of murder.

Parks switched back to a control question, throwing a curveball to see how she would react. 'You're wearing blue today, aren't you?'

'What? Oh. Yes.' Faye looked confused and even glanced down to confirm that her blouse was really blue.

'There were other people on the boat that night, weren't there?'

'Yes.' True.

'Were they,' Parks said, glancing at his notes, 'Miss Laura Keaton, Mr Tim Fowler, and Mark Sanders?'

'Yes.' True.

'Was there anyone else on the boat, to the best of your knowledge?'

'No.' True.

'Did you write the ransom notes?'

'No!' True again.

Parks glanced over to Morton as if to ask if he had any follow-up questions. Morton quickly scribbled one down on a piece of paper and passed it over.

'Miss Atkins, when you were convicted four years ago, did you do it?'

'No.' True again.

'Thank you for your time.'

Parks began to remove the apparatus from Faye. When he was done, Rafferty quickly scooped her up and escorted her from the room to take her home.

'Well?' Morton said when the two women were gone.

'Chief Inspector, in my expert opinion, she was telling the truth. There were a couple of small blips–' Parks indicated point on the graph where Faye had failed the name question, and the curve when she had been asked the control question about dishonesty. 'But that's to be expected. All of her responses were consistent with someone telling the truth.'

'Do you really believe that polygraphs are accurate?' Morton asked.

'At least eighty percent of the time,' Parks said. 'The reality is that one can learn to pass a polygraph by exaggerating responses to the control questions. Miss Atkins didn't do that.

Her control questions are consistent with her real answers. It's easy to fudge a guilty response to look inconsistent. It's much more difficult to fudge a guilty response to look totally honest. I like to think of answers as comparative. People who lie tend to make blanket denials. Faye admitted to lying to get out of trouble. That speaks to her innocence.'

'That's your verdict, then,' Morton said.

'That's my verdict. Faye Atkins is not your killer.'

***

Faye sulked that evening. She said little to Rafferty, despite Rafferty's best efforts.

'Faye, I'm sorry. I wasn't doubting your innocence. My boss wanted to make sure. At least we can rule you out now. Isn't that a good thing?' Rafferty implored.

'No. I always knew I was innocent.'

'Faye, I–'

'We thought we could trust you,' Faye said, and then hastily added, 'Fabby and I, that is. But you're just like everybody else.'

Rafferty held up her hands in surrender. It was like arguing with a child – and that child was right.

Chapter 43: Who, What, and When?

Tuesday 28th June, 09:00

The coffee was boiled, and then stewed some more. The four officers found themselves sitting once more around the conference room table, bleary-eyed and out of ideas. The investigation was hitting wall after wall, and little progress had been made.

The suspects were the same suspects they'd had since day one: Faye Atkins, Jake Sanders, Tim Fowler, Laura Atkins, and Pip Berryman. Their names were still on the whiteboard in Mayberry's meticulously neat handwriting.

'Ignore Jake Sanders for now,' Morton said. 'I don't think he did it. Even if he did, justice cannot reach beyond the grave.'

'And ignore Faye too,' Rafferty said.

'Polygraphs don't prove a thing,' Morton grumbled. But he still nodded, and Mayberry got up to put a red X through her name on the whiteboard.

'And that leaves us with three,' Ayala chimed in. '*And* we're still nowhere on proving which of them did it. We've got the mistress, her boyfriend, and the guy from work. Which suspect do you fancy?'

'Pip Berryman has to be the least likely. Ayala, go talk to him. Take Mayberry with you,' Morton ordered. When Ayala remained seated, Morton added, 'Now would be a good time for that, gentlemen.'

Ayala and Mayberry scarpered from the room, pausing only to snatch up their jackets.

'What do you want me to do, then?' Rafferty asked.

'I want to look at the not-so-happy couple. Tim and Laura had the same access to the boat. They had the same meal. They share a common cause by way of motive. Laura is the mistress betrayed, and Tim the lover cuckolded.'

'Didn't Tim leave first that night?' Rafferty asked.

'That's his story, yes. If Tim really did leave first, then Laura must become our prime suspect.'

'Unless Tim returned, or Mark didn't die on Sunday evening,' Rafferty countered. 'Mark could have died on Monday or Tuesday, according to the coroner. We just don't know the precise timeline.'

'True,' Morton conceded. 'And if our timeline is off, then our suspects' alibis go out the window, and we have to start afresh. I find it unlikely that he wasn't seen at all for days after going missing. No calls, no bank charges, no witnesses. None of our suspects could reasonably have held him hostage.'

'So, where do we start?'

'Let's start with the CCTV,' Morton said. 'You go get the footage from Tim's building. That ought to show both Tim and Laura returning home after the dinner party. Get the time-stamps, check they didn't leave again, and look for any exits from their building which are not covered by cameras.'

'What are you going to do?'

'I'm going to see what cameras are near the mooring site, and see if we can find any evidence at all that Mark Sanders was still alive on Monday 13th June.'

***

There was no answer when Ayala buzzed the door for Berryman Financial Services Ltd. They had to be buzzed in by a neighbouring business just to get into the building. From there, it was a simple case of walking in the front door unannounced. So much for security.

They found out why nobody was paying much attention to the doorbell the moment they entered the Berryman offices.

Pip Berryman was in the middle of a screaming match when Ayala and Mayberry arrived. He was yelling so loudly that the entire office had fallen silent. Ayala had expected to find the normality of an office: quiet, calm, and efficient. Instead, the boss's son was ensconced in his father's office, having a rip-roaring argument.

The staff of Berryman Financial Services had paused their work to listen. Not one person was paying attention to their computers or the phones ringing off the hook. Nobody was even bothering to hide it.

Ayala turned to one woman who was listening intently from her desk. 'What's going on?' he asked in a hushed tone.

'Pip's yelling about his inheritance. Daddy's finally cut him off.' She seemed to be very pleased with this news. It was clear Pip was not a popular fixture among the staff, for this look of rapture was replicated on the faces of everybody listening.

'Why?'

The woman whispered back, 'Because he's feckless and an embarrassment to the family name. That's what Mr Berryman said, anyway. Shh, I'm trying to listen!'

Ayala gave up trying to talk to her and strained to make out what the Berrymans were arguing about.

'I'm not you, okay? It's not like when you were my age!' Pip screamed.

Mr Berryman Senior's retort was swift and cutting. He spoke in a deep, rumbling voice which carried throughout the office. 'You ungrateful little shit! I gave you everything! The best schools, the best clothes, the nicest cars. You know what I had at your age? *Nothing.* I worked sixty hours a week to build this firm from the ground up. I ate rice and beans for years before we made a real profit. Get the hell out of my office, you entitled, whiny, self-centred, feckless moron. You're fired.'

'Fired? No! I quit!'

Berryman Senior smirked. 'Fine. Then I don't have to give you a severance package. Get out, or I'm calling security.'

Pip Berryman fled from his father's office, tears beginning to stream down his face. The office watched in silence at first, and then the jeers began. He sprinted past Ayala and Mayberry and made a beeline for the stairs.

'Come on,' Ayala said to Mayberry. 'We've got to follow him.'

***

The crush of peak time at Canary Wharf tube station hit Rafferty as she disembarked from the Jubilee Line. The crowds were jostling for position on the platform, every man for himself. By and large, it was men: big, hairy, suited men carrying Italian leather briefcases, browbeaten expressions, and egos the size of minivans. They flooded onto the train as Rafferty fought to escape past them. The stench of too much cologne and man-sweat hung in the air. It was small mercy that Rafferty only had to escape the tube station rather than wait for a train.

By the time Rafferty found herself on the street, she felt like she needed a shower. The tube had been built for the Victorian era, and the builders had never expected to cram so many people inside such a small space. It had been standing room only from Green Park. Rafferty found herself jammed in between two commuters whose armpits were inconveniently located at nose height.

There was a light breeze in the air as Rafferty headed towards Westferry Road. Laura Keaton and Tim Fowler shared a penthouse apartment in one of the ritziest towers on the Isle of Dogs, the Medici building. It was a crescent-shaped development with views over the water, and was home to some of the wealthiest financiers, who prized it for its proximity to Canary Wharf, the river views, the helipad, and the private dock on the Thames. Even a studio in the Medici building would set the buyer back a cool three million pounds.

Morton had given Rafferty two tasks: find out what time Laura and Tim had returned home on the night of June twelfth, and then see if there was any way out of the building without being seen or heard.

She took the second task first, encircling the whole building on foot. There was one main entrance foyer, guarded by a smartly dressed doorman who eyed her cautiously as she walked by. Around the back, there was a small communal garden with a fence surrounding it. Behind the garden, there was an alleyway for taking out the rubbish.

Rafferty found access to the alleyway easily enough. It ran in the shadow of the next building and was just wide enough to push an oversized rubbish bin along. There was one metal gate from the doorway into the inside of the complex. It had a single padlock securing it which could be accessed from either side.

'Fifteen seconds?' Rafferty mused, wondering how quickly she could pick the lock. She knew Morton would disapprove, but she had to find out. She produced lock pins from her handbag and went to work. It took just thirteen seconds before she heard the satisfying click of the padlock coming undone. She swung the gate open and took a quick glimpse inside the garden.

It was empty. Despite the sunshine, none of the building's occupants had taken to the garden. There were no lounging employees, no summer jugs of Pimm's, not even a smoker lingering in the doorway.

Rafferty clicked the lock shut behind her and headed for the back door of the building. Locked. She loitered, fishing in her handbag, acting as if she was looking for a smoke. If the garden had been busier, she might have been able to tailgate her way inside the building. After fifteen minutes of waiting for someone to emerge, Rafferty gave up on that plan. It didn't really matter how hard it was to get into the building. What mattered was how easily Tim or Laura, or both, could have left without being seen. There was no CCTV on the back door, and it seemed there would have been few witnesses.

She glanced up. Above the gardens were the private balconies of the flats. There might have been someone sitting out on their balcony who could have seen someone coming and going. Or there might not have been. Tim and Laura had returned late in the evening on a Sunday, hardly a popular time to be gazing down at the gardens below.

The gardens provided access. If Tim or Laura had a key to the lock, or it had been left unlocked, or either of them knew how to pick a lock, then it was a short hop from there to the City Road Canal where *The Guilty Pleasure* had been moored up. Rafferty put the padlock back as she made her way out of the garden.

Back at the main entrance, Rafferty flashed her badge at the doorman and demanded to be escorted to see the CCTV tapes for the front door.

'I can't do that, ma'am.'

Rafferty glanced at the doorman's name badge. 'Look, Eric. I'm investigating a murder. I don't care about your residents' privacy, your CCTV policy, or anything else. I need those tapes.'

Eric glanced down at his shoes. 'My apologies, ma'am. If it were up to me, I'd give you them. But our CCTV is all in the cloud. I don't have access to it.'

'Then, who does?'

'Westferry Security Services. They're based nearby. But you'll need a warrant, I'm afraid. Is there anything else I can do for you?' Eric asked.

'Actually, yes. Are you here full-time?'

'Every weekday, ma'am. Seven in the morning 'til eight at night.'

Damn. He wouldn't have been working on Sunday 12th. 'Are there night staff?'

'No, ma'am. We have a weekend porter, but no night service. At night, the residents simply use their keys and door code to get access to the building. The weekend porter keeps the same hours that I do.'

Rafferty thought back to the time that Tim and Laura would have left *The Guilty Pleasure*. The weekend porter would have been long gone by the time they got home that night.

'Eric, are you acquainted with Mr Tim Fowler?' Rafferty asked.

'Of course,' Eric said. 'He has the penthouse, ma'am.'

'Then, you know his girlfriend?'

Eric bit his lip. 'I am... familiar with Miss Keaton.'

'You don't like her?'

'I couldn't possibly say, ma'am.'

'Just blink twice if you don't like her.'

He blinked. Twice.

'Thank you, Eric. Can I ask a delicate question?' Rafferty said.

'You can ask. I may not be allowed to give you the answer.'

'Has Miss Keaton brought another man home before?'

Eric's face remained impassive. He blinked twice.

'Thank you, Eric.'

Rafferty made her way outside. Westferry Road was almost exactly five miles away from where *The Guilty Pleasure* had been moored up on the City Road Basin. It was too far to walk easily, but not far by taxi. At that time of night, with no traffic, it would have been well under half an hour. There were black cabs in the area, though they might well be less frequent on a Sunday, when the banking crowd wasn't on the Isle of Dogs. Either Laura or Tim could have doubled back to the boat, and there was no CCTV to prove it either way.

***

The nerd sitting behind the big desk wasn't the normal guy. Instead, his place had been taken by a large gentleman with furious ginger hair and the bushiest beard Morton had ever seen.

'Where's Zane?' Morton demanded.

'Who?' the man asked in a Glaswegian accent. 'There's naebody here by that name.'

'I can see that. Where is he?'

'Gone, laddie. Off to work fer Google or summat. You're stuck with me. Noah Brodie. I'm the new guy.'

Great. Another novice. 'You any good?'

'Try me,' Brodie said, flashing a toothy grin.

'I've got a murder on a narrowboat on the canal. I need a broad search of any local authority CCTV cameras in the area.'

'Facial recognition? Have ye got photos of who we're looking for?'

Morton had come prepared. He handed over a thumb drive. 'Here. Mug shots for each of our suspects, home locations, possible travel routes, known credit card numbers, the lot. I need to know where each of them has been, and exactly what they did from June 12th onwards.'

'Leave it with me, laddie.'

'It's Detective Chief Inspector,' Morton said as he turned to leave. 'If you want to work here, you'll do well to remember that.'

'Aye, I will,' Brodie said, and then added under his breath, 'Laddie.'

***

The offices of Westferry Security Services were only a few minutes away, as the doorman had promised. They occupied a tiny unit on the third floor of a communal office block.

As it turned out, Westferry Security Services was really just one woman: Jamie Black. She reluctantly buzzed Rafferty into the building and was waiting for her at the top of the stairs.

'Miss Black, I'm Detective Inspector Rafferty. I understand you run the CCTV for the Medici building.'

Black nodded. 'That's right.'

'I need to see the recordings of the front entrance on the night of June 12th.'

'I can't.'

'Can't or won't?' Rafferty asked. 'I was told you're the person I need to talk to. I'll level with you. I'm working a murder enquiry, and I need this footage.'

'I can't...'

'Miss Black, my boss is a very old, very white, very old-fashioned guy. He doesn't think I can cut it just because I'm a woman,' Rafferty lied. 'If I can't get this footage, it'll prove him right, and I'll be in trouble. Can't you help a sister out?'

She could see Black wavering. 'I really can't... Can't you come back with a warrant?'

Not with the way the mags have been lately. 'Jamie – I can call you Jamie, can't I? I can go get a warrant, but it'll take time, and I'll have to come back and search your premises with a team, and you know the guys will take the credit for my work. I don't want to see you out of action for the rest of the week.'

Black's hands began to tremble. 'But my clients...'

'Your clients pay you to look after their privacy and security, don't they? I can't imagine you ever agreed to help cover up a crime. And your clients don't want to see the police poking around here, do they? Imagine how bad it'll be if there are marked police cars outside. Jamie, you seem like a really nice person. How about you let me take a peek at the footage, and, if there's nothing there, I'll be out of your hair in half an hour.'

'And if there is?' Black asked.

'Then, I'll get a warrant and come back – and I'll make sure we keep the disruption to a minimum, in light of your co-operation.' Rafferty smiled sweetly. She had her on the ropes.

'Promise?'

'I promise,' Rafferty said.

'Alright. Follow me.'

Jamie Black led the way to her desk, booted up the computer, and began to search through her archives. She easily found the video files from the evening of June 12th. 'Fast-forward to ten o'clock onwards, please, Jamie.'

'You got it.'

Rafferty watched at 30x speed as people zoomed in and out of the building. 'There! Go back a minute.'

Black rewound and hit play at normal speed. There was Tim Fowler wearing a sports coat and jeans.

'That's my man. 23:03. Now, can you forward a bit more?'

The tape was fast-forwarded once more. 'There! 23:47. That's Laura.' Rafferty snapped a quick picture on her phone for the team, then turned back to Jamie. 'Thank you, Miss Black. We'll be in touch.'

The timings lined up with what the witnesses had said. Tim had left first, leaving Laura to chat with Mark. She arrived just forty-four minutes later. It didn't seem like much time to commit murder.

But Rafferty still couldn't prove whether they had stayed in. Either of them could have doubled back in plenty of time for Mark to disappear by the morning.

Chapter 44: Interrupted

Tuesday 28th June, 12:00

They found Pip in The Green Man drowning his sorrows. He hadn't been hard to find. The younger Berryman had fled the offices of Berryman Financial Services and headed straight for the nearest bar.

He was ordering a double whisky, straight up, when Ayala and Mayberry accosted him.

'Pip Berryman?' Ayala asked.

'Who's asking? Did my father send you?' Pip looked accusingly from Ayala to Mayberry and then back again.

'Metropolitan Police,' Ayala said, flashing his ID. 'This is Detective Inspector Mayberry. I'm Detective Inspector Ayala.'

Pip downed his whisky and motioned for the barman to pour him another. 'He's got the Met at his beck and call now, has he? Haven't you anything better to do? I only smashed his precious lamp. He fired me, you know!'

Mayberry shot Ayala a look that clearly said, "What an idiot."

'Sir, you've just confessed to criminal damage. I'm afraid we're going to have to take you in for questioning.'

'Really?' Pip said disbelievingly.

''Fraid so. Stand up, turn around, and put your hands behind your back, please.'

Ayala waited for him to comply, then slapped cuffs around his wrists. It was incredibly satisfying to see Pip's face as they clicked tightly shut.

***

A knock on Morton's door startled him. He had been filling out paperwork for most of the afternoon, a task which seemed to take more and more of his time with every passing year.

'Enter,' he called out.

Noah Brodie bounded in with the manic energy of a man possessed. He took a seat without waiting to be asked and slammed his laptop down on the desk.

'Sit down, why don't you?' Morton said dryly.

Brodie grinned sheepishly.

'I take it you have some CCTV footage for me?'

'Nope, none.'

'You came all the way up to my office to tell me you couldn't find anything.'

Brodie chuckled. 'I ain't that much of a bampot. I got your boat.'

'You what?'

'Yer boat. The Canal and River Trust log the boats. They've all got a unique number, don't they? I can show you when and where the boat went. Does that help?'

Morton paused to think. They knew *The Guilty Pleasure* had travelled from east to west and that the body dump site was probably somewhere along the way. The body could have floated or been dragged under another boat, but it showed she could have done it.

'Can you look up any boat?'

'Course I can.'

'Where has Jake Sanders' *Mobile Office* been? Was he anywhere near the location where we discovered the body?' Morton asked.

'Gimme a sec.'

Brodie opened up his laptop and began to type furiously. For a few minutes, Morton's office fell quiet, with only the click of keyboard actuation punctuating the silence.

'Is this going to take long?'

'Hold ya horses, Detective Chief Inspector laddie,' Brodie said. 'And... here we go. Yep. Blimey, this one's been busy. He did move down that way. Now, the logs aren't perfect – they're recorded manually, so ye only get a snapshot – but it looks like *The Mobile Office* was moored up next to *The Guilty Pleasure* on Monday 13th, early in the morning.'

'Jake never left until the next morning?'

'Nope,' Brodie said. 'He was seen again later that day, way over in Limehouse. Then again at King's Cross. He's a busy laddie.'

'Both of them were there?' Morton mused. That suggested Jake had had better access than they had thought. But he was dead, and dead men told no tales. 'Has he done that before?'

'Gone to Limehouse?'

'Moored up near *The Guilty Pleasure*,' Morton said.

'Hang on...'

Brodie once again began tapping. If this was a one-off, it suggested Jake had stayed for a reason. If it was habitual, then perhaps Jake had simply moved the boat the next morning to avoid moving it after an afternoon beer with his brother.

'He's done it before. Lots of times. There aren't as many logs – Jake's not a continuous cruiser, and the Canal and River Trust lot don't have to worry about him overstaying when he's got a permanent mooring, too – but it looks like a pattern to me. Wherever *The Guilty Pleasure* went, *The Mobile Office* followed.'

Habitual, then. Jake could have done it. Any of them could have done it. Yet again, the evidence was inconclusive. Morton wanted to bash his head against the desk in frustration. Would they ever catch a break?

**

Pip Berryman fidgeted awkwardly in his seat. His brow was furrowed, and there were visible sweat patches under his armpits. He looked as if he'd never set foot in a police station before, let alone an interview suite at Scotland Yard.

Morton eyed him up through the one-way mirror in the corridor. He was of two minds about the dandy man-child waiting to be interviewed. Pip was certainly nervous, but he hadn't, however, asked for a lawyer.

Looks were often deceiving in Morton's line of work. Innocent men and women told lies to conceal secrets that had nothing to do with the crime at hand. Guilty men and women told lies to cover up their guilt.

What never lied was the evidence. A cursory glance at Pip was enough to persuade Morton that he probably wasn't the killer. He looked too scrawny to have ever been in a fight, and his hands were the palest white and perfectly manicured. They were the hands of a man who had never done an honest day's work in his life.

Morton kept him waiting for another ten minutes. Poor Pip grew visibly more agitated as Morton watched. He was fidgeting in his seat and looking anxiously from the door to the one-way mirror and back. Every now and then, he glanced at his wrist. His watch looked expensive, but it was a brand Morton didn't recognise. When the ten minutes were up, Morton walked in casually and took a seat opposite Pip.

'You know why you're here, don't you, Pip?' Morton said.

'Yes. And I'm sorry.'

'You're sorry? What for?'

'For yelling at my father,' Pip said. 'For smashing his precious lamp. I shouldn't have done it, and I'm sorry. There. Can I go now? You're not really going to press charges over this, are you?'

Morton paused. Was Pip leaping to the lamp out of genuine concern, or was he trying to play the victim? He stared at Pip, letting the silence build awkwardly in the knowledge that Pip would feel compelled to say something – anything – just to keep the interview moving.

Pip broke sooner than Morton had expected. 'It was a damned lamp, all right? I'll buy Daddy a new one. He can't be this mad at me. Do you really waste your time on petty criminal damage? Don't you have real criminals to look for?'

Daddy? Morton tried not to laugh. It was almost inconceivable to hear a grown man call his father Daddy in public – and even more laughable that a murderer would do so. Unless it was an elaborate act.

'No, Pip. I don't care about the lamp. Tell me about the man you killed.'

'K-killed? You can't seriously mean... me? You think I killed Sanders?' Pip was hesitant at first, almost on the verge of nervous laughter, but his voice grew stronger as he spoke. He seemed to take pride in the idea that someone might think him capable of murder.

'You hated him, didn't you?'

'Hated him?' Pip echoed. 'I wanted to be him. He was tall, handsome, charming. He got sales that nobody else did. He made my father proud. I've never had that. I so badly wanted to impress Daddy. That's why I stole Mark's client. I didn't know he'd been murdered. I wouldn't have wanted it to be like that.'

Morton watched Pip well up. His remorse seemed to be genuine. If he was acting, Pip Berryman deserved an Oscar.

He thought back to the broken lamp. 'What was the argument with your father about?'

'He found out. Someone tipped him off that my big new client – the first time he'd ever patted me on the back, the first time he'd proudly told his friends that I was his son – wasn't my client. He wasn't pleased that I'd picked up the slack when Mark didn't – couldn't – turn up at the meeting. He was angry that I'd, like, that I'd taken credit for the whole deal when it wasn't really mine.'

'And that's when you broke his lamp,' Morton said.

'Exactly.'

'Then, where were you on the night of Sunday 12th June?'

Pip paled. 'I was... at home. On my own.'

'Can you verify that in any way? Did you order take-out? Did you make any phone calls?'

'I don't think so,' Pip said.

He was lying. Morton knew it in his gut. But why? What was he hiding?

'Okay,' Morton said slowly. 'Thank you for coming in, Mr Berryman.'

'Am I free to go?'

'Oh, no. You confessed to criminal damage. I'll have a constable come in to take your statement on that front in a moment. Are you sure you don't want that lawyer?'

***

Tuesday 28th June, 17:45

Morton made it home early that night. He was cooking when his wife came home from her psychology course. They cracked open a bottle of Barolo and settled at the dinner table to enjoy an evening meal of smoked venison loin, pickled radish, pea powder and Swiss chard with chestnut pomme puree. It was a lot of work, but oh so worth it.

Sarah smiled as she tried the venison. 'Mr Morton, are you trying to impress me?'

'Always. Even after all these years. Every day with you is a privilege, not a right, and I'll never forget that.'

She punched Morton's arm gently. 'You old softy.'

'Hey! Less of the "old". You're my age, you know.'

'Nope. You're several months older than me,' Sarah chided him with a pout. 'I'll always be the young, pretty one in this relationship.'

'Yes, you will.'

Morton leant over the table to kiss his wife. She was his one rock, the constant presence, the only thing that seemed to be the same every year. No matter how bad a day he'd had, she was always there with a sympathetic ear.

'Come on, spit it out,' she said. 'You're dying to tell me about this case. Have you got another impossible murder to solve?'

Morton rested his chin in the palm of his hand. His chin was rough with stubble. In all the hubbub of the last few days, he'd forgotten to shave that morning. 'Forget impossible. It's much *too* possible. Any of them could have done it. Every single suspect has a motive, everyone has means, and nobody has an alibi. There's no way we've got anywhere near enough for an arrest, let alone a conviction.'

'Who do you think did it?'

Morton took a bite of his venison while he gathered his thoughts. 'The girlfriend, Faye. She was on the boat. She had access to the dump site. She had motive because he cheated on her. She was on the boat when it crashed, taking with it any lingering evidence. The live-in spouse is always suspect number one.'

'But?'

'But she's passed a polygraph test, and forensics are certain she couldn't have written the ransom note. Rafferty's adamant that Faye is just a victim of circumstance.'

Sarah cocked her head to the side and looked at Morton. 'You trust Rafferty, don't you?'

'Of course, but–'

'But what?'

'But I trust my judgement more.'

'Shouldn't you trust the evidence?' Sarah said.

'If I had any, I would.'

'Then, find something. You always do.'

Chapter 45: Pointing Out the Obvious

Brodie ambushed Morton on Tuesday evening as he was about to head home. 'Laddie!'

Morton spun on his heel. 'How many times have I told you not to call me that?'

'Sorry,' Brodie grinned. 'Won't happen again... sir.'

'What do you want?'

'Jake Sanders didn't have a gambling problem.'

Morton felt himself frown. 'Come again? I've seen the betting slips.'

'Then, ye'd better look again.'

Brodie led Morton down to the forensics department. All of the slips had been digitised and put on the big screen for Morton to see.

Morton squinted at the fine print. 'What am I looking at? They look like betting slips. Winners? Losers?'

'Losers. All losers. Jake kept the winners, shredded the losers,' Brodie said with a hint of pride.

'Why is that unusual? All gamblers want to win, and shredding the losers isn't unreasonable.'

'Not when they're money laundering. He wasn't stealing to gamble. He was gambling to steal.'

Morton felt his jaw slacken. He knew something hadn't been adding up. Jake was an accountant by profession. He had to know gambling was a fool's errand. 'He used the betting shops to turn money he'd stolen into legitimate tax-free winnings?'

190

'Exactly, laddie. Jake had a system, alright. He chucked his money on the best bets where he could lose the smallest amount. I spent yesterday calling round to confirm, and by my best guestimates, he was funnelling nearly half a million a year into twenty or so betting shops and getting eighty-five percent back.'

Morton was impressed. Jake had turned stolen money into legitimate winnings with only a minimal cut lost to the laundering process. 'Hang on. Where's the money now, then?'

Brodie held out his hands palm-up. 'That, laddie, is one for you to answer.'

***

Faye was trying to sleep when she heard the key in the door. The lights were off, and everything else was quiet. Faye shot bolt upright, startling the two cats, which darted underneath the sofa bed in the blink of an eye. The clock on the wall said half past six. Rafferty couldn't be home this early, could she? She'd gone out not more than half an hour earlier. Hadn't she said something about dinner with somebody? A man? Faye couldn't remember exactly what Miss Ashley had said.

The door opened with a creak. A man's silhouette was visible in the doorway, and his height cast an enormous shadow across the lounge. Faye felt her muscles tense up, her heart rising in her throat. Her pulse raced. She darted her eyes around the room looking for something – anything – with which to defend herself. She briefly considered running for the kitchen, where she knew Rafferty would have sharp knives on the countertop next to the microwave, but there wasn't time.

There. On the table. It was only a corkscrew, but it would have to do. Faye leapt up off the sofa as the man came through the doorway carrying two bags full of groceries.

If she'd taken a moment to pause, Faye would have realised just how much the man looked like Miss Ashley. She might have had time to consider that few aggressors bring groceries into the places they're robbing. She might even have simply slammed the door shut and pushed across the dead bolt.

Faye was like an animal possessed. It was as if instinct had taken over her entire body. Her heart had accelerated so fast, it felt like it was going to thump right out of her chest. Her muscles had tensed up, poised and ready to strike. She felt powerful, feline, capable. It was fight or flight, and there was nowhere to run. The corkscrew was in her hand before she knew it. It was one of those corkscrews made of solid stainless steel with a bottle opener at the top and two ratchet arms along the side. There was no flimsy handle to break or any good place to hold. Faye held it with the ratchet arms folded up and the screw point facing out like a dagger.

She planted a foot on the coffee table. The intruder was taller than she, easily over six foot, and broad along with it. She needed every advantage she could get. She seemed to move without thinking. With her right foot planted firmly on the oak coffee table, she pushed downwards to launch herself into the air. She seemed to hang in the air just long enough to see a startled expression form on the man's face. He dropped the bags of groceries, spilling their contents all over the floor.

Faye landed on him with the momentum of her leap behind her. She stretched out, still holding the corkscrew, aiming for the man's neck.

The point of the corkscrew pierced his shoulder, eliciting an almost inhuman yowl of pain. He roared and threw Faye off of him, leaving the corkscrew embedded where his neck met his left shoulder.

The man staggered forward. For a moment, it looked as if he might fall to his knees. Faye looked around the room, desperately searching for another weapon.

And then the man howled again as he yanked the corkscrew from where it had been embedded in his shoulder. He held it out in front of him, staring shell-shocked at the sight of his own blood dripping from the metal. Blood poured from his shoulder where he had been impaled, turning his white shirt crimson.

***

Patrick Rafferty fell to his knees. One moment, he had been walking through the front door of his little sister's flat, and the next, he was collapsing on the floor drenched in his own blood.

He couldn't see the girl. He could barely see anything. His mind was concentrating on the burning pain. Then he heard footsteps. The front door was still open, and the neighbours must have heard him screaming.

'Paddy! Paddy! What happened?'

Patrick could have sworn it was his sister's voice. He turned to see her kneeling above him. 'Stabbed,' he whispered hoarsely.

'Who stabbed you?'

'Some... girl.' Patrick tried to raise his arm, to point towards the girl, but his arm wouldn't listen. He looked up, his vision growing increasingly blurry, and then... nothing.

***

The door was open when Rafferty made it home. She saw her brother on the floor, surrounded by the groceries he had bought to cook them dinner. He shouldn't have been there. He had made it to the Elephant before she did, and that never happened. The one time he was early, and this had happened.

'Paddy! Paddy!' Rafferty shouted at her brother. 'What happened?'

He seemed to twist and writhe, turning his head towards her. He whispered something, his voice hoarse and raspy with pain. Rafferty couldn't make out what he saying.

Paddy seemed to be trying to look towards the bedroom. Rafferty followed his line of sight. 'Is there someone in there?'

Fuck. Rafferty tore the sleeve off her shirt and wrapped it tightly about Paddy's shoulder. She did so as quickly as she could. If there was someone in the bedroom, she had to find out. Satisfied that Paddy wouldn't bleed out before she could return, she hit 999 on her mobile.

It was answered immediately. 'DI Ashley Rafferty. I've got a stab victim bleeding out. I need an ambulance.' Rafferty reeled off her address and then chucked the phone down on the floor.

'Paddy! Stay with me, Paddy. You're going to be okay,' Rafferty said, her voice full of false confidence.

Paddy's eyes were glazed over, and his expression was one of agony. Good. All the time he could feel pain, he was still alive. The endorphin rush would kick in soon.

'Paddy, you've got to stay awake. Whatever happens, fight this. You've got to stay awake, do you hear me?'

Rafferty kept glancing towards the bedroom. Faye should have been home. Had she been hurt too?

'Paddy, I'm going to check on Faye. Stay with me. There's an ambulance on the way. Just stay awake.'

Rafferty rose, and then, with one last glance at her brother, she headed for the bedroom. The door was pulled to, but not properly shut. Rafferty held her breath so she could hear if anyone was inside. Someone was definitely breathing inside the room.

In one fluid motion, she kicked the door open, yelling 'Police! Freeze!' as she did so.

The lights were off. She flicked the light switch. The lights flickered on, revealing Faye sitting on Rafferty's bed with her legs tucked up beneath her chin and her arms wrapped around her shins. She was shaking and covered in blood.

'Faye! What happened?'

Faye looked up at the sound of Rafferty's voice. Her eyes were wide and wild. 'I... I don't know.'

The hairs on Rafferty's neck stood on end. Hunches were normally Morton's domain, but something was telling her that Faye had been involved somehow.

'Faye, can I see your hands?'

The younger woman uncurled her arms and sat up. Rafferty's hunch was right. The blood started at Faye's right hand and had been smeared by transfer to her shirt and trousers. Faye had been the one to hurt Paddy. There wasn't an intruder to be found. The attacker was the woman whom Rafferty had invited into her home.

Rafferty forced down the bile in her throat. The betrayal could wait. She needed to deal with Faye quickly. Paddy was bleeding out on the living room floor, and Rafferty hadn't yet heard the paramedics arrive. She did the mental arithmetic. The nearest hospital was St Thomas' in Lambeth, a little over a mile away. In traffic, that was a nine-minute ride. By that math, Rafferty had three or four minutes to take Faye into custody.

'Faye, could you move to the other side of the bed, please?' Rafferty said, her voice deadly calm.

'Why?' Faye asked in her sing-song voice. She was like a child who didn't understand that it was not normal to be sitting on someone else's bed covered in yet another person's blood.

'Please, just do it.'

Faye did. She shuffled to the right-hand side of the bed, next to the wall – and next to the radiator.

'Okay, Faye, stay still for me.' Rafferty approached Faye slowly. With one hand, she reached around to her back pocket and pulled out her handcuffs.

Then, as slowly and deliberately as she could, she clicked the handcuffs about Faye's right wrist and then the other half to the radiator. Faye looked utterly confused, as if she had been the one betrayed.

'Stay here, okay?' Rafferty said.

She turned and sprinted back to where Paddy was lying on the floor. She knew he couldn't hear her, but she kept talking to him, telling him everything was going to be alright.

'Where are those damned paramedics?'

Chapter 46: Seventy-two Hours

Tuesday 28th June, 21:00

He was curled up on the sofa when the page came in. Sarah was leant against him, her head resting on his shoulders. She sighed when the phone went off.

Morton arched his back so he could squeeze his hand into his jeans pocket and retrieve his phone. He glanced at the screen and exhaled loudly. 'Fuck.'

'What's wrong?'

'Rafferty's brother, Paddy, has been attacked. It doesn't look good. He's on his way to St Thomas' Hospital now.'

Sarah lifted her head off his shoulder and turned to face him. 'What happened?'

'My murder suspect attacked him with a corkscrew,' Morton said. 'Want me to drop you off at the hospital on my way to Scotland Yard? I've got to go see what's up with Faye Atkins, and I know Rafferty could do with some moral support.'

Before he'd even finished the sentence, Sarah was grabbing her coat and heading for the door.

***

With Sarah dropped off at St Thomas', Morton headed for Scotland Yard. At this late hour, he easily found a parking space in the underground car park. Ayala was waiting in reception when he got there.

'What's going on, Ayala?' Morton asked by way of greeting.

'It's Faye, boss. It looks like she was startled by Paddy when he let himself into Rafferty's flat. He was there to cook dinner for him and his sister, and had an armful of groceries with him. He barely got the door open before she freaked out, jumped him, and stabbed him in the shoulder with a corkscrew. He wouldn't have even seen it coming.'

'What's Faye's story?'

'She says she can't remember a thing.'

Morton folded his arms. 'That's convenient.'

'Yep, and we can't question her, either. When she said she couldn't remember anything, they called in medical. Medical said she's physically fine, and they kicked it over to psych, some guy called Doctor–'

'Jensen,' Morton finished for him.

'Yep. That's him. He's got her in interview suite one now. She seemed hyper-nervous at first, but she's calmed down a bit.'

Morton set off for the interview suite at a jog.

'Boss? Where are you going?'

'To watch.'

***

Faye was sitting in the chair cross-legged. She was staring attentively at Dr Jensen as if she was sizing him up. She seemed wary, leaning back with her arms folded across her chest. *Guarded,* Morton thought. She had changed out of the clothes she had arrived in and was now wearing the plain clothing provided to all detainees. Presumably, someone had retained the bloodied clothes for evidence. Morton made a mental note to have Mayberry follow up on that. She'd been cleaned up, too, though there was still dried blood on her.

Morton flicked the little switch by the side of the one-way mirror to turn on the speaker.

Jensen's voice sounded patient, but there was a bite to it, as if he had been asking the same question since Faye had arrived. 'You've said that, Faye. You don't remember anything about Patrick Rafferty. What *do* you remember?'

Faye gave the doc a withering glare. 'I don't remember anything.'

'This amnesia – how long did it last?'

'I don't remember.'

'What's the last thing you do remember before the amnesia?' Jensen asked.

Faye's eyes seemed to glaze over. When she opened them, she looked around the room in surprise. 'Where... where am I?'

Jensen turned to the glass and rolled his eyes. Then he turned back to Faye. 'You're in Scotland Yard.'

'The... police?' Faye said. 'Why? Where's Miss Ashley?'

'I'm Doctor Jensen. What's the last thing that you remember?'

'Doctor? Is there something wrong with me?' Faye said.

Morton watched the verbal ping-pong go back and forth. The medical exam had concluded that there was nothing wrong with Faye at all. Either they were wrong, or she was playing a very weird game.

Jensen looked as confused by Faye's sudden dislocation as Morton felt. Jensen's hands were clasped so tight that his knuckles had turned white, and his eyes were narrowed. He clearly didn't believe Faye's act.

'You're telling me you don't know why you're here? What is the last thing you remember?' Jensen asked again.

'I was at home – Miss Ashley's, that is – and a man broke in,' Faye said. She looked around nervously, and gasped when she saw herself reflected in the one-way mirror. 'Is that *blood*?'

'It's not yours,' Jensen reassured her. 'You're healthy as an ox, Miss Atkins. Tell me about what happened when the man broke into the flat. What were you doing?'

'I was in bed. I haven't been sleeping well. I heard someone at the door. Miss Ashley wasn't due home, so I got scared. Then, there was a man in the doorway. He was big, really big. He filled the whole doorway.'

'And then?'

'I don't know. I must have blacked out. And then I woke up here.'

'When was this?'

She looked puzzled, as if it was a stupid question. 'When I started talking to you.'

'Just a moment ago?'

'Yes,' Faye said. 'What's going on? Can I talk to Miss Ashley? I'm scared.'

Morton watched Jensen turn to the mirror and give an almost imperceptible shrug.

'Let me go find out,' Jensen said. He left Faye in the interview suite and locked the door behind him.

'So, you've been having fun,' Morton said.

'Fun? She's totally infuriating. But, as far as I can tell, she's not lying.'

Lying was Jensen's specialism. He studied micro-expressions to look for those tiny glimpses that belied what a suspect was saying.

'She's not? So, she's genuinely lost her memory?'

'It would seem so. There's nothing physically wrong with her. Mentally, she's all over the show. She acts lucid one moment, and she's unaware of what's going on the next. It's like a TV that keeps flipping channels.'

'So, what do we do?'

'We put her on a seventy-two-hour psych hold and see what we can find out.'

***

Rafferty was trying to stay calm. She was sitting in a waiting room at St Thomas' Hospital, where Paddy had been in surgery for almost two hours, and she was desperate for news. She still didn't understand how it had happened. Why had Faye attacked Paddy? It wasn't as if she hadn't warned Faye that Paddy would be visiting. She had mentioned it at least a dozen times. Could she have forgotten to mention to Faye that Paddy had a key?

'Here,' Sarah said, pressing a cup of hot chocolate into Rafferty's hands. 'You look like you need this. I always find that something sweet helps with the shock.'

Rafferty tried in vain to smile. 'Thanks, Sarah. For everything. You didn't have to come down tonight.'

Sarah took the seat next to her. 'Of course I did. David would be here too if he could be.'

'Why'd she do it?' Rafferty lamented. 'She knew he was visiting. I just can't believe she would be startled by Paddy. She had no reason to want to hurt him. She'd never even met him.'

'I don't know. We can worry about that tomorrow. Tonight, all that matters is Paddy.'

Rafferty set her cup down, stood, and stretched her legs. She had spotted a nurse wandering past in the corridor. 'Excuse me! Nurse!'

The nurse turned around. 'Yes?'

'Is there any news on Patrick Rafferty?' Rafferty said. At the nurse's look of consternation, she added, 'He's the man who was stabbed in the neck.'

'I'm afraid not. He's still in surgery, and he's lost a lot of blood. The surgeon will come and find you as soon as we know anything.'

Rafferty thanked the nurse and returned to the waiting room to pace up and down.

***

Jamie Black was pacing in her office. The detective wasn't answering her phone, and she'd ignored Jamie's voicemails asking for a call-back. She was tempted to give up. She didn't have to tell her what she'd found.

One more try? Jamie wondered. She picked up her phone and called again, and for a moment she thought it had gone to voicemail. Then the call was answered.

'Inspector Rafferty? This is Jamie Black from Westferry Security Services. I have some information for you.'

'Hi, Jamie. Is this urgent?'

'I think so. I can prove someone left Tim Fowler's apartment on the night you asked about.'

'How?' Rafferty said.

'The lift to their penthouse is a private lift. Only they can use it. I can see the lift was called for the first time that Monday at twenty past midnight.'

'So, somebody left the flat?'

'That's correct.'

'Thank you, Jamie.'

***

Jensen thought he might go crazy himself if he didn't figure this out soon.

Faye was sitting exactly where she'd been left, sitting motionless on her bed and staring blankly at the opposing wall. She hadn't said a word since they'd put her on a seventy-two-hour psych hold.

'What do you think, Doctor Jensen?' the attending nurse asked.

'She's clearly dissociative,' Jensen said. 'She's not suffering any sort of organic mental disorder, there's no indication in her bloodwork that she's suffering the physiological effects of drugs or alcohol, and she's not in withdrawal, either.'

'Is that smart-person speak for "I don't have a clue"?'

'Pretty much.'

'So, why can't she remember anything?' the nurse asked. 'Is she just pretending?'

'She's not lying, not that I can tell. Normally, when someone says "memory loss", you think physical trauma, stroke, sleep deprivation, drugs, or some underlying physical illness. She isn't sick, not physically, at least.'

'What about early onset Alzheimer's?' the nurse suggested.

'It's not Alzheimer's,' Jensen snapped. 'She's not confused, nor is she sun-downing. She does seem to have personality swings, though you can't tell that from all the time she's refusing to speak.'

'It was just an idea, Doctor Jensen. I'm only trying to help.' The nurse shuffled off, leaving Jensen alone with his thoughts.

There was something wrong, something unusual. If Faye was genuinely losing time, there had to be a reasonable explanation.

***

Paddy Rafferty got out of surgery in the small hours of the morning. Rafferty was still waiting, with Sarah napping by her side, when the surgeon appeared with news.

'Patrick is stable, though he's not out of the woods yet. The corkscrew penetrated his neck between zones two and three.' The surgeon indicated the lowest part of his neck. 'You did well to contain the blood loss as much as you did.'

'What's the prognosis?'

'Patrick suffered neurogenic shock. We've got to keep an eye on his blood pressure. There's a risk of contralateral hemiparesis causing some issues, though we won't know the extent until Patrick is fully conscious. But he'll live.'

'Can I see him?' Rafferty asked.

'Not yet. He's in recovery, and we'll move him to the Intensive Care Unit when he's ready. Go home, get some sleep, and come back in the morning. Your brother's doctor will be able to answer any questions you may have. He'll be in the ICU for the next day or two, at least.'

The surgeon disappeared back through the doors marked 'Medical Personnel Only', leaving Rafferty in the waiting room.

'You awake?' Rafferty prodded Sarah.

Sarah smiled. She'd been awake the whole time but had been trying to give Rafferty some privacy while she talked to the surgeon.

'I knew it,' Rafferty said. 'You can go home if you want. I'm going to wait here.'

'You sure? I don't mind sitting up with you.'

'Go. It's fine. Say hi to David for me.'

'Will do,' Sarah said. 'Ash, why don't you take a day or two off? I'll talk to David for you. The boys can cope without you for a couple of days – I hope.'

Rafferty forced herself to smile. 'Thank you.'

Chapter 47: Unexplained Absences

Wednesday 29th June, 08:15

The CCTV didn't lie. According to the footage, nobody had gone out the front door of the Medici building that morning at just after midnight. Somehow, either Tim or Laura, or both, had slipped out of the flat on the last night Mark had been seen, and they'd done it without going past the CCTV cameras.

Ayala knew he had to find out which of them it was.

There was no point in talking to either of them again. They'd just deny it – unless Ayala could confront them both at the same time. It was too early to find them together. Tim would no doubt be hard at work in his office in the City, and Laura would be... Where would Laura be? Nobody had said anything about her having a job.

A thought struck Ayala. They had Laura's mobile number. If her mobile was on, they could trace her whereabouts. He dialled the new IT guy.

'Brodie.'

'This is DI Ayala. I need a look-up on the location of a suspect, Laura Keaton.'

'It'll cost you, laddie. I'm not on the clock 'til nine.'

'Cost me what?'

'Twenty quid? Nah, I'm just messing with you, laddie. I'll call you back in five.'

***

Laura was at a five-star hotel on the south side of Hyde Park in Knightsbridge. Ayala arrived on the scene while the breakfast service was in full swing. Guests were coming and going from the dining room to the background noise of clattering plates and cutlery. Ayala followed the crowds. If Laura was here, as her mobile phone location suggested, then the crowded dining room was the best place to look for her.

Liveried serving staff dashed back and forth, carrying pots of coffee and jugs of freshly squeezed orange juice.

'Room number, sir?' the host prompted Ayala.

'Oh, no, I'm just looking for someone.'

The host looked put out, as if he was unsure what to do with a man loitering in the dining room. Ayala watched as he glanced over to reception, discreetly summoning security to escort Ayala out.

'I'm a police officer,' Ayala said quickly. 'I have reason to believe one of my witnesses is among your guests, and it's urgent that I find her.'

'Okay. What's her name? I can tell you if her party has arrived for breakfast yet.'

'Laura Keaton,' Ayala said. 'That's K-E-A-T-O-N, Keaton.'

The host looked bemused, as if he was insulted that Ayala had felt the need to spell it out. 'That's K for knot, is it?'

'Yes... Wait, no. Everyone's a comedian, these days. Is she here or not?' Ayala demanded.

'I'm afraid we've no record of her, sir. Are you sure she's a guest? If so, could the reservation be under another name?'

'She's definitely here somewhere. Could I show you a photo of her?' Ayala asked. He pulled out his phone from his breast pocket and began rifling through the police database for Laura's file.

'You can show me, sir,' the host said, 'but I see thousands of people every day. I probably wouldn't recognise her, even if she's here.'

Ayala showed him anyway.

'Sorry, sir, I don't recall seeing her,' the host said. When Ayala didn't immediately walk away, he added with a little more bite, 'Why don't you try asking at the front desk, *sir?*'

'Right. Thanks for your time.' Ayala didn't need a second hint. Behind him, the queue to be seated had grown ten deep, and Ayala had to fight to get back to reception. 'Excuse me, coming through!'

The receptionist at the front desk was no use. She couldn't find a guest in the system by the name of Laura Keaton, either.

It was possible Laura had checked in under an alias, or she was there with someone else, or maybe the new IT guy had got it wrong. Ayala picked up his mobile. 'Hey, Siri, call Brodie.'

For once, it worked flawlessly.

'Laddie, did you find your lady?' Brodie said.

'No,' Ayala said. 'There's no sign of her.'

He heard Brodie typing again in the background. 'Her mobile's still there. North side of the building, probably in a room facing the park.'

'Any idea which floor?'

'Nay, laddie. GPS doesn't give me altitude. You're on your own for that one.'

Brodie hung up.

Rude! Ayala thought. He turned back to the front desk. 'What's on the north side of this building?'

'Those are our premium hotel rooms there, sir. Each has a full-width balcony with a view over Hyde Park and a whirlpool bath.'

'I don't need a sales pitch,' Ayala spat. 'Are there any communal areas on that side of the building?'

'We've also got a rooftop bar and a ground floor spa.'

A sauna? 'Do you have to be a guest to use the spa?'

'No, sir. We allow day guests to partake of our spa as well as residents.'

'Thank you. Which way is it?'

No sooner had the receptionist pointed out the right corridor than Ayala was off.

***

Laura was in the spa. The receptionist at the spa recognised her photo immediately.

'She's getting a mud wrap right now, sir. Can I interest you in one?'

Ayala hesitated. It did sound good, but he knew he'd never hear the end of it from Morton if he tried to expense a mud wrap to the Met. 'How long will she be?'

'Another half an hour, sir. Would you like me to let her know you're here?'

'No! I mean, don't do that. I'd like to, err, surprise her.' Ayala grinned. He wasn't usually that quick on his feet.

'We have a juice cleansing bar just over there, sir. Perhaps you'd like to take a seat in there? I'm always willing to comp the Met's finest.'

'How'd you know I was a policeman?'

'What else would you be?'

The juice cleanse was awful. It was an ungodly concoction of spinach, lettuce, cucumber, kale, parsley, and ginger. Ayala downed it and pulled a face. If that was being healthy, he'd rather enjoy a cigarette and go out while he was still handsome.

There was a woman sitting across the bar. She laughed at Ayala's expression. 'That bad, huh? You should have gone for the tropical cleanse. It's just pineapple, orange, and vanilla yoghurt.'

'You could have told me that two minutes ago.'

'Where would the fun be in that?' She proffered a handshake. 'I'm Rachel.'

'Bertram.'

'Wow. Did your parents not love you or something?'

Ayala rested his forehead on the bar. Could he ever catch a break? The same jokes. Every. Last. Time.

'Hey, I'm just kidding. So, what're you doing here, Bertram? You're clearly not a juice cleanse regular. Waiting for someone?'

'You're very astute,' Ayala conceded.

'I should be. It's my job to watch people.'

'You're on the job?'

Rachel laughed. 'Close. I'm a PI.'

'And you got to follow someone here?' Ayala looked away from the bar. There was a large glass window with a view of the swimming pool and Hyde Park beyond it. The place was deserted.

'Yep. Some poor sap thinks his girl is cheating on him.'

'And, is she?'

'Damned if I know,' Rachel said. 'I've been watching her on and off for a month, and all I've got on her is a crafty cigarette and the occasional spa day on his credit card.'

Ayala's mind flashed back to the first time he'd met Laura. She had a brilliant smile, but one that was tinged with the yellow of nicotine. 'Hang on. Your mark – she's not Laura Keaton, is she?'

Rachel's jaw dropped.

'I'll take that as a yes.'

'This just got interesting. How about a quid pro quo? You help me, I'll help you?' Rachel said.

'What do you want?' Ayala asked warily.

'Tell me what dirt you've got on her – and you must have some, if you're following her around Knightsbridge at nine a.m. on Wednesday morning – and I'll give you a copy of everything I've got on her.'

The press had already put most of the details out there. An early edition of *The Impartial* had run a second article less than a week ago, when the boat was destroyed, so Ayala wasn't at risk of disclosing anything confidential. 'Alright. She's a suspect in a murder investigation.'

'No! Her? But she seems so... boring!'

'Really? In what way?'

'She never does anything. She shops, she gets her hair and nails done, she goes home.'

'To the Medici building.'

'Yep.'

'You wouldn't happen to have been following her on Sunday, June 12th, would you?' Ayala asked optimistically.

'Hang on.' Rachel opened her oversized handbag and drew from its depths a digital SLR. She powered the camera on and scrolled backwards from her most recent images. 'June 12th... June 12th...'

'Anything?' Ayala prompted.

'Aha!' Rachel said. 'Here we are. I was watching her part of that afternoon. Has your phone got Bluetooth? I can airdrop you everything I've got from here.'

'Yep.' Ayala swiped his thumbprint to unlock it and passed his phone over. 'I'm not very tech savvy.'

'And not very security conscious, either, if you're willing to give a private investigator your phone.' Rachel flashed him a toothy smile.

'I've got nothing to hide.'

'That's what they all say. There you go, everything's copied over. Anything else I can help you with?'

'Could you email me any other pictures you have of Laura?' Ayala asked.

'Sure, but there's nothing interesting in there.'

'Then, I'll let a junior officer sift through those.' Ayala handed her a card. 'And thank you.'

Chapter 48: Nowhere to Run

Wednesday 29th June, 10:00

Faye continued to maintain her stony silence. She moved only to sleep, eat, or use the bathroom. Jensen watched her movements and her expression, and there was only one way to describe her: weird. That wasn't the technical term, of course, but it was how Jensen felt. She was unlike any other patient he'd ever examined.

It hadn't taken long to find out about Faye's past. She'd grown up in a broken home with a loving mother and an abusive stepfather. Rafferty's old notes described her meeting the girl in their run-down Victorian terrace in Ilford, where the walls were damp, the furniture worn, and the family terrified but unwilling to talk about it.

Her stepfather had got away with it. The team from Sapphire had been certain there was domestic abuse. They hadn't been able to prove it, and so the case had been turned over to Child Protective Services, where Faye had slipped through the net, another unknown victim.

If Rafferty's suspicions were correct, they explained a lot. Early childhood trauma could easily cause complex post-traumatic stress disorder, and Faye's silence was textbook avoidance behaviour. So, too, was her reliance on Rafferty. For her to take one brief encounter with "the nice policewoman", as she had called Rafferty, and turn that into a dependency lasting into her early adulthood suggested that she had nowhere else to turn.

None of which explained her amnesia.

Rafferty arrived at midday. She looked tired but relieved.

'Any news?' Jensen asked.

'He's going to be fine. It looks like he was lucky with where she struck him. He's confused, angry, and upset. Nothing he can't handle.'

'Don't be so quick to dismiss how he feels,' Jensen said. 'Men rarely get the chance to express themselves. Bottling up that sort of emotion can be more damaging than any stab wound. If you'd like, I can talk to him.'

'I think another white coat would send his blood pressure through the roof. Thanks for the offer, though. What've you learned about Faye?' Rafferty looked at him expectantly, as if he should have all the answers already.

'Very little. She's done virtually nothing, said even less, and I just don't have much to go on. That's why I asked you to come here.'

'You want me to try to talk to her?' Rafferty asked.

'Not quite. I want you in the room. For whatever reason, Faye sees you as a safe space. She opens up around you. She trusts you. If you're there, her personality might shine through, and then we can work towards a diagnosis.'

'You want me to pretend to be her friend, her big sister? After what she did to Paddy? You're the one who's out of your mind, Doc.'

Jensen met her steely gaze with one of his own. 'Yes, I expect you to pretend. This girl is not right, and, without help, we may never find out why. She's been losing time, forgetting chunks of her own past, and that is most definitely not normal. She could well hold the key to solving your murder enquiry. I'm not asking you to like her, to be sympathetic, or to do her any favours. I'm asking you to help me work out what's going on. If she is lying – and that's not impossible; I've been wrong before – then we need to prove she's sane so she can face charges for hurting Paddy.'

'Okay,' Rafferty said reluctantly. 'Let's give it a go.'

***

Faye perked up the moment that Rafferty walked into the room. She went from being sullen and withdrawn to smiling and eager-to-please in a heartbeat.

Jensen trailed in in Rafferty's wake and then gestured for her to sit between him and Faye.

'Morning, Faye. Do you remember me?' Jensen asked.

'Doctor Jensen?' Faye said. Her voice was calmer, more certain.

'That's right. And you remember Detective Inspective Rafferty, too, don't you?'

'How could I forget Miss Ashley?' Faye asked.

'How are you feeling today?'

'Sad.'

'Why is that?'

Faye pulled a face. 'I'm stuck in here, and I don't know why. You keep saying I hurt someone, but I didn't!'

'You mean you don't remember doing it. Do you often forget things?'

'Sometimes I wake up places, and I don't know how I got there,' Faye said.

Jensen made a mental note of that. It sounded almost like borderline personality disorder, but Faye wasn't showing any of the other symptoms. There was no somatization, she wasn't engaging in revictimisation, nor was she risk-taking. It was a chal-

lenging area. There were no hard and fast checklists for dissociative disorders. Symptoms could come and go almost at a moment's notice.

'How long has this been happening?'

'Ever since I was little.'

That chimed with Jensen's suspicions of post-traumatic
stress disorder. Everything went back to Faye's childhood. 'And
this has happened a lot since?'

'Mostly when I was in prison. I couldn't keep track of time.
Days blurred together. I ate, and I slept. I slept, and I ate.'

Jensen had heard that before. The monotony of life inside
meant there was seldom a difference between Monday morning and Friday afternoon. The prison was the prison, the harsh
fluorescent lights were on all day with no hint of sunshine, and
the food was on a two-week rota that rarely changed.

'Is it just things you've done that you forget? Have you ever
forgotten a person or place?'

'No...' Faye said. Her face contorted for a split second, the
kind of micro-expression that Jensen usually associated with
falsehood.

'Are you sure?'

'Well... there was this one woman who thought she knew
me. She kept calling me Leah.'

Jensen glanced at Rafferty to ask if the name meant anything to her. 'When did this happen?'

'The day after I got out of Holloway.'

'Interesting. What about things? Have you ever bought
something and forgotten about having bought it later?'

'Hasn't everybody?' Faye asked.

'Okay. Maybe they have,' Jensen conceded. 'Faye, have you ever heard voices inside your head?'

'You mean, like, when I'm thinking?'

'Yes,' Jensen said. 'Have you ever heard a voice that isn't yours?'

Faye shook her head. 'I don't think so.'

She wasn't lying this time. That ruled out schizophrenia. It was time to shift the conversation to Faye's childhood and see how she reacted. Jensen gave Rafferty a nod to let her know that he was going to do so. They'd discussed it in the corridor, as there was the possibility that Faye could turn violent again.

'Faye, would you say you had a happy childhood?' Jensen asked, starting with the broadest possible discussion point.

The effect was immediate. Faye's smile vanished. She leant back in her chair, clearly trying to physically distance herself and the question. She didn't answer.

Rafferty patted Faye's knee. 'It's okay, Faye. You're safe here, okay? Nobody is going to hurt you.'

And with that, Faye switched back again. It was like watching someone hopping TV channels. One moment, she was the childlike Faye who was eager to please, and the next, she was sullen, sulky, and withdrawn.

Jensen had never seen anything quite like it. 'Faye, could you tell me a bit about your stepdad?'

She switched again, her eyes flashing darkly. 'I don't want to talk about *him*.'

'Is that when you started missing time? When your stepfather first moved in?' Jensen kept his voice pleasant and airy. If it weren't for the seriousness of the discussion, he could have been chatting about the weather.

'I suppose so,' Faye said. 'That man deserves to burn in hell for all eternity.'

The linguistic switch was immediately apparent. Faye had become more confident, more articulate, and much angrier. There was a darkness to this Faye.

'Like Patrick Rafferty?' Jensen asked.

Again, Faye seemed to change. 'I'm sorry, did you say something?'

'Do you think Patrick Rafferty deserves to burn in hell?' Jensen repeated, echoing her narrative.

'N-no... Why would I? Have I met him?'

Jensen shook his head. She still seemed to be telling the truth. She was either the best actress he had ever met, or she was an utterly unique case of dissociation.

'Thank you for your time, Faye.' Jensen rose and motioned for Rafferty to follow him.

When they were in the corridor, Rafferty slammed the door behind her. 'Why'd you pull out of the interview?'

'She's not going to give us anything. Every time we touch upon something traumatic, she withdraws somewhere inside her own head. Whatever she says can't be relied upon. She could have implanted false memories to cope with her trauma. Most of the time, she's simplistic, shallow, childlike. Then she has moments of micro-amnesia. She's there, and then she's not.'

'So?'

'So, she's not fit to stand trial for attacking Paddy. But I can't give you a diagnosis. I'm going to need some time to research what's wrong with her. In thirty years of practice, she's totally unique. I have never seen a case quite like hers.'

'What's going to happen now?'

'Right now, we're holding her on a section 136 psychiatric hold. That gives us seventy-two hours from when she was brought in on Tuesday. I need to make the case for detaining her pursuant to section thirty-five, which would buy us twenty-eight days. There's one snag.'

'What's the snag?'

'We have to show she couldn't be treated while on bail. I don't think I can prove that yet. She's only a danger when she feels threatened. This isn't a violent psychopath. This is a traumatised young woman who is fighting to protect herself in the only way she knows how.'

'She attacked Paddy!'

'When she thought he was an intruder. She'd forgotten everything you said to her about him coming over, so, when he entered your flat, Faye felt threatened. Look at the circumstances. She didn't lie in wait to attack him. It wasn't premeditated. She used a weapon of opportunity, and she didn't flee the crime scene. Does that sound like any criminal you know?'

'No, but...'

'But, nothing. She's a victim, not a criminal, and she needs our help. I'm sorry Paddy got hurt, I really am. But we can't fall into the trap of pigeonholing the mentally ill as being violent and deranged. If Faye can be found a safe space, perhaps in a women's shelter or living with someone she trusts, then there would be no reason she couldn't be treated while on bail.'

'And if you can't find something...'

'She'll be out late Friday night.'

Chapter 49: Lady of Leisure

Wednesday 29th June, 10:00

Laura's spa session seemed to last all morning, despite the fact that Ayala had been assured she'd only be another half an hour. By the time Ayala spotted her emerging from the massage suite, he and Rachel had become fast friends. The private investigator had emailed over a copy of everything on her camera, and Ayala had ensured that Mayberry was cc'd in.

Rachel sighed when Laura emerged. If it was just a girl's spa day, there'd be no money shot for Rachel. Tim was paying her the big bucks to check if Laura was playing around, and she couldn't prove it.

'You going to keep following her?'

'Yep.'

'Even though she'll just be with me?' Ayala said.

'Ah, what if it's all a ruse? What if you're not really a police officer, but you're her bit on the side?' Rachel joked.

'Then, I hope you'll photograph my good side.'

Ayala bid Rachel farewell and made a beeline for the hotel lobby so he could cut Laura off before she made it to a taxi.

'Laura! Wait up!' Ayala shouted after her.

She turned, looking around as if she hoped to see a friendly face, and frowned when she saw Ayala. 'You, again!'

'Yep!' said Ayala cheerfully. 'Me again. Nice place. Tim must be generous.'

'He is.'

'Good for him. Can we have a chat somewhere private? Do you have a room here?'

Laura looked offended. 'Why would I have a room? You think I'm cheating on him, don't you? Like that silly brunette who keeps following me around. She thinks I haven't noticed. What do I care if she's photographing me?'

If Laura knew, it was possible she'd changed her behaviour to hide whatever she was up to.

'Right,' said Ayala. 'How about the hotel bar? It should be deserted at eleven o'clock in the morning.'

It wasn't. By the time they had bought a round of drinks and found a snug hideaway in the corner, the bar was filling up with the early lunch crowd, the late mimosa crowd, and the perpetual alcoholics.

'So, what do you want this time?'

'You lied to us, Laura. You left your apartment that night.'

'No, I didn't.'

'Will Tim confirm that?' Ayala asked. 'Surely, he notices when you're not in the same bed.'

Laura said nothing, opting to take a sip from her chai tea instead.

'So, you did leave the flat, then. Why?'

'I was smoking, okay? Tim doesn't know it, but I sneak downstairs to have a crafty cigarette in the gardens.'

'Why wouldn't you just smoke on your balcony?'

'Tim would see me there,' Laura said. 'It's a huge pet peeve for him. His nan died of emphysema or something, so he end-lessly lectures anyone who smokes. Can't a girl have a secret cig-gie every once in a while?'

Ayala shrugged. He wasn't one to talk. His own addiction to nicotine had been a lifelong battle, and it wasn't a battle he was winning. 'So, you didn't go back to the boat that night?'

'No, of course not. I had a few ciggies and then came back inside because it was cold.'

'Why were you gone from the flat for so long?' Ayala asked.

'So Tim wouldn't notice,' Laura said. 'I was giving him enough time to fall asleep so I could slip back inside, gargle some mouthwash, stick my jumper in the washing machine, and slip into bed.'

'That sounds like a lot of work just to keep smoking a secret.'

'I've got a lot to lose, okay? Tim has been wonderful for me. He got me out of Ilford, he puts me up in his penthouse flat, and I get to spend every day shopping and seeing London. I can't lose this life.'

'Give up the ciggies, then.'

'I'm trying.' Laura rolled up her sleeve to reveal a nicotine patch on her upper arm.

'When was your last one?'

'A week ago. I'm dying for a smoke. I didn't kill my best friend. I wasn't sleeping with Mark. I just like a cigarette. Now, will you get off my case? I've got a lunch date with the girls to get to.'

And with that, she gulped the last of her chai tea, fixed her sleeve, and left Ayala alone in the hotel bar.

It could be an elaborate lie, but it tallied with what Rachel had told him. Ayala pulled out his phone and texted Mayberry: *Keep an eye out for any shots of Laura smoking among the photos that you've been emailed. See if any of them are more recent than last week. Cheers. B.*

***

The big guy was scary. He had a beard that made him look a bit like a lumberjack, and a booming voice that carried across the room even when he wasn't talking particularly loudly.

Mayberry approached him cautiously. 'E-excuse m-me?'

'What d'ya want, laddie?'

'I n-need to sort th-through these ph-photos.' Mayberry handed the big man a thumb drive onto which he'd copied all the photos.

'Let's have a look, then, laddie.' Brodie took the USB and plugged it in. He then motioned for Mayberry to grab an empty chair from the other side of the room and pull it up beside his desk. 'Right, here we are. Good lad, you've kept the metadata intact. That'll make this a bit easier. What're ya looking for?'

'N-not sure,' Mayberry stammered. 'Can you use f-facial recognition to group the photos by the p-people in them?'

'I can, laddie, but it'll take a while. You good to wait?'

Mayberry nodded, and Brodie got to work. The photos began to whizz across the screen, each file flying into a folder based on whom the program found in each image.

Brodie turned away from the computer and pulled a biscuit tin from a drawer on his left. 'Biscuit, laddie?'

Mayberry took one, stammered his thanks, and bit into a piece of butter shortbread.

'It's good, isn't it? My lass makes it for me every week. Don't know what I did to deserve such a woman. It must be the beard.' Brodie mimed stroking his beard, almost like a Bond villain, making Mayberry laugh. 'You got a lady, Detective Mayberry?'

Mayberry nodded. Brodie was probably the only person in the building who didn't know he was engaged to the chief's daughter.

'Keep a tight hold on her, laddie. There's nothing in this world like being with the right woman.' At the sound of a beep, Brodie turned his attention back to the screen. 'Right. That's done. Want me to go through these with you? I assume you want to start with your murder suspects? Don't look at me like that. I'm not some clueless nerd, laddie.'

'P-please.'

They found Laura easily enough. She was in most of the photos. Just as Ayala had said, she was a smoker. 'C-can you f-find the m-most recent photo of her s-smoking?'

'One sec. Yep. Last Thursday.'

Almost a week ago. Mayberry texted Ayala back with the confirmation. That made Laura's story credible. If she had been smoking the night Mark went missing, it wouldn't take much to stretch that narrative into reasonable doubt.

'W-what about p-photos from the n-night of the m-murder?'

Brodie clicked through again, this time using the metadata to isolate only the pictures taken that night. He displayed a handful of shots taken that afternoon side by side.

'Th-that one!' Mayberry pointed. 'C-can you make it b-bigger?'

He did, and *The Guilty Pleasure* came into view. Laura could be seen through an open window, as could Tim. Brodie zoomed in on the people.

'No!' Mayberry cried.

Brodie looked confused, but he zoomed back out. Mayberry pointed to the edge of the picture.

'The other boat?' Brodie said. When Mayberry nodded, he zoomed in. It was Jake Sanders' boat *The Mobile Office* moored up by *The Guilty Pleasure* stern-to-bow.

At the edge of the frame, Mayberry could see Jake. He was with a woman on board the boat. They were kissing, with her hands snaked up around his neck. She was much older than Jake, with grey hair, veiny hands, and a brow marked with lines.

Who was she? Had she been there all night?

'Are there a-any more of h-her?'

'That's your lot, laddie. I take it she hasna come up in your investigation before?'

Mayberry shook his head. There was another suspect, after all.

Chapter 50: Who Is She?

Wednesday 29th June, 13:00

They reconvened in the Incident Room after lunch to discuss Mayberry's findings. Rafferty was notably absent, though Morton wasn't surprised to discover that his wife had been behind that. Sarah was always putting people first and his investigations second. A day or two wouldn't hurt too much, though.

'We need to find this woman,' Morton said bluntly. 'No ifs, no buts. Has anyone seen anything that might explain who she is and why she was aboard *The Mobile Office* with Jake on the night of the murder?'

'Could it be his mum?' Ayala suggested.

Morton mimed being sick. 'You kiss your own mother like that? No. Definitely not. Besides, his mother is dead. Cancer took her years ago. She went before their dad did.'

'The Sanders family name seems cursed,' Ayala said. 'Dad's dead. Mum's dead. Big brother is murdered. Little brother offs himself. That's seriously bad juju.'

'No kidding. We need to find her. I want you both looking through Jake's correspondence.'

'Again? We already did!' Ayala protested.

'Yes, but last time, you were looking for evidence of financial malfeasance. This time, you're looking for any messages he could have sent to a lover. They had to arrange their meeting on the boat somehow, so start with his phone. Check WhatsApp, Messenger, Jake's email, whatever the kids are using these days. Find out who she is and bring her in. Do it fast, because if she can alibi Jake, we're running out of suspects.'

Chapter 51: Freedom

Friday 1st July, 21:00

The seventy-two hours of Faye's psych hold seemed to fly by. Faye would not say another word, no matter what Jensen did. She ate, she drank, and she slept. She ticked all the boxes for 'able to look after herself', but, as far as Jensen could tell, she didn't fit neatly within the illnesses defined in the so-called Psychiatrist's Bible, the fifth edition of *The Diagnostic and Statistical Manual of Mental Disorders*.

She wasn't, in Jensen's opinion, a danger to anyone. She was quick to anger and would no doubt lash out if a threat presented itself, but that alone wasn't enough to preclude her release, whatever Rafferty might think.

There was a small mercy. She had nowhere to go. The women's centres nearby were too full, or so they said. Few would want to take on the liability of a woman with an undiagnosed mental illness and a proven history of violence.

At her release, Faye was back to being sweet-natured and quiet. But she abhorred being touched and would not even shake Jensen's hand.

'Where are you going to go, Faye?' Jensen asked her.

She only shrugged and mumbled something about Miss Ashley. Fat chance of that. Rafferty was still livid.

Morton arrived on the scene five minutes before Faye was due to be released.

'David! Don't you have anything better to do on a Friday night?' Jensen asked.

'Don't you?' Morton shot back. 'I assume you've found grounds to keep her here.'

'I'm afraid not. In four minutes' time, we can't legally hold her.'

'Coward,' Morton said. 'That's a bad call, and you know it. She's clearly not healthy. Do you seriously think it's all a big act?'

'I don't know what to think. I've been doing this a long time, and I've never seen a patient quite like her. If it were up to me, I'd keep her in a hospital, study her more, and try to find a way to help.'

'But it's not.'

'No, it's not. Three minutes.'

'Where is she?'

'In her room.'

'Take me there,' Morton ordered.

As the clock ticked down, Faye was pacing in her room. Exactly on time, Jensen opened the door. 'You're free to go,' he said.

'Not so fast,' Morton contradicted him. 'Faye Atkins, you're under arrest for wounding Patrick Rafferty, contrary to section twenty of the Offences Against the Person Act 1861.'

Morton snapped handcuffs around her wrists, watched her puzzled demeanour dissolve into one of steely silence, gave her the standard arrest spiel, and frogmarched her from the building.

***

There was a lawyer waiting when Morton arrived at Scotland Yard with Faye in tow.

'Detective Morton?' she said.

Morton turned to see Genevieve Hollis, a lawyer he'd crossed paths with before. She was known for being scrupulously honest and quick to defend anyone she thought had been denied due process. 'What do you want?' he asked warily.

'I represent Faye Atkins.'

'Impossible! She wasn't arrested ten minutes ago.'

'Quite,' Hollis said. 'I took a call saying you were arresting a woman with mental health issues, and I happened to be in chambers over in Holborn. Is that true?'

'Our experts were unable to diagnose anything wrong with her,' Morton said tersely.

'Then, we shall agree to disagree. Where is my client?'

'Being processed. I'll have her brought up to the interview suite as soon as possible so you can talk to her,' Morton said.

***

Before Morton could face Hollis, he had to do the unthinkable: he had to ruin Kieran O'Connor's Friday night off.

There was no doubt in Morton's mind that Hollis would argue that Faye was unfit to stand trial. It was an odd move to raise it so early. Most lawyers would raise it later on, so as to keep alive the possibility of total acquittal. By making the assertion of mental illness so early on, Hollis was almost, but not officially, conceding Faye's guilt.

There was an inherent contradiction in the assertion. Faye had been examined by a police-appointed psychiatrist and found insufficiently impaired to be detained. She could not be both unfit to plead and fit to look after herself. It was a contradiction Morton couldn't reconcile.

He dialled the prosecutor's mobile number and prayed that Kieran would hear it ring.

***

Kieran arrived a little before midnight. He was almost entirely sober, but his breath smelt of mints.

'Are you sure you're up to this, Kieran?' Morton asked him. 'Hollis and Faye are waiting for us.'

The prosecutor nodded. He'd taken on bigger cases while less sober, not that he'd ever admit that in the cold light of day.

Before long, the four of them were in an interview suite once again. Kieran and Morton sat on one side of the table, while Hollis sat beside her client.

'She's not a mentally disordered offender,' Kieran said.

'I didn't say she was,' Hollis replied, tight-lipped. It wasn't what she'd said to Morton ten minutes earlier.

'You didn't?' Kieran said sceptically.

'No. What I'm saying is that she's not guilty. She has no recollection of the crime you allege she committed. No mens rea, no conviction,' Hollis said simply, referring to the required intention.

'You think that'll work?' Kieran smirked. 'The "I don't remember it" defence? If she's not a mentally disordered offender, and there's nothing physically wrong with her, how are you going to explain her amnesia?'

Hollis slid a piece of paper across the desk. 'This is the formal report that your Doctor Jensen wrote about my client. As you can see, it is dated for today. Could you read the last line for the record?'

Kieran skimmed it, and his eyes narrowed. How had she got hold of Jensen's report? 'Didn't you just deny she was mentally ill?'

The defence barrister's eyes twinkled. 'No. All I said was that I didn't make that claim, you did. I didn't say that she wasn't, either. You inferred that from my silence.'

Morton watched the prosecutor try to spin the wheels-within-wheels logic. She had said she hadn't said it, not that she didn't agree. After having had a few drinks, it was almost beyond Kieran's comprehension, and he took a full thirty seconds to think about his next move.

'Then, do you agree that your client should be found a place in a mental hospital to be given treatment?' Kieran asked, trying to avoid anything too combative.

'I think she should be put somewhere where she can safely be given treatment. I think that place is at home.'

'At home? She sank her home,' Kieran said.

'That is none of your concern,' Hollis said. 'According to your own expert's report, pursuing criminal charges "may lead to a considerable worsening of the patient's mental health". She's not fit for trial, and you know it. As I see it, you've got two choices: let my client go, or face the mother of all civil suits. Which will it be?'

Jensen had back-stabbed them.

Kieran looked accusingly at Morton as if to ask why he'd been dragged in if this report existed. 'I'll need to get an independent copy of this report.'

Hollis gave Kieran a contemptuous glare. 'You don't have your own expert's report? My, the Crown Prosecution Service is disorganized.'

'Interview terminated,' Morton interjected, 'at 11:51 p.m., Friday July 1st.'

Kieran and Morton left the room, and Kieran began ranting.

'What the feck was that all about? Why didn't I know about this report?'

'I didn't know, either,' Morton said darkly. 'But, I guess we now know who tipped Hollis off. Jensen.'

'We're going to have to let her go,' Kieran said.

'Rafferty won't like that.'

'Then, nail her for the murder. You still think she did it, don't you?'

Morton didn't have an answer anymore.

Chapter 52: Old Friends

Saturday 2nd July 03:00

Laura and Tim were awakened by an unexpected visitor. When the buzzer went off, neither of them stirred straight away.

'You going to get that, babe?' Laura asked eventually.

'Only if it doesn't stop,' Tim replied sleepily.

It didn't, and five minutes later Tim was scrambling to get dressed. He buzzed Faye in and met her in the lobby.

'Faye, what're you doing here?'

Faye looked tired. There were bags under her eyes, her hair was a mess, and she was soaked through. 'I've got nowhere else to go, Tim. Can you help me?'

'Come on,' Tim heard himself say.

She looked so pitiful that he doubted anyone could have refused her request. He led her into the elevator, swiped his wallet against the contactless security reader, and then they ascended in silence.

Laura was waiting for them at the front door. 'Faye!' She rushed over to hug the bedraggled woman. 'What happened?'

'The boat... it sank,' Faye said.

'Oh my God. Tim, fetch some blankets from the airing cupboard, would you? And a towel. Oh, and one of my spare dressing gowns. She can't stay in wet clothes.'

'Can I have a word with you, honey?' Tim asked. He motioned for Laura to follow him into the kitchen.

'What?' Laura demanded. 'She's got nowhere else to go.'

'What if, y'know, she's the one who killed Mark? I know I didn't do it. You know you didn't. That doesn't leave many people, does it?' Tim said.

'Don't be silly,' Laura said. 'I've known her since I was a toddler. Faye wouldn't hurt a fly. I'll bet it was Jake. He's the one who was going to benefit from the life insurance, wasn't he? And he was in financial trouble.'

Tim looked aghast. 'Didn't Jake's dad die a while back? And he got a fat insurance pay-out then, too.'

'Mr Fowler, are you suggesting that Jake did both of them in? You're quite the detective, you know. If you let little Faye stay for a day or two, I might let you arrest me.' Laura winked.

'A day or two, but no more,' Tim said.

He didn't believe it even as he said it. He watched Laura as she bounded from the kitchen. He'd do anything for that woman.

Chapter 53: Grey Justice

Saturday 2nd July, 09:30

Mayberry found her easily. The woman's name was Virginia Williams, and she was a resident of the London Borough of Hammersmith and Fulham. The old lady was property-rich, cash-poor, and terminally ill.

Jake had been calling her for months. Mayberry suspected it had been business at first. She was in his client files and had seemed to be working on giving away as much of her wealth as she could while she was still living.

It was probably a good thing that there weren't any text messages. Mayberry wouldn't have wanted to read them.

The phone calls progressed from a few minutes long during business hours to many hours late in the evening and at night. Sometime during the last few months of his life, Jake had begun a relationship with a woman forty years his senior.

Jake's motivation was obvious: in that part of town, a four-bedroom detached house was worth just shy of two million pounds. That was enough to pay off his debts and set him up for life – if he didn't gamble it all away.

He certainly wasn't dating her for her looks. She was sixty-six and looked more like eighty-six. She had a hunched back, sagging skin, and a smoker's rasp.

Mayberry knew he ought to go talk to her, but he really didn't want to do it alone. Morton wasn't answering his phone, and Rafferty was still on leave to care for her brother, which only left Ayala.

***

Saturday morning breakfast was usually a celebratory affair. Tim worked long hours and compensated for it by trying to extract as much life as he could out of his weekends while the markets were shut.

With Faye in the picture, it wasn't the idyllic eggs Benedict that Tim had hoped for. She sat at their dining table looking sullen.

'You okay, Faye?' Laura asked for the tenth time.

Faye gave a small shrug, as if she were indifferent to the world.

Tim exchanged glances with Laura. It was to be expected. Faye had lost everything – her boyfriend, her home, and with them, her life. It couldn't be easy to be suddenly so adrift.

'So,' Tim said. 'Any idea what you'll do now?'

Tim thought it was a fair question. She couldn't sleep on his sofa forever, and he certainly wasn't going to turn his home office back into a second bedroom.

Laura clearly disagreed. 'Tim!' she scolded. 'Be a bit more sensitive, please. She's in shock, that's all.'

Tim cocked his head to the side, then went out to the balcony to admire the view across the Thames. As he sipped his coffee, he heard the French doors open behind him, and Laura's arms soon snaked up around his chest from behind.

'I know it's hard, babe, but she won't be here forever. I want our Saturday mornings back, too,' Laura said.

'She's not right, Laura. And she's not telling us everything.'

'What makes you say that?' Laura asked.

Tim passed her a copy of Saturday's edition of *The Impartial*. 'Turn to page thirty-seven.'

When she did so, Laura found a half-page spread about the sinking of *The Guilty Pleasure* and the *Arcadian*. 'So? It's no surprise this rag would run a story about something so trivial.'

'Look at the date.'

Laura did. It was last Saturday's edition.

Where had Faye been for a week?

Chapter 54: Confrontation

Saturday 2nd July, 13:00

Ayala and Mayberry found the house and stopped to stare in wonder. It was in Melrose Gardens, a part of the Melrose Conservation Area, just a hop and a skip from Goldhawk Road Underground Station.

It was Victorian in style, with high ceilings and enormous bay windows covering two-thirds of the front of the house. It probably wasn't very energy-efficient, but for a buyer with two million pounds or more to spend, that was unlikely to be a concern.

Virginia Williams answered the door in slippers and a dressing gown. Obviously, she hadn't been expecting company. 'Not today, thank you!' She jabbed a finger at a sign hanging beside the door. It read: "No Hawkers, No Canvassers, No Junk Mail, No Charity Bags, No Exceptions."

'Ma'am! We're with the Metropolitan Police.'

'Why didn't you say so?' Virginia said. 'Come on in, and mind the step there. Come on, the sitting room's this way. Kick off your shoes as you go, please, if you'll be so kind.'

They divested themselves of their shoes. Ayala took a moment to look pitifully at Mayberry's high-street work boots next to his own Italian leather loafers. Some people just didn't have any semblance of style.

'What can I do for you gentlemen today?' Virginia asked with a toothy smile.

'Are you familiar with a Mr Jake Sanders?' Ayala asked.

'Familiar with him? I'm engaged to him!' Virginia flashed her ring finger, where the cheapest, gaudiest ring was on display. It looked almost as if Jake must have won it at a fun fair.

'Engaged?' Ayala echoed disbelievingly. 'Since when?'

'Last month. He's such a sweet man. He looks after me ever so well.'

Ayala winced. She was referring to him in the present tense. She didn't know he was dead. 'Miss Williams, I'm sorry to have to be the one to tell you this, but I'm afraid that Jake took his own life a week ago.'

'No, no, it can't be,' she said firmly. 'You've got the wrong man. My Jake wouldn't do that.'

'I'm afraid he did, Mrs Williams. When was it you last saw him?'

'The Saturday before last, I think. But he can't be...' Her eyes were beginning to water as she realised the truth of what she was being told.

Ayala delved into his top pocket. He got a lot of flak for carrying a pocket square, and had gotten even more from Morton when the boss had learned it was monogrammed, but it was perfect for occasions like this. Ayala passed it over and then rummaged in his inside pocket for his spare.

'Thank you,' Virginia sobbed. 'What happened?'

'His brother was murdered.'

'No! He never told me. Are you sure you haven't got the wrong man?' Virginia had a glint in her eye again, a tiny ray of hope – one which Ayala would surely have to crush.

'I have a photograph of the two of you together aboard *The Mobile Office*.' Ayala showed her a crop of the picture Mayberry had found.

'Oh God, it's him!' Her tears began to flow, and her sobbing soon became a wail.

'Miss Williams, I'm sure this is difficult for you. Is there anyone we can call for you?'

She waved him off while still holding his pocket square. 'No, there's no one. I'm all alone in this world now.'

'I'm sorry for your loss,' Ayala said, and he meant it. 'But I have to ask you a few questions. Do you remember the day this was taken?'

'June twelfth,' she said sharply. 'We spent a magical evening together.'

'Evening? Until when?' Ayala asked.

She smiled coquettishly. 'Until the next morning.'

Mayberry looked like he wanted to puke. Ayala suppressed his own gag reflex. 'Are you sure, Miss Williams?'

'Quite sure. That was the night he proposed to me.'

Jake Sanders was not their killer.

***

Morton had Laura and Tim brought in to Scotland Yard that Saturday afternoon for two reasons. Firstly, he felt obliged to warn them. He knew Hollis had driven Faye to their home because he had followed closely behind to see where Faye was going. They deserved to know what they were letting themselves in for.

Secondly, he needed to know if either of them could have done it. If, as Morton suspected, Laura was only hiding a cigarette addiction, then their alibis for each other covered all but the forty-odd minutes Laura had been aboard *The Guilty Plea-sure* with Mark.

It struck Morton as unlikely that Laura could kill in such a short time frame, especially without waking Faye, who had allegedly been asleep in the other room. Mark Sanders was a big man, physically strong, and he would have resisted. The pathologist's best guess – and it was barely more than a guess – had been asphyxiation. It would have taken speed and force to kill him while he was wide awake.

Morton had been apprised of their trip to visit Virginia Williams. With Jake officially ruled out on account of his newfound alibi, Morton had just three serious suspects left.

Tim and Laura were escorted in to Scotland Yard by Ayala. Morton had them shown to the largest interview suite, offered refreshments, and then he left them to stew for half an hour.

A waiting period wasn't the nicest of interview techniques, and Morton wasn't expecting miracles from it, but he could hear them bickering as they waited. It was obvious that Tim was not happy with their new house guest.

Eventually, Morton graced them with his presence.

'Good afternoon,' Morton said. 'Thank you for volunteering to come in today.'

'We volunteered, did we?' Tim said. 'It didn't feel like it when your boy came to pick us up at my flat unannounced.'

'My apologies. You're free to go if you don't wish to be here.' Morton watched Tim stand. 'But I'd strongly suggest you give me five minutes, at least. I think we can clear at least one of you of murder today.'

'One of us?' Tim echoed.

'At least,' Morton repeated. 'I'd like to go back over the timeline.'

'We've already told you,' Laura said. 'Tim left first, and I wasn't far behind him.'

'Indeed. Approximately three-quarters of an hour. Why did you stay behind?' Morton asked.

'I was chatting with Mark.'

'Do you do that a lot?'

'Well, yeah, he's my friend,' Laura said tersely.

'And nothing more than that?' Morton prompted. He had hit a nerve.

Tim looked at Laura accusingly.

'Nothing happened, okay?' Laura said. 'We were just chatting that night.'

Tim seemed to latch on to the phrase "that night" instantly. He continued to glare, but he said nothing.

'So, you left later. When you got home, was Tim there?' Morton said to Laura.

'Of course.'

'And you were together for the rest of the night?'

Tim looked at Laura suspiciously again and then interjected, 'No. She wasn't there all night. She left for a bit just after midnight. Where did you go, honey?'

Laura averted her eyes. Morton almost felt sorry for her. She hadn't killed anyone, at least not during that absence.

'I can answer that.' Morton produced a photo of Laura smoking in the garden. It wasn't on that night, but the timings fit, and Morton wanted to provoke the two of them. If one of them had a temper, the result would be interesting.

'Where did you get this?' Laura demanded of Morton. 'Were you following me?'

'Not me. You should ask Tim about that.'

The cat was truly among the pigeons now. They both started yelling simultaneously, and it looked like Morton might have to pull them apart. The tape was catching everything. Their argument was indecipherable hearing it live, but Morton would have Brodie play it back with their voices separated out in case they said anything interesting.

'Enough!' Morton yelled after a few minutes. 'You can see a relationship counsellor on your own time. You,' he said, jabbing a finger at Laura, 'smoked and hid it. And that's not even the worst of it. Does Tim know that you sent Mark inappropriate texts?' He pushed a folder across the table to Tim. It contained copies of all the messages Mark had been sent. 'And you,' Morton said to Tim, 'hired a private investigator to follow your girlfriend. Who does that? You two are idiots, and you're perfect for each other because of it. Now that we've got that out of the way, Laura, did you see Tim leave the flat that night?'

'No.'

'And you were standing by the back door the whole time you were smoking?'

'I was,' Laura confirmed.

'Then, Tim, you're a free man. There's no way out of the Medici except for the front and back doors. You didn't go out the front, as we've got the security tapes, and you'd have passed Laura on the way out the back.' Morton discounted the remote possibility that they had in fact worked together on the basis that they had not even bothered to properly alibi each other.

'And what about me?' Laura asked.

'Was Mark alive when you left?'

'Yes, but I can't prove it.'

'But you were having a relationship with him,' Morton said. If only she'd admit it, he could warn her to get tested.

'No. It was just the texts,' Laura said firmly.

'Did anyone see you leave?'

'I don't think so. Maybe Jake did, but–'

'But he's dead,' Morton finished for her. 'Which is either very inconvenient for you, or the perfect way to fake an alibi.'

'Are we done here?' Tim demanded.

'You were always free to go,' Morton said again. 'The door's over there.'

This time, they left.

***

Faye felt much more like an intruder than a guest in Tim's flat. She had been told in unequivocal terms not to stray into their bedroom or his home office, not to use the kitchen when they were out, and never to answer the phone.

It was a lonely place. The usual noises of London faded in the executive lift up to the penthouse. The décor was so minimalist, so white, so boring, that it felt more like a waiting room than a home. There were even magazines, unread, on the coffee table. Not that *The Economist* was Faye's cup of tea.

She'd taken to browsing the streaming services on the television in their absence. The children's films were her favourites. They reminded her of a better time.

The lift creaked into life, which meant that Laura and Tim would be up in less than a minute. The lift emptied out into a small foyer with the front door to the flat opposite the lift. Faye hit the off switch on the television remote and turned to wait for them.

They were whispering when they came through the front door. Faye couldn't quite make out what they were saying. Laura and Tim fell silent as quickly as the television had when they saw Faye sitting on the sofa waiting for them. They smiled briefly, but it looked more like a grimace than genuine pleasure. Without a second glance, they took a hard left and made their way into their bedroom. The door clicked shut behind them, they locked it, and the whispering resumed in earnest.

Faye's curiosity got the better of her. She got up, tiptoed over to the door, and pressed an ear against it to listen.

Chapter 55: Only We Know

Saturday 2nd July, 17:00

Tim locked the bedroom door behind them. Faye was still in the living room, still just sitting there on the sofa.

It had been a rough taxi ride over. Tim knew he hadn't done it, and Laura now knew too. If Tim trusted Laura – and, despite their arguments, he did – then the only logical suspect left was the woman on their sofa.

'What do we do?' Laura whispered once they were in the privacy of their own bedroom.

'We've got to get her to leave,' Tim said. 'Tonight. I can't sleep knowing there's a murderer in my living room!'

'Aww, babe, you know it wasn't me, then.'

'Of course it wasn't you. And I don't care about the cigarettes or the dirty messages as long as you're all mine now.'

Laura hesitated a moment too long, so it sounded hollow when she said, 'Of course.'

'Let's talk about this later. How do we get her out of here?'

'Ask?' Laura suggested tentatively.

'Or we could wait until she goes out, change the locks, and pretend she never existed.' Tim smiled for the first time since the police had picked them up earlier in the day.

'That could work.'

'Alright, I'll go tell her it's time to move on. We only promised her that she could stay a couple of days, anyway, so it's not like she shouldn't have seen this coming.'

***

Faye had her ear pressed to the bedroom door, and she heard everything. They thought she was the killer. She began to shake as she heard her best friend plotting to betray her. Didn't Laura know her better than that?

She hunched over and began to cry in silence. She wasn't sure what she was crying for. It could have been for losing Mark, for losing Laura's trust, for losing her home, or everything at once. The world had become overwhelming, unbearable, a place devoid of hope.

And then she straightened up. She arose a new woman, filled with purpose. She would never go back to prison. The world would know her strength, her resilience, her determination.

She darted into the kitchen, where there was a knife block on the countertop.

If Laura and Tim were out to get her, she'd have to get them first.

***

Tim made the mistake of being the first to leave the bedroom. He didn't see Faye immediately. She wasn't sitting on the sofa, nor was she in the open-plan kitchen on the other side of the lounge.

He stepped forward to look for her, and she sprang into action. The first thing he felt was the sheer weight of Faye launching herself at him from behind. Tim felt his knees give way under their combined weight, and he fell forward to land on the hardwood floor with a crack.

He twisted to try to see what was going on. Faye had a knife – his favourite *gyuto* knife from his kitchen – clutched in her left hand.

Before he could stop her, Faye had the knife to his throat.

'Give me one good reason why I shouldn't,' Faye said.

'I... Laura! No!' Tim cried as Laura appeared in the doorway to see what was going on.

Time seemed to freeze. He pleaded with her with his eyes, begging her to run, to turn tail, to save herself. She locked eyes with him for an instant, and then time seemed to unfreeze. The bedroom door slammed shut with a bang, and then Tim heard the lock engage. At least Laura was safe.

The knife was cold against his throat. He knew first-hand just how dangerous the blade was. He'd bought it in Tokyo a few months back, and it had only just been professionally sharpened. It was folded powdered steel, hardened to Rockwell C64, and was finished to a razor-sharp edge. One slip of the hand, and Tim would be gone in minutes.

'Well?' Faye demanded. 'I'm waiting.'

Tim closed his eyes. If his life could end at any moment, he didn't want to have to watch it happen. 'Please, I didn't do anything. I'm not trying to hurt you, Faye.'

'You think I did it. You want me to go back to prison!' Faye's hand wavered dangerously, the knife grazing his neck. She was unsettled, and he was powerless to stop her.

'If it's prison you're worried about, don't you think murdering me will send you straight back there?' Tim said, his voice straining with emotion despite the self-evidence of his logic. 'Besides, the three of us are the only suspects in Mark's murder.

Even if you got away with whatever you do to me, you'd be the last one standing. The police will figure it out.'

Faye seemed to pause to think about this. Tim knelt in silence, his throat millimetres from the blade and his knees aching against the hardwood floor.

'By that logic,' Faye said slowly, 'I should get rid of any witnesses.'

'No!' Tim shouted. 'You can't. You'd never hurt Laura. You can hurt me all you want. Just leave her be.'

There had to be something he could do. His whole life, Tim had felt powerful. He was rich. He was white. He was a man. Life had been far too easy for far too long, and it was only now, at the point he might lose it all, that he suddenly saw just how quickly his assets had become liabilities.

Faye hadn't had what he'd had. She'd grown up in a broken home with no money and none of his privilege. He needed Faye to see him as human. All the time he was just "the rich guy", he was inhuman, even disposable.

'I'm sorry,' Tim said.

That confused her. 'What for?' Faye asked, her expression quizzical.

'I'm sorry you haven't been given a chance yet. You've never been treated the way every human being deserves to be treated. You've been taken for granted, abused, and left to fend for yourself, all the while watching the rest of us live like kings. That can't have been easy.'

'No... it wasn't.'

'Then, let's change that,' Tim said. 'You don't have to do this. You can walk away from this apartment today a free woman. I won't call the police, and neither will Laura. Do you see that painting over there on the wall?'

Tim saw the shadow of Faye looming above him shift as Faye looked over to the wall where Tim's favourite painting hung. It wasn't anything particularly special, nor was it very valuable. Tim had bought it on eBay with his first-ever pay cheque, and it had come with him every time he'd moved ever since.

'Yes,' Faye said.

'Behind the painting, there's a safe. I keep twenty thousand pounds in cash in there. It's my bolt money. Take it and go find somewhere you can be happy. We won't follow you.'

'What if I don't want to go anywhere?'

'There's nothing here for you, Faye,' Tim said, still eerily calm. It felt wrong to be so nice to her, but he knew it was his best chance of getting out of the situation alive. 'Mark's gone, Jake's gone, and it'd be pretty hard to stay friends with someone you've taken hostage.'

***

Laura paced frantically. There was no way out of the bedroom except through the door. The windows were tilt-only, and she didn't fancy a sixteen-storey drop even if she could break them.

Damn! Why did she have to leave her mobile in her handbag on the kitchen counter?

She could hear everything they were saying. She wanted to try to say something, to calm Faye down, but the girl Tim was talking to wasn't the Faye she'd known since preschool. She was different, somehow.

There wasn't much in the bedroom, nothing she could use as a weapon to stop Faye. She could try swinging a chair at her, she supposed, but she doubted she could do it quick enough to stop Faye hurting Tim.

If only she had her phone. She needed to call the police.

She could scream. There was bound to be someone at home in one of the flats below. Would they hear? Would they call the police? Or would Faye panic?

Tim's laptop was on his desk. Laura booted it up. Windows immediately prompted her for a password. Shit.

123456? Nope. Qwertyuiop? Wrong again. 1q2w3e4r5? It wasn't that, either. Laura kept trying, hitting the keys as softly as she could to avoid alerting Faye to what she was up to. She tried her own name, Tim's, and various combinations of their names and dates of birth.

She was getting nowhere. Out of desperation, she looked around his desk for inspiration. Tim had hung photos of them together on the wall. There was a photo of her moving in with him, a picture of them curled up on the sofa, even a selfie taken in the back of a taxi on the first night they'd gone out as a couple. He'd kissed her that night after a magical evening at Clos Maggiore.

Could Tim be that sentimental?

Laura quickly typed in the date of their first kiss. Nope. Then she tried ClosMaggiore, no spaces.

Bingo! She was in.

Now what?

It was hard to think straight. Laura typed "email police" into her search bar. She clicked the first result and landed on the generic police website. It read, "In an emergency, dial 999." Duh.

Farther down the page, Laura found a list of local forces' websites. Some local forces had email contacts. The Metropolitan Police's website said exactly the same: "In an emergency, dial 999." There was a contact form – as long as you didn't need a response any time soon.

Out of the corner of her eye, Laura spotted social media icons. The police were on Twitter!

On the Met's Twitter profile was the same message again: "In emergencies, always call 999."

Laura cursed her bad luck. It seemed life could no longer exist without a mobile to hand.

She could hear Tim still talking quietly to Faye. He was trying to persuade her to go. He'd offered her money, he'd complimented her. Soon, he'd run out of things to say.

And then it hit her: Skype. She quickly Googled "Skype emergency calls". The first hits were discouraging: Skype didn't appear to support emergency calls. Then Laura noticed that all of her results were about US users wanting to dial 911, so she appended "UK" to her search.

It was possible to dial 999. The Skype website warned against relying on it, and advised her to use a mobile phone whenever possible, but she could do it. Tim already had Skype installed. She opened it up, found the "dial by number" option, and hit 999.

Chapter 56: VOIP

Saturday 2nd July, 17:16

As a veteran of twenty years, Brian had seen all kinds of 999 calls. There were the pranks, the silent phone calls, the suicides, and the occasional crime in progress. Whenever he got a really traumatic call, management were always quick to offer counselling and support.

The weirdest calls were from the regulars. Brian had a handful of repeat customers who seemed to call out of boredom or loneliness, and every time, Brian had to follow proper procedure in case this time there was a genuine emergency.

He'd never taken a call about a hostage situation in progress.

When the call came in, his screen flagged the origin: it was a VOIP call. Brian almost dismissed it immediately. The vast majority of anonymous online calls he dealt with were kids playing pranks. They thought they could hide behind their anonymous online accounts and waste operators' time.

The voice belonged to a woman. By his best guess, she was in her late twenties and was probably a smoker.

'Send the police. I'm being held hostage. She's got a knife,' the woman whispered so quietly, she was barely audible. Brian turned up the volume on his headset, closed his eyes, and listened intently.

'What's your location?' Brian asked.

'The Medici building on Westferry Road. We're in the penthouse. Hurry!'

'Okay,' Brian said. With a couple of keystrokes, he issued an emergency dispatch to get boots on the ground. 'Can you tell me who she is?'

'Her name's Faye Atkins. She's a murder suspect you let go. Now, she's threatening to get rid of the witnesses.'

Brian stared, dumbstruck. Had he really just heard what he thought he'd heard?

'Did you say she's a murder suspect? Which murder?'

'Mark Sanders. She was his live-aboard girlfriend. I've got to go. She's got a knife to my boyfriend's throat.'

'Ma'am, stay on the line, please,' Brian said.

He was a moment too late. The line went dead.

***

Mayberry returned to Jake's boat, *The Mobile Office*, that Saturday. It was empty and had been left in Jake's home mooring untouched since it had last been searched.

If Jake had had hundreds of thousands of pounds, it had to be hidden somewhere. That kind of money didn't just disappear. And yet, nothing on the boat suggested that Jake had had access to that sort of money. He had lived inconspicuously, with few luxuries. The boat was old and in need of repair. His belongings were nothing special. He hadn't spent the money on travel or property, so it had to have been stashed somewhere. Jake had gone to great pains to conceal the stolen funds as legitimate winnings from bets. The boat had already been searched. If there were valuables around, then they'd have found them the first time.

How could Jake make nearly half a million pounds just disappear? He had to have done something with the money.

Mayberry paused. How would he hide the money? It had to be something liquid.

Liquid... Could it be that simple? There were both a water tank and a diesel tank on *The Mobile Office*. If Jake had hidden something inert in either tank, it could stay there unseen without anyone being any the wiser.

Mayberry Googled the size of a small gold bar and then did the maths. Four hundred bars weighing one ounce each would be worth about four hundred grand. At 50mm by 28mm by 1.5mm each, four hundred could fit in a shoebox with space left over for a pair of shoes.

The water tank was easy enough to search. Mayberry was disappointed to find it empty. The next place to search was the diesel tank. Was it possible to store gold in diesel? Mayberry searched online for the answer and found nothing. There was nothing for it but to drain the tank and see. Thankfully, Jake had a number of jerrycans on board that had been used for filling up the tank.

Mayberry found a syphon in the kitchen. He washed it quickly, dipped it into the tank, and sucked the end to get the diesel flowing. The diesel, which was dyed red, quickly began to spill out.

Mayberry glanced inside the tank. Nothing.

He was about to give up when an idea struck him. No. He couldn't have. Could he? Mayberry swallowed his pride and headed for the centre of the narrowboat, where the tank for the pump-out toilet was.

Mayberry was wearing evidence gloves, which offered scant protection for the task. He opened up the tank, took a deep breath and counted down from three. Three. Two. One.

He thrust his arm in – and hit literal gold.

Chapter 57: Ride Along

Saturday 2nd July, 17:20

When Morton's phone rang over dinner, he knew it was trouble. After the last emergency, Sarah had begged him to set up different ring tones for different caller IDs. The *Mission: Impossible* theme tune was Morton's warning sign that an emergency operator was trying to get hold of him.

The phone hadn't rung more than twice before Morton fumbled the answer button.

Morton listened in silence for nearly a minute as the operator explained the situation, eliciting a curious look from Sarah. Then he said, 'I'll be right there.'

He turned to Sarah, looked longingly at the rack of lamb on the dining table, and sighed.

'Duty calls?' she asked.

'Duty calls.' He kissed her goodbye, and then he was gone.

***

Westferry Road had turned into a circus. It was an A road, a main artery around the Isle of Dogs, and on any other day, it would have been thronging with the hum of traffic. Today, the road was closed from Westferry Circus in the north to Cuba Street in the south. It would cause tailbacks for miles, as the diversion route went out of the way to avoid the docks. No doubt the Canary Wharf Security Guards, a private group responsible for patrolling the area just north of the Medici building, would be pulling their hair out and wondering why traffic had suddenly come to a complete standstill.

Morton was waved through the police road block with little fanfare. He parked in the middle of the road next to everyone else. There was a silver BMW X5 parked near the Medici building, which Morton recognised as being an Armed Response Vehicle from the distinctive yellow circles on the windscreen and the asterisk on the roof. He'd always wondered why they had an asterisk there, until someone from the Air Support Unit had explained that it was there so they could easily identify ARVs from the air.

Morton could see one of the three officers from the ARV standing in front of the building, ushering people out. He was dressed in black, armed, and relaying information back via radio. If proper protocol had been followed, the other two members of his team would be securing the scene as best they could. From what Morton knew of the Medici, that probably meant one man in the lift stopped on the floor below the penthouse, and another in position on the fire escape.

There were more cars pulling up behind Morton. He looked around to see if the rest of the team had arrived yet. It didn't look like it. Morton recognised negotiators from the Hostage and Crisis Negotiation Unit who were talking to Jensen.

Now was not the time for Morton to have it out with the psychiatrist. Morton swallowed his pride and walked over to introduce himself to the negotiators.

The lead negotiator briefly shook his hand. 'Joshua Stuart.'

'DCI Morton. What's the plan?' Morton asked.

'The firearms officers are standing by,' Stuart said. 'She's not coming out of the penthouse. The Medici building is on lockdown, and all known civvies have been evacuated. The ARV team is armed, but only with Glocks. I wouldn't trust them to make that shot if they need to.'

'Is there an SFO en route?' Morton asked, referring to a Specialist Firearms Officer. The Met had just over a hundred of them in their employ, and they were almost all assigned to the Counter Terrorism Command. Only Specialist Firearms Officers underwent advanced weapons training.

'There's one on the way, but not here. The penthouse faces out over the Thames. Any distance shot would have to go through the balcony.'

'From where?' Morton looked incredulous. There was nowhere to shoot from.

Stuart shuffled awkwardly. 'The other side of the river. There's an apartment block there of about the same height. If she can get in position, she'll have a clean shot straight through the patio doors on the balcony.'

She? Morton was impressed. There were very few women among the ranks of Specialist Firearms Officers.

'That's got to be twelve hundred feet away!' he protested. It was an impossible shot, even on a sunny day with no wind. The SFO's weapon of choice was the Sig Sauer SG 516 Marksman rifle with an eighteen-inch barrel. Morton had seen a briefing when they were introduced, bragging about their maximum range of a thousand yards. Not once had he seen someone actually make that sort of a shot.

'More like thirteen hundred. We've also got a bird in the air,' Stuart said, pointing up. There was a Eurocopter EC-145 half a mile above them. 'She can get us visuals, but it'd be too dangerous to shoot from a moving chopper when there are two hostages.'

'What about a drone?' said Morton.

'To do what? We can't shoot a civilian with a drone.'

'No, but it would get us a view inside the flat. What you're telling me is that our options are to shoot from an absurd distance, storm the building, or talk a crazy person off a ledge,' Morton surmised. He turned to Jensen. 'I presume that's why you're here.'

'You presume correctly,' Jensen said.

Morton looked at him disapprovingly. 'And what will you be doing to keep her calm? You didn't have much luck the last time you were in charge of her.'

'We have new information this time,' Jensen said. 'She's in a dissociative state. She's lashing out, and she's trying to protect herself.'

'By taking two innocent people hostage?' Morton said incredulously.

'In her mind, she's doing what needs to be done. We need to understand that to understand her. She isn't acting logically, David. You can't treat her like a normal suspect. She will not respond the way you would expect.'

Morton felt his pulse rising. The doc was really getting under his skin. 'Is that why you tipped off a defence lawyer when I arrested her?'

Jensen nodded. 'She was my patient. I owed her a duty of care. She deserved to have an advocate to fight for her best interests.'

'We'll discuss this another time,' Morton said through gritted teeth. 'What's the plan?'

'We open up communications,' Stuart said. 'The doc, here, will be with us the whole time, and we'll radio in the ARV team, our sniper, and the boys in Air Support. I'm setting up in the lobby.'

Ten minutes later, they were ready to roll.

Ayala, Rafferty, and Mayberry arrived together. Ayala was carrying a tray full of sandwiches and a thermos full of coffee.

In the calm before the storm, Morton took Rafferty to one side.

'Are you okay?' he asked. 'How's Paddy?'

'Fine, and fine. Let's do this.'

Chapter 58: Ring Ring

Tim was still on his knees, and Faye still had a knife to his neck. He could hear movement below, and if he could hear it, then Faye could, too.

'Faye, you've got to let me go,' he pleaded. 'If the police come up and see you holding a knife to my throat, they will shoot you.'

It was infuriating how long she took to respond. Every second, Tim could feel his heart thundering in his chest. He wanted to be somewhere else, anywhere else, more desperately than he'd ever wanted anything in his life.

'I'd rather be dead than go back to prison,' Faye said.

'You don't have to do either,' Tim said quickly. 'Take the money from the safe and go, now, before the police come up.'

Faye hissed in his ear, 'Do you think I'm stupid? I can hear them on the stairs outside. We're surrounded.'

The building was oddly quiet. It was like that Christmas a few years earlier, when the snow was terrible and London had become a ghost town. Tim had no doubt that it was just the three of them and the police left in the building. He thought he could hear the whir of a helicopter somewhere out of sight, but he didn't dare turn his head to look out the window. The blade was too close to try that.

'Faye, think about it. You're not you right now. If you let me go, then maybe the police can find you some help. Don't you want to get better?'

'There's nothing wrong with me!' Faye yelled right in Tim's ear.

He tried not to shy away from the noise, but it was automatic. He felt the knife graze his throat just a millimetre or two.

'Okay!' Tim held his hands up in surrender. 'Then, what do you want? You don't want to kill me. I'm not here to hurt you at all.'

'I want to go back to how things were yesterday.'

'And I'd like to be twenty-one again, have all my hair, and not have to worry so much about dietary fibre. Yesterday is gone. What can you do now to get where you want to be? Think about it. Your best bet of walking away from this is pretending to be crazy.'

Tim rolled his eyes. *Pretending*.

'And then what? Spend my life in a hospital with actual lunatics? I'm *not* crazy.'

'Okay, but if you had the right lawyers, maybe you'd be found not guilty. The money I offered you could buy you a really good lawyer. Rich people get away with a lot.'

Faye was about to answer when the landline rang.

'It'll be for you,' Tim said. 'It's probably the police. Do you want me to answer?'

'No. Not you. Stay where you are. Laura! Laura! I know you can hear me, Laura. Come out here.'

Tim prayed for Laura to ignore her, for Laura to stay safely behind the locked bedroom door.

'Come on out, Laura, or I'm going to kill Tim right now.'

***

Laura froze. She knew opening the door was reckless. She knew she should stay exactly where she was and wait for the police to burst in. That was what Tim would have wanted her to do.

She found herself reaching for the lock. Faye couldn't threaten both of them at once with one knife, could she? What was the door really doing, other than making her feel safe?

'Come on out, Laura, or I'm going to kill Tim right now.' Faye's voice was muffled by the door. It was so strange to hear her best friend's cheerful lilt twisted and contorted into something undoubtedly evil.

Laura opened the door.

'Good girl,' Faye taunted. 'Now, answer the phone. It's got a speakerphone option, doesn't it? Don't lie. I've heard Tim using it.'

Walking the ten feet across the living room to the phone seemed to take forever. Laura's eyes darted from Faye to Tim and then across to the window. No matter where she looked, the image of her boyfriend with a knife to his throat followed her.

She answered the phone with a quivering hand and pressed the speakerphone button.

Chapter 59: Clean Shot

Keira Thornton both loved and hated her job.

What she loved was the challenge. Hitting a target as small as a human hand from hundreds of metres out was no easy feat. But the moral quandary was always there, hiding in the back of her mind. Taking a life weighed heavily on her each time she had to pull the trigger. Whenever she could, she'd aim for a non-lethal shot. That didn't happen often.

If the order came down, today's shot would be the hardest she'd ever had to take.

She'd located herself atop a block of residential flats opposite the Medici building. It didn't have a fancy name or fancy residents. It just had a clean view straight into the penthouse.

The hostages were in plain sight. One was on his knees with a knife held to his throat by his captor. The other was standing no more than ten feet away. To see that the captor was a woman was a surprise. Most women killers used passive methods, like poison or smothering. Keira had to give it to the captor: she was pretty badass.

The main challenge was distance. At thirteen hundred feet away, Keira had to take gravity into account, as well as the curvature of the earth. Then there were wind speed, humidity, air temperature, and barometric pressure.

The Coriolis effect was the hardest to account for. By the time the bullet travelled the thirteen hundred feet, the earth's rotation would have moved the target by a couple of inches. Combine that with the need to fire above the target to account for gravity, and it was a hard shot, though nowhere near the world record.

Keira had her DOPE book with her. It was her personal record of how her equipment had performed in the past, and she used it to help calibrate her shots.

Even with the best data, Keira couldn't predict everything. The wind could change, rain could pour down from the sky, or the target – or worse, one of the hostages – could move during the half-second or so the bullet would take to travel. The odds weren't great, as it was so windy. If the wind died down, Keira knew she could make the shot. The key would be to aim at a larger hitbox. It would be impossible to guarantee hitting the medulla oblongata, or "apricot" in sniper parlance, the part of the brain which controlled motor function. Hitting that exact spot would prevent any further movement before death, and thus stop the hostage-taker from slitting her victim's throat. Sometimes, hitting the second vertebrae was enough to do the same, but standard operating procedure was to hit the apricot.

She radioed the negotiators on the ground. 'In position, over.'

Chapter 60: Not Feeling Yourself

Saturday 2nd July, 18:00

Stuart heard little for the first few seconds after the landline was answered. He had a directional microphone pointing at him so that only his voice would be picked up while the rest of the gathered police stood around him with bated breath. Jensen the psychiatrist was sitting next to him, his original report on Faye open on the desk.

A live video feed was streaming at potato quality from the helicopter to an LCD television. There was a little lag between real time and the video feed. In the situation, it was the best they could do.

'Faye, this is Joshua Stuart. I'm with the police. Can you tell me what's happening?'

'Go away.'

'I can't do that, Faye. You must be having a tough time in there. Is there anything I can do to make things easier? Are you hungry?' Stuart's own stomach rumbled as if to emphasise the point. It was dinner time.

'No.'

'Could you tell me what you do want?'

'No.'

She wasn't making this easy. Stuart looked around the room for encouragement. He caught Rafferty's eye. She mouthed, 'Ask her about Mark.'

'You must be missing Mark,' Stuart said. 'What would he say if he were with you right now?'

'Yes. I do miss him. He was good to me.'

It wasn't much, but he had wedged open the door just a little bit. Stuart shot Rafferty a quick thumbs-up.

'You say he was good to you. In what way?'

There was a pause before Faye replied. The video showed her face softening. She didn't look quite so animalistic, so wild, anymore. 'He looked after us. We lived on a nice boat, we ate nice food, and he always made me tea in the morning.'

'That must have made you feel safe. It makes me feel safe when I know people are going to be okay. Would you consider letting one of your two friends go?'

'No.'

Damn. She was back to blanket denial.

Stuart tried something less contentious. 'What was it like, living on a boat?'

'Cosy.'

Stuart knew he had to steer the conversation back to something she couldn't give a one-word answer to. 'I bet it was exciting, wasn't it? Travelling the waterways with Mark?'

'Not really.'

Stuart felt Jensen tap him on the shoulder. Jensen pointed at himself and then the microphone.

It couldn't hurt. Stuart shuffled over so Jensen was directly in front of the microphone.

'Faye, this is Dr Jensen. You were saying how nice it was to feel safe. Didn't you feel that way around Miss Ashley?'

They watched the television stream with bated breath as Faye seemed to zone out for a moment. She looked around wildly, and then focussed back on the task at hand as if she'd almost forgotten where she was.

'Miss Ashley?'

'She's here with me. Would you like to talk to her?'

'Yes. Yes, please.'

Rafferty was corralled over. She squeezed herself between the negotiator and the psychiatrist. 'Faye, this is Ashley Rafferty. Why don't you tell me what's going on?'

'They... they did it. They hurt my Mark.'

Jensen squinted at the screen. He couldn't make out enough detail. There was no way he could analyse micro-expressions from that source.

'Who did, Faye?' Rafferty asked.

'T-Tim! And Laura! They must have.'

Rafferty settled on cold, hard logic. 'What do you think about me coming up and getting them, then? If they're guilty, we'll prove it.'

'No! No, you won't! You think *I* did it. Even though I didn't. I did your lie test and everything.'

Rafferty was about to reply when her nose crinkled up in confusion. She reached forward and hit the mute button on the microphone.

'What is it?' Morton asked from the side.

'This video footage... is it like a phone camera?' Rafferty asked. 'You know, back to front.'

They all looked around for a technician. 'No. It's not mirrored, if that's what you're asking.'

'Why?' Stuart asked, bamboozled.

'She's holding the knife in her left hand.'

'And?' Stuart said, not understanding the significance of that.

'Faye Atkins is right-handed.'

Jensen leapt up as if he had suddenly made a breakthrough. 'Her speech today. Is that how she normally talks? Long, complex sentences?'

Rafferty cocked her head to one side, considering it. 'No. She's usually really quiet, simple.'

'And what about her body language? Would you say she's self-assured, confident, cocky?' Jensen was speaking faster and faster.

'No. She's usually withdrawn, diffident, and hates being touched.'

'And yet.' Jensen grinned. 'She's strong enough to hold two people hostage?'

He motioned for Rafferty to shuffle over, pushing Stuart even farther away from the microphone. He leant forward and unmuted the microphone.

'This isn't Faye, is it? Who am I talking to?'

***

Morton felt his jaw slacken. It wasn't often that he felt like the dumbest man in the room, but right then, he knew he wasn't keeping up. He looked from Mayberry to Ayala. Neither of them had a clue, either.

The speakerphone crackled as Faye replied, 'I'm Leah.'

Twins? Morton scribbled it on a piece of paper and held it up so Jensen could see it.

The mute button was pressed once more. 'No, David. Not two people. Two personalities. One is Faye, the sweet innocent girl whom Rafferty got to know. The other is Leah. She's your killer.'

'But, she passed a lie detector!'

'Leah didn't. Faye took the lie detector test for her. Think of it like two totally different people in one body. Faye had no idea what Leah was doing. She was just the little personality, the core, the sweet, harmless girl who trusted everyone. Leah is the alter.'

'And who or what is Leah?'

The doc took a sip of water and dove in. 'Leah is the hostage-taker. If I'm not mistaken, she killed Mark. We already know Faye was in an abusive home. If I'm right, Faye split into two personalities, Leah being the second personality, when she was four or five years old.'

'When her stepfather was abusive?' Rafferty said sharply.

Jensen nodded. 'I think so. That would explain everything. Leah is the protector personality. Leah is aware of Faye, but Faye has no clue that there's another person in her head. She thinks she's been blacking out. That's what she described before. Every time Leah took over, she'd wake up somewhere else with no recollection of how she got there.'

'But, why does Leah exist?' Morton asked.

'To take the pain, the stress, and make the difficult decisions. She deals with the things Faye cannot cope with. That's why Leah is holding Tim and Laura hostage. Laura and Tim know they didn't kill Mark. You know they didn't do it. You also know Jake didn't do it, because he had an alibi. Who does that leave? Poor little Faye. Innocent Faye. The protector personality is trying to reconcile Faye's innocence with the possibility of going back to prison.'

'But the note! The handwriting!'

'Different personalities, different writing. I'm sure you saw Leah's handwriting on the ransom note. As you can see, she's left-handed. They're not the same person.'

Morton had never felt less sure of himself in his life. 'So, what do we do now?'

'We make Leah think we believe she's innocent, and hope that's enough to convince her to let Tim and Laura go.'

Chapter 61: De-escalation Point

The plan was simple: persuade Leah that they thought either Laura or Tim had killed Mark.

The danger was obvious. If they managed to convince Leah, she might lash out at the person they had shifted the blame onto. They would become a symbol of her rage, and if she used the knife, then the situation would end badly. Laura was the logical candidate. Leah would know that Laura had been the last one to leave that Sunday.

Jensen motioned for hush. He needed to concentrate.

'Leah, we know you didn't do it.' It was a risky opening gambit.

'Finally! Now you listen to me.'

'We're sorry, Leah. We didn't know. Laura was alone with Mark that night, wasn't she? Tim left nearly an hour before she did. You're holding an innocent man hostage.'

'You're trying to trick me, aren't you?' Leah taunted them. 'How'd she do it? I was in the other room. Wouldn't I have heard something?'

'Leah, you were asleep, weren't you?' Jensen said. He was reading from notes Morton was passing over. 'If Mark was standing outside, she could have hurt him without you knowing. It's not your fault.'

'Then, I should kill Laura, shouldn't I? She deserves it.'

Jensen looked horrified. He cast his gaze downwards as he felt the heat of everyone in the room staring at him. 'No! You don't want to do that. Let us arrest her. A life behind bars is more miserable than a quick death.'

'But, wouldn't Tim have to have known? He would have seen her come home after killing Mark.' Leah continued to taunt them in Faye's singsong voice.

'If he did, we'll arrest him too,' Jensen promised.

'Hmm. I'm hungry. I think I'll have Laura make me a sandwich. Can you call back later, please?' And with that, she hung up.

There was a mad scramble the moment the line went dead. Everyone burst into conversation with those nearest them. Two personalities? Were they innocent? Few of those present had all the facts.

'Enough!' Morton shouted. 'We have a crazy suspect here, not a hardened criminal. If there's an innocent personality involved, how do we get her to come out? I want to hear ideas on how we can save the most lives here.'

'We can't kill Faye,' Rafferty said flatly. 'If Leah is the criminal, then the pair of them belong in an asylum.'

'So, what do you suggest?' Ayala piped up.

'We need to make a show of being willing to arrest Laura,' Rafferty said. 'Can we show Leah the CCTV of Tim getting home first? If we can convince her to let Tim go, there will be a moment between him being released and her crossing the room to get Laura. That ten seconds would be enough for the ARV team to get up the stairwell, into the flat, and contain Faye.'

'Someone would have to take the CCTV footage up there,' Morton said. 'We could load it onto an iPad.'

'I know. I'll do it,' Rafferty said. 'I'll take it up. She trusts me.'

Chapter 62: Finger-pointing

Rafferty was quickly fitted with a Kevlar vest and given an iPad to show Faye. The technician in charge of the live feed attached a microphone to her collar so they could hear everything, even if the phone line was cut again.

Jensen telephoned ahead. 'Leah, we've got you video proof that Tim is innocent. We're going to send it up with someone you trust. You know Miss Ashley won't hurt you, right?'

'Miss Ashley, Miss Ashley, dear old Miss Ashley. Send her up. Unarmed. She can come to the doorway, but no farther.'

'Okay. Whatever you say.'

Rafferty made her way through the lobby, oblivious to the well-meaning backslaps she received from those around her. Morton followed close behind her.

'You didn't think I'd let you go in alone, did you?' Morton smirked.

He pulled on his own armoured vest, and they headed for the lift. It took a few seconds to come down, and when it opened, the second member of the ARV team was waiting for them.

'When you go in there, don't do anything stupid. I know you. You'll want to get them out alive. She's got that knife much too close to Tim's neck to risk anything. I'll be down the corridor out of sight when you knock on the front door, but if you need me, I can be there in ten seconds.'

'Thanks, boss. Stay safe.'

When the lift door opened at the penthouse, Rafferty and Morton stepped out, and the doors shut behind them. Morton crept down the hallway out of sight of the front door and motioned for Rafferty to go on without him.

The door was only a few feet from the private lift. The hallway was more of an entrance chamber, with a large chandelier and a comfy sofa for guests to sit on while they waited.

Rafferty hesitated at the front door to the penthouse. The whole situation just seemed so surreal. It explained both everything and nothing. She'd been right: Faye was innocent. It had to have been Leah who had panicked and attacked Paddy that night. There had been a killer sleeping on her sofa, and she'd been none the wiser. What sort of detective missed that?

She shook herself. Self-doubt wouldn't help the situation. She had a job to do. The CCTV footage exonerating Tim was on the iPad, and Faye, or Leah, or whoever the hell she was, needed to see it.

She knocked three times and waited. Eventually, the door swung open. Laura was behind the door. Faye and Tim were perhaps ten feet away.

'Give Laura the iPad, then turn around and go,' Leah said. 'Don't try anything unless you want to see Tim, here, bleed all over this lovely oak floor.'

Rafferty handed it over. 'If it locks up on you, the passcode is 1234. There's a timestamped video of Tim getting home that night, and a second of Laura getting home nearly three-quarters of an hour later. They didn't leave until the next morning. Tim didn't do it.'

'Laura, shut the door behind her,' Leah said, smiling sweetly. 'Now, hold the iPad up so I can see the video. Stay five or six feet away. No closer, unless you've decided you don't like poor Tim anymore.'

***

Leah watched the video three times. Each time, she looked down at Tim questioningly. Each time, the knife never moved from his neck.

'Why'd you do it, Laura?' Leah asked. 'You're the only one left.'

'I didn't!'

'Wrong answer. If I didn't do it, and the police say I didn't, and Tim here is a good boy, then who did it? You killed my Mark, didn't you? Is it because he wouldn't fuck you anymore? Oh, yes, I know all about that. You can pull the wool over dear, sweet Faye's eyes, but I'm always watching out for her.'

'I wasn't... I didn't...' Laura looked pleadingly from Tim to Leah and back again.

'If you wanted to keep your sugar daddy sweet, you shouldn't have been hitting on my boyfriend. I trusted you, and you betrayed me.'

'Fine. I slept with him. So what? You were in prison for four years. I was going to break it off. I love Tim.'

Leah put her free hand on her right hip. 'Star-crossed lovers, I'm sure. Him, a rich but ugly and boring banker. You, a dirty whore from Ilford. I can't wait to see the movie. Who'll play you? You won't. You'll be behind bars, won't you? How about you pick up that phone, call the police back, and give them your confession right now?'

'I couldn't do it. How would I move Mark's body? He's big, and I'm not strong.'

'You could have rolled him off the boat.'

Laura tried again. 'And, how did I kill him? You heard DCI Morton. There wasn't a mark on him.'

'You smothered him.'

'While he was awake?' Laura gave Leah an incredulous look. 'How did I get the body to the place it was found? I don't have a boat. You do, and you've clearly thought a lot about how he died, haven't you?'

Leah's mocking smile disappeared. Her eyes became steely. Her hands trembled. She roared in anguish.

Chapter 63: Take It?

Morton and Rafferty heard everything from the hallway. Then Morton's radio began to buzz.

He flicked on the channel reserved for the negotiator and the ARV team. Stuart's voice came through whisper-quiet: 'Morton, what's your call? You know her. Will she kill?'

Time seemed to slow down. It was now or never. He could give the order to storm the building from the fire escape. That would almost certainly get Tim killed.

He could do nothing. Leah had been holding them hostage for over an hour. If she was going to kill, why hadn't she done it already?

Or he could order the sniper across the river to take the shot. It wasn't an easy shot, and success wouldn't be guaranteed. The sniper would have to hit Leah in the head from over a thousand feet away. If she missed, she could kill one of the hostages with a stray bullet, or force Leah's hand. The odds were against them.

Even if they succeeded, Morton would forever be the man who had ordered the cold-blooded execution of a mentally ill woman. There was no good choice to make.

Morton needed to weigh up Tim's life against that of Leah/Faye, and then factor in the odds of success.

The radio crackled again. 'Morton, do we take the shot? We need your answer. Now! Over.'

Morton raised the radio to his lips, ready to reply, and then he hesitated.

***

Keira Thornton was watching everything go down in real time. She didn't have access to the video feed from the Air Support Unit. That would have been a distraction. She'd tried turning on only the audio, but the lag between things being said and the audio stream was unbearable. It was easier just to lip-read as best she could.

The delay in streaming was giving her a migraine. If the police view of the situation was this far behind live – and in a situation like this, every second counted – then it would take forever for any order to get to her. The man on the ground would have to watch the delayed feed, make his decision, and then radio it in. In those thirty seconds, the hostage-taker could kill both her hostages.

Thornton's duty was clear. If the situation headed south, she'd have to make the call herself. She was authorised to "use such force as is reasonable to prevent a crime". It was, in Keira's opinion, a cop-out. Virtually anything could be spun to be reasonable or not.

In theory, there was no "shoot to kill" policy. The default position was that she should "shoot to incapacitate". That was what the bosses always told her. The quickest way to neutralise someone was a shot to the heart. Not many suspects ever survived that neutralisation.

Most of her work with the Counter Terrorism Command didn't play out that way. They wore body armour, so the head was the only option. It was the same here, except that instead of body armour, Faye had a hostage to use as a human shield. Anything less than a perfectly timed shot to the medulla oblongata, the part of the brain that controlled movement, would give the target enough time to use the knife.

The radio blared with Stuart's voice. 'Morton, do we take the shot?'

Thornton felt her pulse quicken in anticipation. She had never told anyone how much she enjoyed the adrenaline rush that went with her work. Those few seconds before the order was given were the build-up, the crescendo, the rising anticipation of a perfectly timed shot from the greatest markswoman in London.

The radio fell silent. She thumbed her own radio. 'Control, what are my orders? Over.'

Only static answered her question. She watched as the knife teetered closer to the man's throat. The hostage-taker's expression was unmistakeable. It was the unbridled rage of someone about to kill.

In that moment, Thornton knew she had to make the call. She took a deep breath, steadied her hand, and laid a perfectly manicured finger across the trigger.

And then, with a gentle squeeze, she took Morton's decision into her own hands.

***

Morton and Rafferty heard the shot over the police radio. There was no mistaking the ear-splitting screech of a bullet being launched from a Sig Sauer SG 516 Marksman.

For a moment, confusion reigned below. Morton imagined everyone in the testosterone-soaked makeshift incident room hearing the gunshot and then only seeing it thirty seconds later.

The ARV team member burst out of the lift and shot past them at a sprint. Morton imagined that his colleague on the stairwell was doing exactly the same from the other side of the flat.

'Go!' Morton yelled. He and Rafferty were hot on the heels of the Authorised Firearms Officer.

Chapter 64: Time

Keira watched the bullet strike the hostage-taker. The bullet hit her in the head, no mean feat from this distance, but Keira had missed the apricot. The hostage-taker's brain matter exploded out of the back of her head, painting the wall behind her as Keira watched in horror.

The knife trembled as the hostage-taker pulled it closer towards her and across to the left. The blade went straight through the man's left carotid artery.

The man's throat exploded with blood, his heart pumping his blood from his neck at enormous pressure. The pressure held the cut open.

The man had just enough time for his eyes to go wide with pain, to look longingly in the direction of the other hostage, and then his expression went blank.

The man and the hostage-taker collapsed together in a heap.

***

There was no need for the armed officer to have gone first. Faye was on the floor by the time Rafferty and Morton made it inside the penthouse. The time it had taken for them to break the door down was enough for Faye/Leah to have fallen forward on top of Tim.

Even as she burst through the doorway, Rafferty knew Tim wouldn't make it. There were blood sprays emanating out from where he had been kneeling, and his blood was all over the woodwork. Laura was at his side, desperately trying to pull Tim out from underneath Faye/Leah.

Rafferty tried to run forward to help her, but Morton roughly held her back.

'You can't. She could be infected,' Morton said, referring to Mark's HIV-positive status. They still didn't know which of the group he could have passed it on to. 'He's gone. There's nothing you can do.'

The world seemed to go silent but for Laura's anguished wails. Her voice carried through the building as she screamed for somebody to help her. She held a lifeless Tim in her arms as his heart stopped beating and the blood ceased to gush from his neck.

It was over.

Control radioed for the okay to send up paramedics, the pathologist was called, and the roadblock was eventually lifted. Mark Sanders' killer was dead, and so were three innocent people – if Faye was included in that number.

Chapter 65: Guilty

Monday 4th July, 08:00

The fallout was immediate. Morton had failed to make the call, and at least one person was dead because of him. He knew in his heart that he could have done more, tried more, and proved everything sooner. His hunch had been right, as usual. Faye was the only one who could have killed Mark.

The handwriting, the polygraph, the endless pursuit of the other suspects, had all been for naught. How could he possibly have known that two personalities resided in one body?

Now that he knew that Faye had suffered from dissociative identity disorder, everything made sense. He hadn't been wrong, and neither had Rafferty. The young woman Rafferty had been trying to protect had been an innocent in every sense of the word.

The contradictions in the evidence made sense, too. Faye hadn't lied because she hadn't done it. Faye's handwriting didn't match the ransom note because she hadn't written it. Leah had been the killer; the ransom note had been her way of diverting attention away from the murder.

This was one for the books. A genuine Missing Persons enquiry had turned up a murder in which the person searching for the deceased was also the killer. The real person they'd missed was Leah Atkins: protector, alter, and unknown personality.

Even Jensen had missed it the first time. He'd only ever met Leah pretending to be Faye. All the dogged police work in the world had failed to reveal the secret behind the mystery. It had only been Rafferty's personal connection that had broken the case.

The media were all over it. Morton's face had been in the Sunday newspapers, and that was why he'd been summoned to the boss's office first thing on a Monday morning. Three deaths were on his conscience. He was the bad guy, and Roberts wasn't going to let him forget it.

Roberts did his usual trick of keeping Morton waiting outside his office. It was a power display, and an obvious one, at that.

'Come in!' Roberts called out at ten past eight.

Morton walked in expecting a formal dressing-down. Instead, the boss was in civilian clothing. It was strange to see him in corduroy slacks and a Ralph Lauren polo shirt instead of his uniform.

'David, thanks for coming in. How's everything going? I hope you're not feeling too down about the weekend's events.'

Morton was thoroughly wrong-footed. 'Shouldn't I be, sir?'

'No need to call me "sir" anymore. I'm retiring. My five years are up.'

Had it been five years already? The gig, formally known as "The Commissioner of the Police of the Metropolis" was a five-year term with a sweet salary of almost three hundred grand a year. No wonder Roberts was dressed as if he was heading off to the golf course.

'Who's replacing you?' Morton asked.

Roberts said nothing. He merely pointed to the doorway where Anna Silverman was waiting.

It was like stepping into an alternate reality. The new commissioner was a woman – the first in the Met's history – and Morton's old boss, at that.

She looked authoritarian, powerful. Her languorous height filled the entire door-frame. Her silver hair was tied back in a neat bun, and she was wearing a women's version of the uniform, complete with a crown above the Bath star and a gorget patch.

Roberts greeted her warmly, kissed her on the cheek, and smiled. 'This old place is your responsibility now. Good luck keeping her shipshape. Especially with this one.' He indicated Morton with a tilt of his head.

'Oh, I know how to handle David, don't you worry.'

'Then, I'll leave you to it.'

Roberts picked up his briefcase, paused to look nostalgically around his office one last time, and left Morton alone with the woman he had once nicknamed The Shrew.

'Close the door behind you, David. And take a seat.' Her tone was serious.

He sat down, feeling a little bit like a child in the headmaster's office, just waiting for the hammer to drop.

'Saturday was a fuck-up, wasn't it? You froze, and innocents died. I'm not sure I can trust your judgement. You didn't even spot the money-laundering going on under your nose. Detective Mayberry had to work that one out. At least we found that in time to seize the money as proceeds of crime, no thanks to you.'

Morton opened his mouth to protest. She was baiting him to see how he'd respond. He decided to stick to the facts. 'I have the highest closure rate of any Murder Investigation Team in the Met's history.'

'Indeed, you do. I think that's why you'll find this new assignment most fulfilling. I want your... ahem, expertise to see more use than ever before.'

She opened her bag, fished out a folder, and passed it over. Morton opened it. 'Teaching duty?'

'Our new recruits deserve the best. September's intake start on the first. You'll be teaching them just how you've managed to achieve such a high closure rate. I'll even let you bring your team with you. No doubt they contribute to your success.'

She had him. She'd never liked Morton, not since they'd worked together twenty years earlier.

'And if I don't think this is the right assignment for me?'

'There's always retirement,' Silverman said with a crooked smile.

Desk duty. Morton cursed.

It was going to be a difficult year.

A Note from the Authors

Thank you for reading **Missing Persons.** We appreciate how valuable your time is, and we're delighted you chose to spend it finishing our novel. If you have a spare moment, we'd really appreciate it if you could leave a review on the site where you purchased this book. Honest reviews help other readers find books they will enjoy, and let authors know what their readers want.

If you'd like to send us an email, or find out when we release new eBooks, head over to our website at DCIMorton.com[1].

---

1.   http://www.DCIMorton.com

You can also follow us on twitter @DCIMorton[2], or like us on Facebook at fb.com/DCIMorton[3].

---

2.   http://www.twitter.com/DCIMorton

3.   http://www.facebook.com/DCIMorton

Also by Daniel Campbell & Sean Campbell
Dead on Demand (DCI Morton #1)
Cleaver Square (DCI Morton #2)
Ten Guilty Men (DCI Morton #3)
The Patient Killer (DCI Morton #4)
Missing Persons (DCI Morton #5)
The Evolution of a Serial Killer (DCI Morton #6)

Printed in Great Britain
by Amazon

63501247R00175